SPECIAL MESSAGE TO READERS

This book is published under the auspices of

THE ULVERSCROFT FOUNDATION

(registered charity No. 264873 UK)

Established in 1972 to provide funds for research, diagnosis and treatment of eye diseases. Examples of contributions made are: —

A Children's Assessment Unit at Moorfield's Hospital, London.

•

Twin operating theatres at the Western Ophthalmic Hospital, London.

•

A Chair of Ophthalmology at the Royal Australian College of Ophthalmologists.

•

The Ulverscroft Children's Eye Unit at the Great Ormond Street Hospital For Sick Children, London.

You can help further the work of the Foundation by making a donation or leaving a legacy. Every contribution, no matter how small, is received with gratitude. Please write for details to:

THE ULVERSCROFT FOUNDATION,
The Green, Bradgate Road, Anstey,
Leicester LE7 7FU, England.
Telephone: (0116) 236 4325

In Australia write to:

THE ULVERSCROFT FOUNDATION,
c/o The Royal Australian College of Ophthalmologists,
27, Commonwealth Street, Sydney,
N.S.W. 2010.

Gwen Moffat's main interests are wilderness areas and the springs of murder, and all her books have featured one or the other, from *Hard Road West* where she followed the trail taken by the American pioneers in their covered wagons, to *Cue the Battered Wife*, a crime novel about an explorer turned mystery writer living in the Scottish Highlands, an upland Eden with serpents.

Moffat has written six travel books and twenty-three novels; she has been a mountain guide and broadcaster, and has written features, short stories, columns and reviews. She has travelled extensively in the Alps, the American West and the wild places of Britain. Currently she lives in the English Lake District.

PRIVATE SINS

Miss Pink, visiting her friend, Sophie, in the Rockies, is drawn into a volatile situation when Sophie's rich, autocratic brother-in-law, Charlie, meets a violent end. The police are satisfied that he had fallen from a horse. The family is tight-lipped, guarding its scandals — until a blackmailer starts to make demands and suspicions grow that the death could have been murder. As a prime suspect is taken out of the river, Miss Pink braves rattlesnakes and subsidence to follow the blood trail to an abandoned copper mine — and returns to confront the perpetrator.

Books by Gwen Moffat
Published by The House of Ulverscroft:

HARD ROAD WEST
LAST CHANCE COUNTRY
GRIZZLY TRAIL
DIE LIKE A DOG
SNARE
THE STONE HAWK
THE RAPTOR ZONE
RAGE
THE CORPSE ROAD
OVER THE SEA TO DEATH
A SHORT TIME TO LIVE
MISS PINK AT THE EDGE OF THE WORLD
THE LOST GIRLS

GWEN MOFFAT

PRIVATE SINS

Complete and Unabridged

ULVERSCROFT
Leicester

First published in Great Britain in 1999 by
Constable and Company Limited
London

First Large Print Edition
published 2001
by arrangement with
Constable and Robinson Limited
London

British Library CIP Data

Moffat, Gwen
Private sins.—Large print ed.—
Ulverscroft large print series: mystery
1. Pink, Melinda (Fictitious character)—Fiction
2. Detective and mystery stories
3. Large type books
I. Title
823.9′14 [F]

ISBN 0–7089–4364–0

Published by
F. A. Thorpe (Publishing)
Anstey, Leicestershire

Set by Words & Graphics Ltd.
Anstey, Leicestershire
Printed and bound in Great Britain by
T. J. International Ltd., Padstow, Cornwall

This book is printed on acid-free paper

1

'KEEP OUT!' the notice screamed. 'Cyanide capsules in place! Cyanide guns set inside. YOU HAVE BEEN WARNED!!!'

'That can't be legal.' Miss Pink was deeply shocked.

'Charlie doesn't care whether it's legal or not. It's his land.'

Sophie Hamilton turned her horse and moved away. Miss Pink pushed after her. 'D'you mean he can put poison down — and for heaven's sake, what is a cyanide gun? Sophie, you don't *approve*?'

They stopped at another small, decrepit structure, evidently masking a mine shaft: a roof of timber and corrugated iron held up by one baulk supporting a massive beam.

'Of course I don't approve.' Sophie was huffy. 'But Charlie could be thinking in terms of insurance and kids coming out from town to explore the mines. These old buildings are death traps: rotting floors, shafts not properly plugged, roofs — look at that roof: held up by one post just, waiting to collapse. On the other hand, Charlie's a great joker.'

'Cyanide's a joke?'

'My dear, anything that causes discomfort is a joke to my brother-in-law.' Sophie caught the other's expression. 'There won't be any cyanide,' she added quickly. 'Only the notices. It's a bluff. I never did like this place,' she went on. 'Ghost towns are fun but old mines can be horrors.'

'Something died here. I can smell it.' Miss Pink was disgruntled.

'A calf, maybe, or a fawn. Bitten by a rattler. Let's get back to the top. I shouldn't have brought you down here.'

They pushed back to the ridge where the air was sweet, scented with sage. Little fair-weather clouds seemed to be stationary in the shining sky and the sun's heat was tempered by a breeze. In the south the mountains were plastered white after a late snowfall. 'This is what I came for,' Miss Pink announced. 'A good horse and a fine day in the Rockies. Blissful.'

'That's great.' The tone lacked conviction. 'I'm so glad. We're lucky with the weather.' Sophie was abstracted. They had reined in facing downhill and a mile or two below was a building too large to be called a ranch house: dazzling white and roofed in red; not one roof, but many at different angles.

'Is that Glenaffric?' Miss Pink asked. She

was being sociable, aware that there was only one house of this size in the vicinity, perhaps in the county.

'Yes, that's Charlie's place,' Sophie said with finality. 'And Edna's,' she added as an afterthought.

It occurred to Miss Pink that she might shorten her visit. Sophie's invitation had been open-ended but she knew a troubled mind when she was in close proximity to one. There had been tension last night, and this afternoon, absorbing those references to Charlie Gunn, the brother-in-law, she guessed she had walked in on a family problem. Her presence could be an embarrassment. All the same, her antennae were bristling; whatever had happened to turn an elegant and friendly lady into a strained and — it had to be said — a dirty person was intriguing to say the least.

They had met when Sophie was exploring Cornwall on her own, something that set her apart immediately: an elderly but well-heeled American tourist in an Armani suit touring in May to avoid the crowds — and in a BMW at that. They'd struck up a conversation over a ploughman's lunch, Sophie had visited Miss Pink's sprawling cliff-top house and they'd kept in touch since, each fascinated by the other's lifestyle. Each had kept something back. Miss Pink had confessed to writing Gothic romances but had mentioned only that she had been on the fringe of one or two murder investigations. Sophie hadn't probed, perhaps expecting that details would emerge later, perhaps thinking that such details would demand a quid pro quo. And Sophie was keeping back a lot, although her confidences would be concerned with her family, not murder. The bits of her background she did reveal were enthralling. She lived in the Montana Rockies, in a small town surrounded by mountains. She owned a dude ranch — dudes were city folk whose idea of bliss was a vacation spent on horseback. Her niece ran the business, so Sophie had all the fun without the grind. When, after that chance meeting in a Mousehole pub, the prospect of riding those ranges was dangled before her, Miss Pink had succumbed, seduced by the memory of big skies and the promise of an Arab mare. They had made excited plans by telephone, had even speculated that they might go elsewhere after Montana: take a horse trailer and ride in Idaho and Oregon, even Canada. It would be a long summer of delights.

The reality had been less inviting. True, Sophie had been waiting at the little local airport but recognition, at least on Miss

Pink's part, was not immediate. She was looking for the chic tourist in designer clothes but the woman who approached — square and solid in old Levis and a flannel shirt — wasn't the Sophie of the BMW and Armani suits. The jeans were sweat-stained, the boots crusted with dung — and she smelled. The eyes, under the peak of a tacky ball cap, were sunken and she looked exhausted. She did explain that she'd been riding, had been held up and had come straight from the ranch to the airport without taking time to change. Miss Pink collected herself, accepted the explanation with equanimity and emerged from the terminal into the velvet night — a moon behind the clouds — to be overwhelmed by the air and the warmth, and the glorious sense of space beyond the airport's lights.

In Sophie's apartment there was no opportunity for questions and no energy. Jet lag struck, and single malt conspired with the lure of a bed after hours shoehorned into a cramped seat to render Miss Pink virtually comatose.

She woke to a brilliant day. Sophie lived on the sixth floor of an apartment block on Ballard's main street. It was an old hotel and its big sash windows looked out over the roofs and shade trees of this small

Western town to alpine ranges. Between the big peaks and the valley there were foothills: long sweeps resembling downland close at hand while, more distantly, higher hills were densely timbered.

Miss Pink had risen so late that she wasn't surprised to find a note from Sophie saying she'd gone out for some sandwich fixings and to make herself at home. The table in the kitchen was laid and coffee was hot in the machine. Miss Pink felt guilty, lying in bed till eleven. When Sophie came home both were apologetic, excited and eager to be out. The tension of the previous night was forgotten — until, from the Bobcat Hills above the old copper mines, they looked down on Charlie Gunn's great house, a place unmistakably built to flaunt its owner's wealth and to dominate the valley.

It was Charlie's father who had made the first of the family's fortunes. *His* father had been a Highland crofter and had emigrated to raise a family in a sod-house on the eastern prairies, but when his eldest son was old enough he had gone to the Yukon and struck gold. He returned to sink his money in sheep, progressing to cattle and horses. He was a good businessman and he forged ahead, buying land and eventually building the house which he was to name after the glen where his people had lived for generations in a two-roomed blackhouse belonging to the laird. The term 'cocking a snook' was coined for Charlie's father.

Miss Pink guessed that what she knew of Sophie's extended family was public knowledge. Both she and her sister had been teachers, but where Sophie had remained single and ended her career as a lecturer in English at the state university, Edna (the pretty one, said Sophie) had married Charlie Gunn, the wealthiest rancher in the neighbourhood.

It was reasonable to suppose that Charlie didn't have his father's devotion to ranching. The cattle and the sheep had been sold and now he concentrated on breeding horses. His land around Ballard had been sold for development, making another fortune for him, but it appeared that no money trickled down to his children. Val, the daughter, was running the pack-trips with Sophie's horses so she must be working hard, at least in the season, and there was something about Clyde, Charlie's son, working as a ranch hand. Sophie chattered about her own ranch but she was reticent about the establishment at Glenaffric and Miss Pink knew nothing of relationships between family members. She had an idea that Clyde was single and she knew that Val had been married twice, and there was a daughter, who would be Sophie's great-niece, but she was away. It wasn't clear where the girl was nor what she was doing, only that she wasn't around. Miss Pink looked forward to learning more, possibly tomorrow when they were to dine at Glenaffric.

They came to the trail-head and stopped. Miss Pink slid down and staggered, her knees locked. She clung to her mare's neck and swung her legs gingerly, watching Sophie unhook the tailgate of the trailer, unable to assist.

'Right,' Sophie said. 'Let's have Barb in first.'

Miss Pink picked up the reins and stumbled forward like a drunk.

'What are you working on now?' Sophie asked politely, easing her Cherokee on to the road.

'I told you: a newspaper column slanted towards senior citizens. I'm hoping it will lead to another travel book.'

'I meant fiction. You must be doing a romance.'

'Not at the moment.' Miss Pink was testy. 'Publishers are down-sizing. I might turn to crime.'

Sophie giggled and then they were both

laughing: two solid old women reeking of sweat and horses. This was more like the Sophie she knew. Miss Pink relaxed happily and settled to enjoy the view. On their left were willow thickets, cottonwoods and a river, on their right Ballard's newest development climbed the slope: raw and opulent houses pointing to steady incomes.

Once a staging post on the cattle trail to the copper mines at Butte, Ballard's fortunes were now reviving with the influx of yuppie commuters from Irving, Montana's Silicon Valley. Each of these new properties stood on several acres of land; as they drove there were glimpses of sleek horses and late-model Jeeps but close to the road a house trailer sat in what appeared to be a junk yard.

The trouble with mobile homes is that they look so shabby as they deteriorate and this was no exception. The general picture wasn't helped by the wrecks of several cars, the skeleton of something — perhaps another trailer — gutted by fire and a yard fenced with branches of trees. It contained two bony horses. A large, florid fellow, his beer gut overhanging slim hips, was at the door of the trailer. He raised a hand and grinned as the Cherokee passed. Sophie nodded to him.

'Friend of yours?' Miss Pink asked.

'I wouldn't say that. He's Val's ex, Paul Skinner.'

'Oh, Jen's father? It is Jen, isn't it?'

'God no! Jen's father is Sam Jardine. Sam was Val's first husband. She should have stayed with him. I never understood why she married this slob.' Sophie's voice dropped. 'Obvious why he married her, of course.'

'Her — expectations?' Miss Pink murmured.

'That's how Skinner saw it. Actually, he was a handsome guy when he was younger, before he put on weight.' Sophie drove slowly, her thoughts elsewhere. 'He thought Val owned the ranch and the stock, but I rent the ranch from Charlie and the stock's mine. And then Charlie could live for years yet; he's only seventy. Skinner wasn't going to wait once he got the picture. Besides, Val soon saw what kind of guy he was. He's got a roving eye and no way would Val tolerate that kind of thing.' Sophie bit her lip. As if Miss Pink had protested she added angrily, 'Well, there was the drink too; what kind of woman is going to spend days living rough in the back country, working her guts out and all to earn money to keep a man in drink while he — ' She checked, breathing heavily.

Miss Pink said delicately, 'But the first husband was different?'

'Sam's all right.' It was bitten off. 'The trouble there was Charlie . . . All the same, if Sam and Val had stayed together maybe none of this would have — but there, we're a different generation. Val says they were both immature, her and Sam Jardine; too immature to settle down, she means, although Sam's settled well enough since, though he hasn't married again. He's got a spread down towards Irving: pedigree Angus. It was Val who didn't want to settle; she's a loner, only happy around horses. Of course, she has to have an interest.'

There's her daughter, Miss Pink thought, but didn't say it. Sophie was thawing gradually; she'd learn the rest in time.

* * *

The ranch had been quiet when they'd started out, now there were horses in a corral, others tied outside a barn. Shrill neighs from the trailer were answered by a chorus of whinnies, and a figure in a ragged straw hat appeared in the doorway of the barn. Miss Pink was introduced to Val Jardine, who must have abandoned her second husband's name along with the man. She was a gaunt woman in her fifties and now, after shepherding dudes on a day trip, the strain showed and she looked older. But there were good bones under the taut skin and her eyes were large: patrician eyes shadowed by the hat brim; she'd be a handsome woman if her face filled out a little. Whatever her age, she looked fit despite the fatigue, and she was good with animals. As Sophie had said, horses came first. After being introduced, Val wasted no time on small talk but turned to a hitched palomino, pasting ointment on a nasty sore. 'The kid riding this one must have tightened the cinch when I wasn't looking,' she growled. 'Rubbed him raw.'

'He'll be fine with a few days' rest,' Sophie said comfortably. 'You can't have eyes in the back of your head. I need to speak with you about that pair I mean to buy from Charlie. Are you happy for me to pick them out?'

'Of course I am. You can do as well as me there.' Val went to work with a hoof pick. Miss Pink watched idly. The woman lowered the leg and moved to the rear end, mumbling to the pony who shifted his weight and seemed to present his hoof before she touched it. Miss Pink turned to help Sophie unload the trailer.

When they'd unsaddled, Sophie settled her guest on the porch, supplied her with beer, told her where the fridge was, and left to help

Val turn out the horses. Miss Pink watched them ride away bareback and reflected that her own offer of assistance had been declined less out of regard for her fatigue than to keep her out of the way. There was an air of tension about Val that recalled Sophie's preoccupation of last night. Well, if what was needed was a family discussion the waiting time couldn't be spent in a more congenial spot.

It was six o'clock and shadows were already forming in the hollows of the hills. Ballard was hidden away to the north and a belt of tall spruce excluded any sound from that direction. Swallows were hunting flies above the corrals and a red-tailed hawk was calling. Eastwards were shapely little hills like flattened cones, the gulches filled with dark conifers. In places where there must be water, aspens caught the sun and flared like emeralds. Beyond the little hills was the line of the Thunder river, invisible in the bottom of its canyon but its presence indicated by a broken escarpment on the far side. Pale crags were seamed by shadowy gullies, minuscule firs silhouetted against the sky. Further south, beyond a great expanse of forest, broken here and there by cliffs, the snow peaks held a glint of gold.

Miss Pink's glass was empty, and so was

the bottle. She got up to find the fridge.

Val's house, little more than a cabin, was the original Gunn home, the first place Charlie's father had put up when he returned from the Yukon and before he built Glenaffric. Basically it wouldn't have changed much, except for the installation of electricity. Val didn't set much store by comfort; there was no table in the kitchen, no dresser, only shelves on the log walls stacked with coarse china and cans of food. There was a sink, an electric cooker that looked as if it were fifty years old and — surprisingly — a new refrigerator and a washing machine in matching shades of green. Everything was functional, even the calendar came from a feed store. The plank floor was bare and the chairs were plain kitchen chairs except for one in wicker with a cushion on which a black-and-white cat was curled, asleep. The only indulgences were photographs of horses tacked to the walls. Animals filled a void for Val. So what was the story behind the missing daughter? Miss Pink couldn't resist a glance into the other rooms: a dim living-room, a couple of bedrooms so similar that from the thresholds it wasn't apparent which was Val's, a bathroom . . . She heard voices and dived for the kitchen to snatch a bottle of beer and emerge as they approached the porch.

Sophie was fussy with apologies for taking so long. Val stared at the visitor as if bewildered to find her still there. For herself, Miss Pink appeared somnolent, allowing the fatigue to show but fully alert.

The older women climbed into the Cherokee. Miss Pink, settling herself, was aware of Val's urgent whisper at the driver's window: ' . . . will be careful, won't you? Don't take any risks.' She was so intense that, feeling Miss Pink's cool stare, the anguished eyes moved — and returned to Sophie without a flicker.

* * *

'You're very perceptive.' Sophie lifted chicken breasts carefully and placed them on kitchen paper. 'Do you have enough lettuce for the salad?'

'Heaps.' Miss Pink added vinegar to the oil. 'Perceptive? That comes with the territory surely. I only said I wish we could find fridges and washing machines in pleasing colours. I haven't seen them in England.'

'You're fishing.' Sophie sliced onions with a lethal-looking knife. 'No one else gives Val nice presents. Charlie keeps a tight rein on Edna's budget and Clyde never has anything to spare. I gave her the fridge and the washer.

Bonuses, you know, after a good season? I believe in rewarding merit and that girl works hard.'

'I could see that.' Val was hardly a girl, but then, to Sophie . . . 'I thought she looked drawn.'

'She'd had a long day.' There was a pregnant silence. Miss Pink fidgeted with the salad dressing, the onions sizzled in the pan. They were self-conscious but neither spoke until Sophie sighed heavily and slammed a lid on the pan. 'There. Half an hour?' She avoided Miss Pink's eye. 'A drink?' The tone was bright and artificial; she'd already had a couple of whiskies. Miss Pink had scarcely touched hers.

They sat at an open window, in the shade because this side of the apartment faced south. They looked over the shadowed street below, over the town and the foothills to the snowfields that were now flushed rosy in the last of the sunshine. Between them, on a coffee table with a surface of Mexican tiles, stood a bottle of Talisker, the level dropping.

'Are you as attached to your nephew?' Miss Pink asked, continuing the conversation.

'Not so much. Clyde's close to his mother, closer than Val is.' She was a little drunk. 'Val . . . me . . . horses: there's a rapport, a bond.'

'Indeed.' Relaxed by her ride, stimulated by sips of single malt, Miss Pink probed cautiously. 'Val isn't a people-person,' she mused. 'That kind of woman doesn't marry. Shouldn't marry. Like me. Like you.'

'How right you are.' Sophie forgot that Miss Pink did enjoy people. 'But she's found her feet now,' she added earnestly. 'Very self-sufficient girl — independent.' Her mind took a leap. 'Pity about Sam. You have to meet him.'

'And there's the daughter.' It was a murmur only.

'You won't see her.'

'What does she do?'

There was silence. Miss Pink's head came round, relinquishing the view. Before that gently demanding gaze Sophie swallowed and glared. 'You'll hear it some time. There's always someone around will make mischief. Like Charlie. Better to hear it from me. Jen left home. Ten years back. Without a word to a soul.'

'Why would she do a thing like that?'

'How do I know? How does anyone know how a girl's mind works? I mean, if her mother has no idea?'

'No idea at all?'

Sophie's eyes slid sideways. 'Well, I told you, that Paul Skinner . . . '

Miss Pink sipped her drink, saddened but not astonished. Stepfathers and nubile girls: a volatile mixture.

'She was only seventeen!' Sophie cried. 'Can you believe that? The child he should have protected — he was her substitute daddy, for heaven's sakes!'

'Does she know?'

'Who?'

'Val. Her mother.'

Sophie stared at her. 'I've drunk too much.' She looked surly. Regretting the disclosures?

'Forget it. Why don't we eat now?' Miss Pink was good at finding escape routes.

'Shoot, the chicken!' Sophie leaped to her feet and rushed to the stove. When she returned she'd taken a grip on herself and sat down with care. 'What I said, implying a relationship between those two, is what I think *could* have happened.' She held Miss Pink's eye. 'I don't *know* anything. No one knows. Jen hasn't contacted any of us since she left. Ten years, Melinda, and not a word!' Her voice had risen again.

Miss Pink had been thinking. 'Then how do you know — ' She left it there but Sophie smiled grimly and finished it for her.

'That she's alive? Because her father — Sam — had this guy working for him around the time she left: Bret Ryan, and Bret and Jen, they had a thing going, just a boy and girl romance, but after she went away she wrote to him, although she didn't say why she'd left home. At least, that was Bret's story. He said he didn't know anything was wrong and he just happened to mention to Sam that he'd heard from Jen — who was in Texas — and Sam, of course, told Val and asked her why Jen had left. The girl was fond of her father but she never told him she was leaving either. And she never contacted him. It was as if she wanted a complete break with everyone from around here.'

'Except this friend — Bret.'

'And she only wrote once to him — he said — but there was an address. Val went straight there: to Dallas, it was. Found the place, a cheap rooming house, but Jen had stayed only a week or two and moved on. No forwarding address. Val never found her.'

'Is it possible she kept in touch with her stepfather?'

Sophie's face hardened. 'He told Val he had no idea where she was.'

'What does he think happened?'

'The family don't discuss it.' Sophie looked out at the sky, now awash with the afterglow. 'Except Val and me.' She added carefully, 'One has the impression that other people think there's something behind it, like a quarrel.'

'Between mother and daughter? It would have to be a sensational quarrel to keep the girl away for ten years.'

'Well, there you are. You see why I think Skinner's involved, although I'd never suggest that to Val. And now, this is the crunch: a friend of Sam's saw Jen in Irving last week, looking at saddles. He wasn't sure it was her — so long since he'd seen her — but the clerk in the store told him yes, it was Jen Jardine. Poor Val is distraught. She only learned this last evening. Sam called her and we discussed what we should do. That's why I didn't have time to change before I met you at the airport. It's why Val is beside herself at the moment, not knowing what to do for the best, afraid I'll take matters into my own hands, go and look for her, maybe antagonise her. You heard her back there at the ranch. Sam says to stay put — Val and me — and he'll try to pick up her trail, but discreetly. I guess he thinks he can get through to her, whereas Val . . . '

'Whereas Val could have been the cause of her leaving in the first place?'

'You mean because of Skinner. You're thinking along the same lines as me. You're suggesting they fought? Over *Skinner*?'

Sophie shook her head vehemently. 'No way. There were other women, and Val was glad to be rid of the guy.'

'Jen might not have known that. And if she thought her behaviour was the cause of her mother's marriage breaking up the girl could have left partly out of guilt, but also because she was frightened of Val's reaction if she ever discovered that there was a relationship between her daughter and her husband.'

'You could be right.' Sophie sighed heavily. 'So what are we going to do about it?'

Miss Pink's shoulders slumped but she rallied. 'She came back; that's a good sign. You said her father is trying to find her; perhaps you should leave it to him.'

Sophie glowered. 'Just so long as someone doesn't drive her away again before Sam can make contact.'

2

Sophie's mood seemed to harden with the new day. She announced that she was going to buy horses as arranged, come what may, so they'd be riding and they'd have a proper breakfast in the restaurant downstairs. Miss Pink accepted that there were to be no more confidences — at least for the present — and made no reference to the previous evening. In any event the food was good and the ambience intriguing; she had no wish to spoil any of it with discussion of other people's domestic problems.

She finished her eggs Benedict and looked around her with approval. 'This place must have an interesting history,' she observed.

Sophie had been absorbed in thought but she responded, if a trifle stiffly at first. 'The Kramers kept its character intact. The Rothbury's one of Ballard's oldest buildings; as a hotel it was famous in the Twenties. You have to meet Russell and Pat; he's a sweet guy. He'll fix shelving, unblock a drain, drive you to the airport, nothing's too much trouble. Pat's all right,' she added quickly, 'but always preoccupied with the business;

that's to be expected, she runs the office — and virtually everything else. Russell says he's the maintenance man.'

'What's their background? Are they ranch people?'

'Bless you, no! I can't imagine Russell . . . high culture, that's him: opera, ballet, you name it. Imagine, in Ballard! They — he flew to New York last winter for *Rigoletto* at the Met. Pat', she added softly, 'used to wait tables here.'

Miss Pink recalled music lovers whom she'd encountered in the sticks and, chatting animatedly, they returned to the apartment. In the top corridor Sophie paused at an open door. 'Hi, Russell,' she called. 'You working on Shirl's carpet? My neighbour's away,' she told Miss Pink. 'He's shampooing her carpet.'

A large, plump man appeared, beaming. He wore granny spectacles, stone-washed jeans and a work shirt. 'Meet my house guest,' Sophie said, introducing them.

Miss Pink shook hands, her eyes straying, listening to a clarinet. 'Mozart,' Russell told her. 'It's the tenant's stereo. Lovely tone, isn't it?' He turned to Sophie. 'And what's the programme for today?'

'We'll see Val and Clyde off first of all. They're going to take the big loop through the Quartz Range and back by way of Black Canyon; they're aiming to clear the trail ready for the first pack-trip. Then we're visiting with Charlie; I need to buy a couple of his animals if we can meet on a price.'

'Such an enterprising lady,' Russell told Miss Pink. 'May one ask what you do, ma'am? I guess you're no more retired than any of us.' Gallantly suggesting they were all of an age when she might give him twenty years.

She confessed that she wrote Gothic novels and the occasional travel book.

'Oh my!' His shoulders sagged. 'And all I can boast is I supervise an apartment building in a cow town. Former cow town,' he amended quickly.

'And a restaurant that's celebrated throughout the county,' Sophie put in.

'Delicious breakfast,' Miss Pink assured him.

He smiled and spread his hands. 'My wife engages the staff. The chef was her choice.' He turned to Sophie. 'How is Val?'

Their eyes locked. 'Sam's looking after things while she's away,' Sophie said. 'He's a good, steady guy.'

'Of course. Did you say Clyde's going too? How long will they be gone?'

'Only three days.'

Miss Pink sensed a hidden agenda behind this exchange. His eyes glazed momentarily, then his attention came back. 'I'm keeping you, ladies. Have a good day. Buy some wild horses.'

⋆ ⋆ ⋆

'Would you have liked to join this trip into the back country?' Sophie asked as they drove out of town. 'We could have gone along. Although they'll be working: clearing the trail of fallen trees, that kind of thing.'

'I love the idea, but sleeping rough, washing in the creeks? Perhaps not. This kind of day is a nice compromise: a ride, good food, sophisticated company, a comfortable bed at the end of it . . . most of all, no mosquitoes. I'm too old for mosquitoes. I'll settle for day rides.'

'You did say sophisticated company?'

Miss Pink looked wary. 'We are eating at Glenaffric this evening?'

'Just my little joke. But I'm afraid it'll be ranch food.'

And the company? She saw that she might need to lower her standards but she consoled herself with the knowledge, culled from long experience, that simple company was likely to be more intriguing than refined. But ranch food? Perhaps after a day on a horse she could eat like one.

* * *

The scene at the old homestead was the authentic West; but for the pick-up in the yard it could have looked the same a hundred years ago except that Val was wearing blue jeans. She was saddling a horse outside the barn where other horses were hitched to the rail and a young man was tying a load on a mule. There was equipment on a tarp on the ground: a zinc food box, felling axes, a saw, ropes, bedding rolls. It looked chaotic. Miss Pink knew it wasn't. In a short time it would all be sorted, and animals and people would be gone. She felt a little wistful.

The man finished with the mule and turned. He was a handsome fellow, a red bandanna at his throat, an old Stetson pushed back, a feather dangling from the brim. His eyes were pale in the dark face — a lined face — he wasn't young at all, just well-preserved. He must be at least forty but he moved like a cat. Broad-shouldered and slim-hipped, he was an exciting image: the archetypical range rider in fringed chaps and spurs.

'My nephew,' Sophie was saying. 'Clyde,

come here and meet Melinda. I'm sorry we're late; we got held up by Russell.'

'And — ?' The pale eyes assessed Miss Pink. She detected a certain wariness, not unexpected in a macho cowboy meeting an old lady, a foreigner at that and an unknown quantity.

'Just talking,' Sophie said airily. 'You know Russell.'

'Enough said. Can you give me a hand over here?'

They moved away, leaving Miss Pink feeling superfluous. Sensibly, she stayed by the Cherokee where she was out of the way. She looked for Val and saw her tightening the hitch on a second mule's pack, not calmly but snatching at it, flushed, her eyes blazing at a man standing on the other side of the beast. At that moment Val came round its rear and confronted the fellow, obviously furious. She gestured, a chopping motion, said something and stamped away. The man glanced about self-consciously. He was around fifty, small and dark, his clothes suggesting a ranch hand. He threw a glance after Val and his lips moved. Miss Pink was reminded of a vicious dog attacking from behind.

The sun was climbing. She collected her hat and camera, and started to circulate, keeping well clear of hindquarters. The fellow who had roused Val's fury was mounting a piebald horse. There was a bedding roll behind the saddle, a rifle in its scabbard. He was staring straight at the camera as Miss Pink took his picture, using the zoom, and then she saw his legs lift as he dug in the spurs. The horse spun round and leaped away, almost trampling the little black-and-white cat — would have done so had it not streaked for a fence just in time. The rider shouted wildly as he galloped down the drive.

Val had dashed over and picked up the cat, fondling it while her eyes followed the rider. Her brother joined her but they were too far away for Miss Pink to catch what was said.

* * *

'Who was the fellow who rushed off in such a state?'

They were watching Val and Clyde ride away, each leading a pack-mule.

'That was Erik Byer, one of Charlie's hands. He thought he was riding out with Val but no way would she have him along. She's got no time for the guy, pushing himself forward like that. He didn't ask, he told her he was joining the party — and then he had the cheek to argue with her!' Sophie was incensed. 'This is the second time; he tried it yesterday when she took the dudes out and she turned him down flat.'

'What's his problem?'

'He's unpredictable. Apart from bad manners — and the dudes are paying customers remember — he goes fully armed: pistol *and* rifle. And Val allows no firearms on pack-trips, except her own.'

'Val carries a gun?'

'Oh, yes. Don't look at me like that. It's for the bears. Grizzlies, Melinda. They come into camp after food; the gun's to scare them off, not to kill them.' Sophie looked down the track where the riders had disappeared. 'And then that Byer, he made a play for Val: eyes on the main chance, like Skinner. Fortune hunters. She saw Byer off, though. I can't stand him, he gives me the creeps. Anyway, who needs him? Val's a strong woman; you don't need more than two guys to clear the trail.'

'How does Clyde come to be working for Val? I thought he worked for his father.'

'It's Friday. He can be spared from Glenaffric for one day and tomorrow he'd be off for the weekend. Besides, he's not working for Val only; the back-country trails have to be cleared for hunters too. Charlie's a great sportsman.' Was it her imagination or did Miss Pink detect a certain irony in that last statement?

They went into the cabin and, told to look around, Miss Pink inspected the living-room, which she had spared only a glance yesterday. It was as functional as the rest of the house: a wood-burning stove, sagging armchairs, an old-fashioned desk — and an electric typewriter. There was no television set but there was a radio and a telephone. The radio would be essential; in this kind of country you listened to the weather forecasts.

'Val doesn't indulge herself,' Miss Pink said as they drank coffee on the porch.

'She'd be content to live in a bunk-house.'

'The long winter evenings must be a bore.'

'Not at all. If you have horses there's always tack to mend and there's the logistics for next season: new routes to be worked out, accommodations to be booked in town, all that. And she's not a recluse; she comes to see me, visits with Clyde . . . she keeps busy.' The words hung in the air. She hadn't mentioned Val's parents. She went on quickly, 'We'll saddle up and ride; we'll keep in the shade where we can, it's going to be a warm day.'

'I was thinking that when the others left.'
'They're going high: a big loop to the south; they'll be in the forest till they reach the tree-line, then they'll have a breeze off the snow.'

When only a few horses were needed the whole herd was brought in to the corrals. After saddling Sophie's grey and the Arab they put the remaining animals back in their pasture and took the trail to Bear Creek, a fine stream that was bridged about half a mile below the ranch. Here there was a stone house with a shingled roof: Erik Byer's home. 'The cellar floods when the creek's in spate.' Sophie was laconic. 'Makes the rest of the house damp. Women wouldn't put up with it but bachelors aren't bothered. Anyway, Charlie's not about to build a new house just because a cellar floods. Every cent has to work for Charlie; he'll not spend unless he sees a return for his outlay. I can tell you, it's going to be a pain haggling over those horses.'

'Why don't you buy them elsewhere?'

They had climbed the far bank of the creek to stop outside a cabin. Sophie sniffed. 'I told you: I don't own the ranch, I lease it from him. Charlie owns everything, Melinda. This is Clyde's home but it's his father's property.'

The cabin was in better shape than Val's, the bargeboards of the gable end roughly carved, reminiscent of a cottage in Eastern Europe. There were the usual corrals and a small barn. A pick-up stood beside the house.

Miss Pink reverted to the point at issue. 'Are you suggesting that Charlie would cancel your lease if you bought horses from someone else?' She was incredulous.

Sophie shrugged. 'He has the best horse-flesh in the county — except for Ali. I do not like that stallion; he has a vicious streak. No way would I buy one of his foals.'

They rode for a while in silence until Miss Pink said, 'You'd think he'd at least do up his daughter's home. He lives in a mansion and she's pigging it in a shack.'

'They don't hit it off.'

'Why doesn't she — I'm sorry, it's not my business.'

'It must seem weird to someone on the outside but there's the background . . . '

'You mean Val's daughter?'

'Actually, the bad feeling between Val and her father goes way back. Charlie's an autocrat, you'll see when you meet him. Edna's a doormat, Clyde's frightened of his father, but Val: she always stood up to him. There were fearful rows when she was growing up — ' She stopped.

Miss Pink suppressed a sigh and looked to the view for consolation. Now through the small sounds of their progress and the background of birdsong there was an undertone: heavy and sonorous like a big plane flying low, but this sound seemed to come from under their feet.

They came to a crest and stopped. Below, the Thunder river poured round a bend. Downstream it was a sepia flood winding through the foothills towards a confluence with its main feeder from the west. Upstream was the start of the Black Canyon, the torrent a mass of foam where it broke through the cliffs of the gorge.

The trail dipped sharply to the river and a swinging suspension bridge. On the far side the path climbed through conifers to join a trail from Ballard, the main route into the back country. This was the way that Val and her brother would return in two days' time. They had headed into the mountains on this side of the river, Sophie explained, would traverse a pass which they hoped would be free of snow and cross the river upstream of Glenaffric's hunting cabin to come down through the Black Canyon, completing a grand scenic loop. 'We'll ride the canyon ourselves,' she promised. 'The meadows round the cabin are stunning in the spring. How about that?'

Miss Pink, looking askance at the white water upstream, said that would be enchanting. They resumed their ride, staying this side of the river, ambling over ground that resembled rolling parkland, and after a while they came on a group of mares and foals. They were deep in a discussion of breeding points when there was a wild neigh from behind them and a horseman came pushing through the sage. 'Charlie,' Sophie murmured, and Miss Pink had her first sight of the local man of property.

Charlie Gunn didn't look seventy years old; he was tall and thin, and sat his horse well, if a trifle stiffly. The animal was a stallion and obviously excited. Miss Pink felt the tension in her mare and she kept Sophie's gelding between them as she was introduced.

The man's face was as angular as his bony frame; it was a face that would tighten in a flash at the wrong word — or was that being subjective, given what she'd heard? The sun struck points of light from the silver conchos on his bridle, from the spurs, from his horse's sorrel coat where it wasn't black with sweat. He smiled, aware of Miss Pink's scrutiny, and she saw where Clyde got his good looks.

When the smile reached his eyes this man was seductive. She was charmed against her will. He asked her how her flight had been, told her she'd brought good weather, implied she was an expert by asking what kind of horse she kept at home.

Sophie's grey fidgeted. She said without warmth, 'We were looking at the new crop of foals. You're doing well, Charlie.'

'Ali here done well.' He patted the damp neck. 'Give credit where it's due.'

Sophie frowned. She'd be thinking of genes; the stallion had a mean eye.

Their ride was over. Charlie wouldn't hear of their continuing; they were to have come to Glenaffric later so they should come now. They started up the slope, Miss Pink giving the stallion a wide berth.

At close quarters Glenaffric was as impressive as it had appeared from a distance, although the effect was achieved as much by its sprawling size as by its architecture. There had been no attempt at an aesthetic whole; a central section was flanked by wings, themselves with extensions at odd angles. There were french windows, bay windows, ill-proportioned dormers, enormous bare stone chimney breasts, blatantly pointed. The walls were dazzling white, the jumble of roofs bright red. The trim — mostly ornamental shutters — was an unfortunate shade of turquoise.

They rode round to the back and left Charlie attending to the horses. Sophie had said that Edna Gunn had been the pretty sister but that now she was a doormat. An image had formed in Miss Pink's mind of a wasted, washed-out woman, perhaps a hypochondriac — pampered? No, not pampered, not Charlie Gunn's wife.

They entered the kitchen where a little dumpling of a woman was on her knees scrubbing the linoleum. A radio played country and western.

The cleaner stood up, red and flustered. She wore crimplene slacks under a hessian apron and an oversize T-shirt with the ghosts of stains down the front. Really, Miss Pink thought, couldn't they dress their servants better?

'I didn't hear the horses,' the woman gasped, rushing to turn off the radio. 'You caught me before I was dressed. So you're the famous authoress we've heard so much about. Please sit down, I'll make coffee . . . '

Sophie introduced her sister. Miss Pink subsided on a hard chair and looked around, trying to disguise her confusion by an interest in her surroundings. A massive cooking stove shone with blacklead and white enamel.

A splashback behind the double sink was tiled, each tile bearing a coat of arms. 'Take a closer look,' Sophie said, seeing her interest.

Miss Pink did so. The arms were those of Scottish clans. 'The Gunns are there,' Sophie said, but without feeling.

'My husband's clan,' Edna put in, smiling.

'Fascinating.' Miss Pink turned back to the scrubbed table, trying to withhold judgement. Crofters were part of the clan too.

Charlie came in from the horses and sat down without removing his hat. 'So did Val get away all right?' he asked carelessly.

'Around eleven,' Sophie told him. 'A bit late but they'll make the first stop-over if there isn't too much timber to clear.'

'Right. I sent Erik down to help out.'

'You *sent* him? You know Val would never consent to have him along. He had his rifle — and the guy's a punk.'

Edna shot a quick glance at her husband. 'A punk?' he repeated, his lip curling.

'He's got no manners,' Sophie protested. 'Val's choosy about the company she keeps and I'm right behind her there. It's my business, after all. Erik *galloped* through the yard; he could have killed someone.'

'Maybe a fly bit his horse.'

Sophie's jaw dropped. She turned to her

friend but Miss Pink had seen Edna's eyes widen. In fear? 'Horseflies are a nuisance,' she said vaguely, biting into a biscuit. 'These cookies are delicious' — gushing to Edna, anything for a diversion. Edna nodded distractedly, her attention on her husband.

'What's Byer's story?' Sophie asked coldly.

'I haven't spoken to him.' Charlie was non-committal. 'I saw him up to the West Forty mending fence but I didn't go up, ask him why he wasn't on the ride. Val won't have him along, that's her funeral.'

'Clyde's with her,' Edna said. 'Between them they — '

'Clyde's never the man that Val is.' He leered and Miss Pink saw the other side of the charm.

When the others went out to look at the horses Edna suggested her guest might like to see over the house. Miss Pink was delighted and, asking to visit the bathroom first, wondered, when she opened the door, if she wasn't being presented with the major glory in advance. Mirrors abounded, the frames wreathed with curlicues; the walls were tiled with images from Egyptian tombs and all the taps were gilded swans.

Despite the vulgarity there were treasures in the house, and Miss Pink was sincere in her admiration even as she suppressed a smile at a Meissen tureen rubbing shoulders with the bronze replica of a cowboy boot, at painted decoy ducks on a Chippendale table. 'Who dusts all these?' she asked in wonder.

'The maids come from Ballard.' Edna ran her finger along a duck's back. 'They're not very efficient. I'd like to have immigrants, Vietnamese maybe, but Charlie won't have live-in help. He gave the women the day off today; that's how you found me scrubbing the floor.' She shrugged. 'I often do that anyway; the maids leave smears.'

Miss Pink shook her head, appalled. All this money . . . 'Who collected these objects?' she asked, pausing at a Delft tankard.

'Charlie's people. They had agents in Europe and they shipped stuff back from all over. Things were cheap after the wars, apparently, and the Gunns have an eye for a bargain.'

You can say that again, Miss Pink thought crudely, eyeing shelves of books in leather bindings, wondering if any had been read by a Gunn.

'We don't use most of the rooms,' Edna went on. 'Charlie spends all his time in the den.' She led the way to an astounding room lined with wood except for a fireplace of stone blocks pointed with yellow cement.

There were animal heads on the walls and stuffed beasts in the corners: two wild goats, a bighorn sheep, a mountain lion. A television set stood in front of the lion and, a few yards away, was what had to be Charlie's chair, constructed of logs. Silver effigies of horses crowded the mantel-shelf and the pictures were Remingtons: cowboys, Indians, stampeding herds.

'Do you ride?' Miss Pink asked weakly.

'Not at my age, dear.' Edna regarded her guest without embarrassment, most unlike the flustered little body whom they'd surprised washing the kitchen floor, and yet the appearance hadn't changed — she was still wearing the grubby T-shirt. 'You've kept your youthful spirit,' she pointed out. 'I — put on weight.' It wasn't what she'd intended to say.

'So what do you do in this splendid mansion?' Miss Pink tried to make a joke of it.

'I supervise the help.' There was a long pause. 'And there's my son, and Val. When you have family there's always something. Do you have family?'

Miss Pink said no, there was no one left, only cousins, and obliged with information concerning her antecedents as they strolled towards the kitchen. Her eye fell on a pair of porcelain perfume bottles in an alcove, decorated with flowers and peacocks. 'These are exquisite.'

'Ah, yes, they're Clyde's favourites.'

'Clyde!'

'My son. Didn't you meet him yet?'

'Yes. I'm just surprised a man should go for something so delicate. I'd have thought the trophies in the den were more — ' Miss Pink trailed off but Edna seemed not to have noticed anything sexist in the words. 'Clyde has an eye for beauty,' she said serenely.

Back in the kitchen Miss Pink kept the conversation on family matters, deploring the fact that as an only child and a spinster she had no nephews or nieces. She envied Sophie in this respect — and then of course, there were grandchildren; did Edna see much of her granddaughter?

Edna plucked at her lips. 'I guess you'll be wanting to see the horses now,' she murmured. Miss Pink thought she hadn't caught the question, but then, 'Jen's away. A lovely girl. Looks more like her Uncle Clyde.' She started to gabble. 'Of course, Val would be a looker if only she wasn't so thin. I keep telling Sophie: you should make her eat when she comes to visit with you, I tell her, cook those rich dishes of yours; that girl needs cream and butter and stuff . . . You know my sister's a gourmet cook? She can do as well as — better than — Pat Kramer's chef.' She looked thoughtful. 'But I guess she eats in the restaurant for the company. There's no pleasure to eating alone. You'll have to excuse me now, I have to start the supper . . .'

Dismissed, Miss Pink went to look for Sophie. She shouldn't have mentioned the granddaughter but wasn't it natural — when you knew that one existed and were not expected to be privy to this family skeleton — to ask after the child? Woman, she corrected, Jen was seventeen when she went missing; she'd be twenty-seven now. But if the explanation for her absence was that she'd had an affair with her stepfather, she should not have asked after her. So why had she?

She stood beside her mare, teasing away at a burr in the mane, frowning, realising that she didn't believe that story about the stepfather. It wasn't enough. Not enough to keep the girl away for ten years, with never a word —

'Hi!' Sophie came striding over from the corrals. 'We have two horses to take back with us. Think you can manage? They're very quiet. Ask me' — as Charlie came up — 'those two were quiet when they were foals.'

'What you gave me for 'em I coulda gotten more if they'd gone for canning,' he said without heat.

'Because they were all I could afford — and then not till you met me on the price. I'm shocked at you asking such a sum from family for a pair of old dude horses.'

Miss Pink thought that there were barbs under the banter. Charlie said, 'You're giving our guest the impression we're a coupla Mexicans driving a hard bargain. I'll tell you the truth, ma'am: she's got two steady animals there and cheap. A quiet horse is what you need on a pack-trip in this kinda country. Did you go through the Black Canyon yet?'

They moved indoors and he served them drinks in a room furnished as a very superior bar, its walls hung with priceless Indian robes and head-dresses of bald eagle feathers. Bald eagles were protected and it was a crime to own as much as a feather.

Charlie was drinking beer from the bottle. 'You'll enjoy the Black Canyon,' he told Miss Pink.

Sophie said, 'I'd like to go in there as Val is coming out. I need new photos for next season's brochure.'

Miss Pink was delighted. 'I'll take some slides. I give little talks back home,' she added shyly, 'and that canyon must make a sensational backdrop. Exposure, you know?' They looked puzzled. 'As in a long drop?' she ventured. 'In climbing jargon a precipice is exposed.'

'It's all of that.' Charlie was with her now. 'We use a quick-release mechanism when we're leading pack animals so if one goes down it don't take you with it.' He grinned. 'And if your mount goes down you got to jump off quick.' He turned to Sophie. 'I have to go in there. Erik says a bear's been at the cabin; it hasn't gotten inside but it's ripped a corner off the roof. I'll go tomorrow, melt some of the fat off that stud.'

'You're never taking the stallion on that trail — not Ali!' Sophie was appalled.

'You suggesting this old man can't ride, lady?' He addressed Miss Pink: 'The meanest animal will go quiet on dangerous ground. He knows if he puts a foot wrong he's gonna roll, and that stud, he's mortal scared of water. I have to whip him through a creek. He'll be terrified of the river a long ways below. No way is he gonna act up on that trail.'

'It's a sixteen-mile round trip to the hunting cabin,' Sophie said. 'You telling me he's going to walk quietly for sixteen miles?'

His eyes slitted. 'He'll walk quiet.'

Miss Pink felt a twinge of sympathy for the stallion.

* * *

They ate in the dining-room, clustered at one end of an immense table. They ate overcooked steak served on Spode bone china and with it they drank a sumptuous claret from glasses with rainbow rims. There was scarcely any conversation. Miss Pink did ask who cooked at other times and Edna, surprised, said she did the cooking. 'She knows how I like my food,' Charlie explained.

By the time the ice-cream was finished Miss Pink was deeply relieved when Sophie announced that they must leave now in order to be home by dark. 'Are they always as quiet at mealtimes?' she asked as they rode back, leading the new horses.

'On a ranch, food is fuel.'

'That's not a typical ranch and I've eaten on working ranches where people talked nineteen to the dozen.'

'Charlie didn't talk, so Edna wouldn't. Anything for the sake of peace. If I'd tried to make conversation with you, she'd have felt she should contribute and he'd have slapped her down. He says she prattles. He can be mean. You only saw the charming side.'

'I had glimpses of the other. And why did he send Erik Byer down to Val's place? Didn't he know she wouldn't have him on the ride? She refused him yesterday too.'

'It's Charlie's way of showing her who's boss.'

'But she's turned fifty. He can't rule grown members of his family like that.' Miss Pink hesitated. 'Or is it because she's living on his property?'

'No, it's my lease — ' Sophie looked flushed but it could have been the wine, or maybe the light. The sun had set and the sky was on fire, flaming in the west, dying to embers in the darkening east. 'She defied him,' she went on. 'Sam was one of Charlie's hands and they fell in love, Sam and Val. They would have kept it secret but Charlie found out — and you can guess who told him; Sam and Erik Byer shared the bunk-house. So Charlie fired Sam and forbade Val to see him again. Of course, she took no notice, went on meeting him, came back late one night and Charlie was in the kitchen waiting up. Edna heard them shouting. Seems he was about to take his belt to her — and that girl was turned twenty! Imagine. And she told him if he touched her he'd never dare turn his back on her again. Edna heard this from outside the door and she told me the way Val spoke made her blood run cold, although she'd always thought the girl had it in her to be as violent as her daddy. But that last was too much for Edna — and the guns were kept too close to the kitchen. She went in there and told Charlie he was driving his daughter at Sam and if she went to him the whole county would be laughing at him: his daughter running off with one of his hands. And while Edna was ranting at him, Val slipped away and she did leave. She had a horse, Sam had a pick-up, they married and set up house over in the Madison Valley, managing a spread for a guy who had no time for Charlie. No one from around here would have dared employ them.'

'But she came back. He must have mellowed towards her.'

'Well, it's history, isn't it? And when she divorced Sam, Charlie would have taken it as a point in his favour, and then he had a soft spot for Jen. That little girl had the pick of his horses to ride and I guess it would have been because of her he let Val move into the old homestead. I had a place down Irving way when I was teaching and after she divorced Sam, Val and Jen came to stay until I worked out the deal with Charlie. I'd lease the old ranch from him, buy some of his stock and start a business with Val to run it. She had a roof over her head and a job, and all the horses she could do with. And then, as the business grew, she took on Paul Skinner. I figure he talked her into marriage . . . However, it wasn't long before she threw him out.' There was a pause.

'Jen was seventeen,' Miss Pink murmured.

Sophie nodded but she ignored the cue. 'And like I said, the child could twist Charlie round her pinkie. She's his blood, after all. Of course, Val is too, but then Val defied him. Threatened him even. That was nasty, for all that Jen seemed to heal the breach. Not totally; he said to me once, after I'd remarked what a good job Val was making of the business, that it was surprising she could do anything right, she couldn't keep a man nor a daughter. I could have killed him. Jen's going broke her heart. And he's got Val where he wants her now; she's on his property and a sitting duck for all his little teases like the business with Byer this morning. I just hope he doesn't try something with Jen now she's back. He could ruin everything. Val's suffered enough.'

They rode in silence until Miss Pink thought to ask what explanation Charlie gave for his granddaughter's absence.

'I have no idea. Edna may know but if she does, she's not talking, not even to me. She says Jen will come back in her own time: a typical Edna remark. She's soft. Always was. She's my sister but she's got no backbone.'

3

Edna called at ten o'clock the following morning. They were about to leave the apartment for the old ranch when the telephone rang. Sophie's end of the conversation was brief. 'Why? We have to check the horses; can't we . . . *Now?* . . . When did he leave? . . . Right, I'll be there' — a surprised glance at Miss Pink — 'I *said*, all right! I'm on my way.'

She dropped the receiver on its rest. 'That was my crazy sister,' she grated. 'She has to see me and — well' — she was rattled — 'she's on her own. Charlie's left for the hunting cabin. That's it. No indication what it's about, but she's flipped. I'm sorry. I have to leave you.'

'Of course you do.' Miss Pink was genial. 'I can amuse myself; I'll visit the library . . . I only hope it's nothing serious.'

Sophie grimaced. 'With Edna, it has to be Charlie. Still, he can't get into much mischief, given his age. It won't be women or money.'

'There's one way to find out.'

'What? Oh, yes. Right, I'm off. I'll have a

word with Russell, ask him to let you have the loan of a car.'

When she'd gone Miss Pink lounged at the open window and allowed her mind free rein. If Edna stipulated that Sophie should desert her house guest then it had to be a serious problem and that meant family. Since the son and daughter were on the trail (and if Sophie were right and Charlie was too old for sexual shenanigans) it could be something to do with the granddaughter. Had Edna heard the news that the girl had been spotted in Irving and felt the need to discuss it with the only member of the family available at the moment? Or had there been a new development? Could Jen be at Glenaffric?

The doorbell rang. Russell Kramer stood in the corridor, beaming. He had no car free for her but she might care to accompany him on a supply run to Irving, this being their local metropolis and well worth a visit. Miss Pink saw that he had his orders: to keep her out of the way. Oh, rubbish, she thought, I'm paranoid; he's just aiming to keep me amused.

He worked hard at it, talking as he drove: about the history of the Rothbury from the Twenties, about the current tenants, the skiers who thronged the restaurant in winter, the hunters and the tourists. When Miss Pink could get a word in she was equally garrulous concerning her visit to Glenaffric, pausing suggestively for his comments, but on the subject of the Gunns and their property he was suddenly taciturn, except in one direction. She returned to Ballard surprised and puzzled at what he had revealed, if unwittingly, but thinking that it could have no bearing on the problem of Jen Jardine.

She had a key to the apartment. She entered, thinking it was unoccupied, to find Sophie in the living-room — and she knew immediately that there was trouble. At two o'clock in the afternoon there was a bottle of Jack Daniel's on the coffee table and Sophie was either drunk or so tense she seemed unable to utter a greeting. She stared mutely.

'Been waiting long?' Miss Pink asked politely.

'Not long.' The other made a clumsy gesture as if wiping something away. 'How was your morning?' The bright tone was at odds with the fixed glare.

'So-so. How did you find Edna?'

'Sit down.' It was brusque: an order, not an invitation. 'A drink?'

'No thanks. I had wine with my lunch. Have you had lunch?'

There was no answer. Miss Pink subsided

into an armchair. Sophie stood up and started to pace, carrying her glass, sipping, pausing before a picture of Yellowstone Falls.

'She called last night. Jen. She called Charlie.'

'I thought it might concern her.'

'Weird!' Sophie turned, flinging out her hands, spilling bourbon. 'We still don't know where she is. There's nothing we can do. Edna doesn't know I told you. The bastard!'

'What did Jen say to her grandfather?'

'It doesn't make sense.' Sophie turned bewildered eyes to the window. 'We don't know what's true any more.' She laughed harshly. 'Did we ever? One of his jokes? No, it can't be a joke. And when he didn't know she was listening, *then* he could have been speaking the truth — but then he never knew she was listening. He's a monster. You know something? I figure mental torture is worse than the physical kind.'

Miss Pink stood up and went to the kitchen, returning with a tumbler. 'I'll join you,' she said firmly and poured herself a drink. Sophie regarded her with astonishment.

'I didn't know you liked bourbon. I'd have offered — '

'No need.' She had offered and had

forgotten. Miss Pink didn't like bourbon; she was trying to jolt this woman into some semblance of normality, of coherence. 'Tell me what happened after we left last evening,' she ordered. 'It had to be afterwards; everything was all right when we rode away.'

Sophie nodded slowly, accepting the need to collect herself. 'Edna was tired and she went up to bed. Charlie stayed in the den watching TV. Edna was reading when the phone rang. She lifted the extension but he still had the television on and there was a lot of shouting so he wouldn't have heard her pick up. When he did switch off the TV she heard Jen's voice. She seemed quite cool, asking after him and Edna — she would have broken in at that point but he said quickly that Jen was to wait, to stay on the line, not ring off, and she heard him put the receiver down so she replaced her own and pretended to be asleep over her book. He must have glanced in, satisfied himself she wasn't listening and gone back to the den.

'She didn't dare pick up the extension again so she crept down the stairs but she only caught the end of the conversation. She heard him say, 'You don't know how she'd take it, sweetie, let's you and me talk it over first, decide what's best.' And then he told her to meet him at the hunting cabin tomorrow. That's today.'

'Did Edna confront him?'

'Oh, yes. He said she was drunk, that she'd been dreaming, she'd imagined it all. There was a row but she couldn't get through to him and they went to bed. Separate rooms, of course. She couldn't sleep and she tackled him again this morning. Would you believe it, he told her the whole story!' Sophie was incredulous. Miss Pink's eyes were narrowed. 'He said that Jen was pregnant all those years ago and she came to Charlie for money. He made her tell him what she wanted it for but she wouldn't name the father. He gave her the money. And he never told a soul. You believe that?'

'Go back a bit. What did Jen want the money for?'

'To go away of course.'

'Yes, but for an abortion or to have the baby adopted — or to bring it up herself?'

'We don't know. Of course Edna demanded he tell her but Charlie says he has no idea either. He knows, I'm sure of it; he knows if he has a great-grandchild nine years old. But how can you force an answer out of a man like that? All the same, Edna says when he comes back she'll find out where Jen is if it kills her.'

'The story's suspect. If Jen was pregnant she'd have gone to her mother — or to you.'

'Not if the man responsible was her stepfather.' They regarded each other thoughtfully, Sophie calmer now. 'And she's come home,' she went on, 'wants to make contact with her mother, if that phone call means anything — and Charlie's trying to prevent a meeting? I hate that man. What are we going to do, Melinda?'

'Is there any way of getting to her before Charlie does?'

'You mean, ride to hunting camp ahead of him? Impossible. There's only one trail from Ballard and he's on it. Besides, the situation's too fraught. How could any of us stop her talking to Charlie? I hate to say this but right now Jen's closer to him than to me, or' — her voice rose — 'even her own mother. And God knows how Val is going to take this. If only we could think of some way of *luring* Jen back without alienating her . . . ' Sophie stared hard at her friend. 'She might listen to a stranger.'

'You're clutching at straws.' Miss Pink knew exactly what was in the other's mind and would have none of it. 'For the moment all you can do is wait, let her make the moves. She left of her own volition, she has to return that way.' And without her meddling old grandfather putting his oar in.

Sophie sat down. She looked a hundred years old. 'I guess you're right: the objective view and all that — which is why I thought — oh shoot, forget it. But we're going in there tomorrow; we'll make a point of calling on Charlie at the cabin, see if he might let something slip about where Jen is. We might even bump into her ourselves, by accident.' She sighed. 'I'm glad you're here, Melinda. I don't know what I'd have done in this apartment all on my own.'

'You'd have consulted Russell.'

Sophie blinked and looked wary. 'Maybe. He's a good friend. What did you make of him? He said he'd ask you to go to Irving.'

'He's amusing. We had lunch in a restaurant on the river bank. Do you know it?'

'My dear! There are so many places to eat in Irving.'

'This was a gay establishment.'

Sophie's jaw dropped. 'I'm amazed!'

'That such a place should exist?'

'No, Irving's much more liberal than Ballard. I'm surprised he should take you there.'

'The food was good.' Miss Pink was poker-faced.

'Did he — What did you talk about?'

'I wouldn't say he told me anything personal. He didn't have to. It isn't common knowledge, then?'

Sophie said wearily, 'I should have known you'd guess, you notice everything. No, it's not common knowledge, definitely not. Only his closest friends know and the obvious people.'

'Like his wife.'

'Of course Pat knows. They have a modern marriage and she leads her own life, presumably. But I suspect Pat's not much interested in sex. She's a businesswoman. He married for respectability and she — well, for security, mainly, although I guess money came into it. This building belongs to Russell. It's worked out. There aren't many married couples you'll find make such an effective working team as Russell and Pat. But the only other person I know he's confided in is you.'

'And Clyde.'

'Now why would you say that?'

'It's obvious. Russell won't talk about the Gunns, with one exception, and then his face softens — '

'Damn! They'll need to watch themselves. Imagine Charlie's reaction.'

'I think he knows already.'

'Impossible!'

'Yesterday he said that Clyde would never be the man that Val is. I thought then that it was a remark with an edge to it, now I see it was loaded. And then there's Edna. Mothers usually know the sexual orientation of their sons.'

'She'll keep quiet about it.'

'I think Charlie knows. They'd have given themselves away. People can easily identify heterosexual couples, why not homosexual ones?'

'Not in Ballard, Montana.' Sophie was grim. 'This is redneck country. They'd know better than to be indiscreet around here. San Francisco's OK, even Irving, although they'd never risk being seen together, even there: too much at stake.'

'I'd wondered about that.'

'Yes, I guess you would.'

'Millions of dollars do tend to intrude on one's mind.'

4

Sophie had to check the horses at the homestead before they could leave next morning and the sun was high by the time they crossed the swing bridge and climbed to the main Ballard trail. Once they were traversing the slopes of the canyon the outlook was stunning: the river way below, while on the far side a confusion of cliffs and boulder fields was threaded with thin game trails. Not a road nor a house to be seen — only once, an osprey's nest on a pinnacle. On their own side they saw few animals other than chipmunks but there was evidence of bears: clawed trees, rotten logs torn apart in the search for grubs.

They came to a landslide that had swept the slope clear, leaving a chute of gravel as unstable as ball bearings. The water was so far below that calculations were immaterial; a hundred feet or a thousand, you were dead if your horse put a foot wrong, yet Sophie's grey walked across the faint line of the trail without breaking stride. The Arab followed as if she were in her home pasture.

'How on earth did Charlie cross that,

leading a pack-horse?' Miss Pink asked on the far side.

Sophie laughed. 'Well, he got across, didn't he? No sign of bodies.'

'There wouldn't be. They'd have gone all the way to the bottom and been swept away.'

'Like Carol Skinner.' It was only a murmur.

'What was that?'

'I'll tell you later.'

The canyon trail wasn't suitable for conversation, the riders forced to move mostly in single file. They rode on and below a steep section Miss Pink emerged from speculation on the fate of another Skinner — Paul's wife? — to sniff the air. 'There seem to be more than two horses ahead of us.'

Sophie paused. 'First time you noticed? There were droppings way back and tracks in the mud where we crossed that creek. It'll be hunters; not hunting, but looking to see where the game is. They have to apply for permits in advance so they need to know whether it's worth applying for a given area. A lot of people come in from Benefit; that's a ghost town back of the rim.' She gestured vaguely. 'We passed the junction but it's easy to miss if you don't know where it is.'

They climbed zigzags to emerge on a crest and stop for a blow. A flash of light glinted on a spur about a mile away. 'Val and Clyde,' Sophie announced, adding, 'I'm not going to say anything about Jen. I'm wondering, if she did come to the cabin yesterday, if she'll be around today. I need to know if Val's seen her without her guessing what I'm driving at.'

'You'll know by her manner, surely. She'd be full of it if she'd met Jen.'

'You're right. It's just that, if she's still in ignorance, I don't want her to know Jen came to the cabin to meet Charlie. There's no knowing what Val might do: gallop back to confront him, gallop home to see if Edna's heard anything more, either way riding hard in this old canyon is the last thing she should be doing, and leaving Clyde to cope with two pack-mules. No, we won't say anything about Jen.'

'We were going to take pictures,' Miss Pink reminded her, a little resentful that this family problem should intrude on such a glorious day.

'So we were. They should look good coming up to this crest.'

They dismounted, tied their horses and prospected for vantage points. It was quiet except for the sound of the river. Eventually

Val and Clyde appeared below, leading the mules. Val saw them immediately and greeted them from a distance. They responded; if you didn't do that the horses could take fright when they realised there was someone — some thing — on the trail. It could be a bear.

'Keep coming,' Sophie called. 'We'll get shots as you pass, then stop there on the top. How're you doing, Clyde?'

Val kept talking. 'Just you two? Hi, Melinda. We've cleared the trail, no problem. There's snow on the pass but we got through, made a sort of trench. It was quite an adventure.' She walked past, Miss Pink and Sophie clicking away. Clyde grinned engagingly for the cameras but made no move to adjust his position. He had no need to, he looked marvellous on a horse.

They stopped on the crest and Sophie made her way towards Val. Miss Pink approached Clyde. 'You met the others?' she asked chattily.

'No.' He looked mystified. 'What others?'

'We've seen fresh tracks. Someone's ahead of us.'

'That'll be my dad. He's at the hunting camp.' He was observing her closely. 'There could be someone else around,' he conceded.

'People come in from Irving, leave their trailers at an old ghost town. It cuts the distance if you want to reach the back country.'

'And they stay at the hunting camp?' She was politely interested.

'No, ma'am. That's private; it's Gunn property.'

'Have the bears done much damage?'

'Bears? At the cabin?'

'That's why your father is up there: repairing the roof where they tried to break in. Didn't he tell you?'

'We didn't see him. The cabin isn't right on the trail. You can see it but it's a hundred yards or so below. The trail stays high. I knew he was planning to come in with the blankets and stuff so I wasn't surprised to see someone was around. There's a horse tied outside.'

Val and Clyde left for the homestead. Miss Pink and Sophie checked to make sure no shoes had worked loose and untied their mounts.

'I take it there's no word of Jen,' Miss Pink observed.

'Val didn't mention her. I did ask whom she'd met and she said no one. No one at all.'

'Clyde said they didn't leave the trail to

speak to Charlie although they saw someone was at the cabin.'

'He was inside — or somewhere.' Sophie was vague. 'Val says his pack-horse was loaded ready for off, so he had to be inside — except that the stallion didn't seem to be around. Val wanted to keep ahead, not have Charlie with her string, not with that spooky animal along. If it'd been me I'd have stopped and let Charlie go first. Now we're going to run into him. When we do, we get as far off the trail as we can. And we'll dismount. I don't want any accidents. I'll tackle him about Jen when we get home. This is no place for a fight.'

They continued, alert for movement ahead, but nothing materialised, not even a deer. The canyon could have been empty of life and it was strange to find the ground levelling off, to emerge to flowery meadows, and see a cabin below them with a loaded pack-horse tied outside a small corral. At their appearance it neighed shrilly.

'Where *is* the stud?' Sophie murmured. 'The cabin door's closed but Charlie can't be far away; that packhorse is ready to go. It must be at least half an hour since the others passed. Charlie could have seen the bear — ah, that'll be it! The brute came back and he's gone after it.'

'I'd have thought you'd need a steady horse to go after bears.'

'True, but you can't chase them on foot. Bears can run fast. We've not heard a shot, though. A shot would resound for miles in this canyon.'

'Are you going down there?'

'No point. He's away somewhere and it's not my cabin. I've no interest in it.'

A mile or so further they came to a small lake cupped in a grassy basin and reflecting the sky. The still water was soothing after the constant rush of the river. They watered the horses, tethered them and moved away, carrying their lunch and cans of beer.

'This is perfection,' Miss Pink exclaimed, making herself comfortable on a log, popping a beer can. A family of teal patrolled the reeds, bees were loud in the flowers, the slopes were drifted with lupins and Indian paintbrush. A thought struck her and she looked round uneasily. 'What about the bear?'

'We haven't seen him so he's made himself scarce.' Sophie wasn't concerned about bears; she was miles away. Miss Pink opened the lunch box from the Rothbury's kitchen and inspected the filling inside half a baguette: 'Salami, ham, cheese, tomato . . . have you got the same?' There was no reply. 'Anyone home?' she asked mildly.

Sophie turned to her, blinking. 'How long has that horse been there?'

'Where do you see a horse?'

'Back there: at the cabin. The packhorse. Didn't the ground look bare, where it was tied? That animal's been there longer than half an hour.'

'You can leave a saddled horse for hours.'

'Not a loaded pack animal. I'm going down there. No, don't panic; I mean when we go back.' She became aware that her friend was waiting to start lunch and her effort to change tack was obvious. 'This is Chef's special Submarine,' she said, opening her own box. 'The bread's home-made, the mayonnaise is his secret recipe. I figure it's white wine, Dijon mustard and sour cream.'

'It looks scrumptious. I've been wondering: why does Charlie have to bring supplies in to the cabin? Why not leave them there?'

'They have to take everything down after hunting finishes because of thieves.'

'You mean bears?'

'Paul Skinner, actually — oh, I shouldn't have said that! It's like this: we've had a rash of thefts over the last year or two; nothing's left in any of the hunting cabins that could be stolen. Charlie maintains Paul

Skinner is the thief but then Charlie would. I've no time for the guy but I have to admit he does get a raw deal. Why, there's even a rumour that he killed his second wife. Yes, you may well look shocked. But Carol Skinner *did* throw herself in the river — well, she was found washed up way below Irving. She was an alcoholic and the last people to see her said she was drunk in a bar close to the river. They say she went out to the car-park and no one saw her again — alive. They found her body two days later.'

'Where was Skinner when she was drinking?'

'He was in a bar in Ballard twenty miles upriver. And he had alibis. But the rumour goes that she could have reached home and he put the body in the river at Ballard. I heard the story first from Charlie; in fact, it would never surprise me to know Charlie started it. It's just the kind of joke he'd enjoy. Oh, forget Charlie, we're supposed to be enjoying ourselves.'

They ate in silence. The surroundings were idyllic and Miss Pink might banish the thought of Charlie's twisted sense of humour, but the image of that cabin wouldn't go away — and Jen Jardine going to meet her grandfather there — and the packhorse standing, waiting to go but so glad to see other horses, neighing wildly as they passed . . .

* * *

The horse didn't neigh when they returned. It wasn't there. 'Well, that's a relief,' Sophie breathed, then suddenly expansive: 'Charlie had me worried there; I mean, he's an old man now — and that stud! The guy's asking for trouble coming in here on his own. He should have brought Byer with him, but it was Byer's day off yesterday, Saturday; he'd have gone to town. However, no harm done. I wonder if he did go after a bear. We didn't hear a shot but then, if he was miles away, maybe we wouldn't.'

Miss Pink murmured agreement. They had stopped and she was staring at the bare patch where the horse had been tied.

'We'll give the landslide a miss,' Sophie went on. 'We can go out by way of Benefit, show you a ghost town.'

That suited Miss Pink, anything to avoid the landslide and that dizzy drop to the river. In the event, the alternative wasn't much better. They climbed to the rim by a line that went straight up: no zigzags; worst of all, no resting places. Once on that slope, you were committed — and the mare was no climber. She lunged and pushed, trying to shoulder past the grey, throwing her head, her eyes wild. The slope was scattered with stunted pines and Miss Pink was slashed and whipped by branches. Once her knee struck wood but there was no time to take breath, to feel pain. At one point, her hand slipping on the wet horn, she gasped, 'I can't stay on!' and 'Nearly there,' Sophie called jauntily.

They came over the lip of the escarpment and stopped, mare and rider shaking uncontrollably. Miss Pink stared at her companion, speechless.

'You came up that nicely,' Sophie told her. 'I forgot to tell you she's inclined to throw her head when she's going uphill. I knew you'd enjoy it, being a mountaineer.'

A narrow path took off through the sage and prickly pear. They were on a wide shelf, still part of the canyon with more crumbling cliffs above, but the trail now mercifully safe; no abyss immediately below, no lethal slopes to traverse. They passed through a belt of big trees, walking quietly on pine needles, and came to a slope where the trail rose gently. At the top they were at last clear of the canyon and ahead there was grassland with aspens in the gulches and, at the head of a shallow depression, a cluster of wooden buildings. Beyond were spoil heaps and a dirt road.

Smoke rose from a chimney. 'Hello, someone's in residence,' Sophie remarked, halting. 'Horses in the corral too.' There was no response. Miss Pink was slumped in the saddle, her feet dangling, easing her aching knees. If Sophie were proposing to go visiting she could go alone. 'Right,' she said, reading the signs correctly, 'we'll give it a miss, come back another time. Besides, I want to get home, find out what happened when Charlie met Jen — if he's talking,' she added grimly.

They skirted the ghost town and picked up a trail that took them to the swing bridge. When they passed his house it looked as if Clyde had come and gone, his door closed and his pick-up absent. On the other side of the creek smoke was rising from Byer's chimney. At Val's ranch a solitary horse hung its head above a pile of hay, the picture of exhaustion. There were panniers on the ground, a packsaddle, a tarpaulin, a sprawl of tack.

'Hi, you guys!' Val emerged from the barn. 'This is Charlie's packhorse. It came in some time ago, must have followed us down.'

'The one that was outside the cabin's gone,' Sophie said. 'You're right, this has to be the same one.'

Val took a halter off the packsaddle and

held up the frayed lead rope. 'Broke free,' she said. 'Maybe that old bear spooked it. So where's Charlie? Did you see any sign of him at the lake?' Sophie shook her head. 'Nor the stud?'

Sophie said meaningly, 'We figure the pack-horse had been standing there rather a long time.'

They thought about it, all three knowing that Charlie might have wounded the bear and was following its trail to finish it off; on the other hand, the stallion could have thrown him. Charlie could be in the canyon. He could be below the trail.

'There was no sign of him anywhere,' Miss Pink said. 'I mean, nothing to show that the trail had given way.'

'We turned off for Benefit,' Sophie pointed out.

'But we went *up* the length of the canyon,' Miss Pink insisted. 'There was no mark even at the landslide.'

'We would have noticed,' Val put in firmly, 'Clyde and me. But there needn't be any sign of the trail collapsing, his horse could have *jumped* off; that animal spooks at shadows.'

'Why would he be on the home trail when he's left his packhorse at the cabin?' Sophie asked and Miss Pink was reminded of the endless, often fruitless speculation that arises with the first indication that a mountaineer is missing. 'I figure he's upstream of the cabin,' Sophie insisted. 'But then again, if his horse threw him, where's his horse?'

Miss Pink said quietly, 'Is it possible he could have had some kind of medical problem, like a slight stroke, and he forgot all about the packhorse? He felt ill and came out to the ghost town as the nearest place to get help? Someone was there.'

'I wonder if those people are on the phone — '

'Someone's at Benefit?' Val put in. 'Who?'

'We'll call Sam, he might know.' Sophie was taking the initiative. 'I'll go to Edna, see if by any chance Charlie's called home — from somewhere, anywhere; if he hasn't we'll send Byer up to the cabin, see if Charlie left any indication . . . Val, you call Sam, ask him who's at Benefit and get their number, then you call them. And ask Sam to contact Bret Ryan, find out if he knows anything.' She glanced at Miss Pink meaningly. 'Melinda, will you explain about Jen and Charlie?'

'What the hell!' Val gaped. '*Jen?* And *Charlie*? What's going on?'

'She'll tell you.' Sophie mounted her horse and cantered down the drive. Val turned to

Miss Pink, wide-eyed and angry.

There wasn't much to tell because she left out the essence of Jen's telephone call, shrinking from being the one to tell the mother that her daughter had been pregnant and had gone to her grandfather for assistance. She said only that Charlie had fixed a meeting at the cabin for some time yesterday. And that was that, she assured the stunned woman; this was all she knew and there had been no subsequent developments — again to her knowledge. That, at least, was the truth.

Val wasted no time asking what Miss Pink knew of her relationship with her daughter, she flung indoors to telephone Sam Jardine. Miss Pink started to unsaddle. She took her time and was still rubbing the mare down when Val emerged to say that no one had any news of Charlie, but that Sam said Bret Ryan had rented a cabin at Benefit and was to start work for him this coming week. Miss Pink looked expectant and Val went on reluctantly, 'Sam says our daughter is around, somewhere.' She assumed an air of nonchalance. 'She could be with Bret Ryan, even at Benefit — that is, if she isn't with Sam himself.' She hardly knew what she was saying. She looked out across the canyon, then her gaze travelled upstream to where the cabin would be and her eyes came back to the older woman. She looked terrified.

Guessing the reason for that terror Miss Pink said, 'The most likely explanation is that the stallion threw your father.'

'I hope so.' Val stared at the other, her eyes unfocused. Was she trying to find a connection between her daughter visiting her grandfather and the man being missing at this moment? She said dully, 'Edna says Charlie hasn't phoned home. Sophie says I have to call Byer, send him up to the cabin.'

Miss Pink glanced at the sky. 'It'll be dark soon.'

'He's got a couple of hours of daylight and then there's a moon. Maybe he won't find Charlie but if the stud's anywhere near the trail he'll come to the other horse; horses hate being on their own out there.'

She called Byer and then announced that she was going to Glenaffric. Miss Pink guessed that she wanted to question Edna regarding Jen's telephone call. She left in her pick-up and Miss Pink, grateful for the chance to relax, dehydrated after a hot day, found beer in the refrigerator and collapsed in one of the porch chairs.

Alone, she became aware of her isolation. There was no house in sight, although she could see the cottonwoods round Byer's place and the tip of the roof that would be Clyde's cabin. He'd left very sharply, she mused, he could hardly have taken time to shower and change after he'd helped Val with unloading.

There was a pounding of hoofs in the dust, the click of steel on stone and the grey appeared. Sophie slid down and eyed her uncertainly. 'This is turning out to be a problem,' she said.

'How is Edna?'

'Difficult to tell. She's a fluffy person until there's a real emergency, then she goes quiet. Val will stay with her. We'll go home; there's nothing we can do here.'

Miss Pink was taken aback. 'Don't bother about me. Shouldn't we stay, in case?'

'In case of what? If he comes in under his own steam: walking because his horse broke its leg, whatever, then that's fine. If he doesn't come in, or the horse comes in without him, there's nothing we can do until daylight. If he's on the trail Erik will find him. If he's off it, he could be anywhere. We have absolutely no idea where to start looking.'

Miss Pink had to accept this. With all those gullies and buttresses dropping hundreds of feet to the river the terrain was rougher than in the mountains proper. You can get out from a big cliff and study it through binoculars but there was no way you could study the Black Canyon — and moonlight only deepened the shadows. She got up stiffly and went to give Sophie a hand with her horse.

* * *

They parked the Cherokee and entered the Rothbury by the back way, a route that took them past the open door of the kitchen. A thickset woman was talking to a man in whites and, catching Sophie's eye, made a gesture to detain her. 'Pat,' Sophie murmured. Miss Pink had the impression that Pat Kramer had been watching out for them.

Introductions were made as they moved along the passage. Russell's wife was no beauty but her make-up was deftly applied, her thick hair well cut and rinsed silver, while her frock in shades of blue was expensive and chic. She looked powerful rather than heavy and every inch the successful businesswoman, except that at this moment she was obviously ill at ease.

The lobby was empty, although the restaurant hummed with activity. Pat lowered her voice as she faced Sophie. 'What happened?' she demanded. Miss Pink's brain raced, looking for connections.

'We don't know.' Sophie showed no surprise. 'Byer's gone up the trail as far as the hunting cabin.'

'There's no sign of Charlie's horse?'

'Only the pack-horse. That broke free and came down alone.'

'But Val and Clyde were there last night. I don't see how, if they were all camped together — '

'They weren't, Pat. Val was several miles upstream. Charlie was on his own.'

'Oh.' The woman turned to Miss Pink. 'I'm not a backwoods person.' She sounded apologetic. 'I envy all you intrepid ladies. The Black Canyon has this reputation, isn't that so, Sophie? You have to be very brave to have gone in there today.' This to Miss Pink again.

'How did you know we were there?' Miss Pink appeared embarrassed, saying the first thing that came to mind.

Pat looked from her to Sophie. 'My husband — Russell — you met him? Of course you did' — she sounded arch — 'you were in Irving with him. He went to Billings on business. We have an apartment there. Val called him.' There was a pause. 'They're friendly,' she added carelessly. Another pause. 'And Russell called me.' Her tone changed, became brisk. 'But you must be exhausted. Let me get you something to drink.'

Sophie declined for both of them. They needed showers; she'd let Pat know if there was any news.

They were quiet in the lift but as soon as they closed the door of the apartment Sophie said, 'You worked it out?'

'Not really. I'm not taking things in. Tell me.'

'When Russell goes to Billings 'on business' Clyde joins him. Pat knows, of course; I told you they have a good relationship, she and Russell. Val knows too. Clyde has to come home now in view of Charlie being missing so Val called the Billings apartment from Glenaffric. Evidently she got Russell just. Clyde hadn't arrived yet. Russell called Pat. Now do you see?'

'It's immaterial. I was merely surprised that Pat should know Charlie was missing virtually as soon as we did.'

'Not *missing*,' Sophie corrected sharply. 'A bit late coming home, that's all.'

But they both knew that every hour that passed without his showing meant that for some reason he was prevented from coming home.

5

Miss Pink tipped her hat brim to shield her eyes from the brilliant sun. 'I have no sense of urgency,' she complained. 'Is it possible that Charlie can be playing some kind of practical joke?'

'He'd never dare go this far.' Sophie was grim. 'It's too public and the guy's vain. Folk would say he was senile if he'd planned a disappearance just in order to annoy his family. And there's the packhorse: what self-respecting rancher is going to leave an animal tied without food or water?'

'Well, you wouldn't.' Miss Pink wasn't really listening, nor was she attending to her horse. Aware that the search could take them over even rougher ground than yesterday, she was mounted on Sophie's grey: old Jake, who plodded like a cart-horse and could be trusted to avoid holes. So she wasn't watching the ground, she was thinking. 'In different circumstances,' she said, 'you might suspect a staged disappearance to avoid creditors or as an insurance scam, that kind of thing. But Charlie's a rich man.'

'He's had an accident. We'll find him; we

have enough people looking.'

That was doubtful. Hundreds wouldn't be enough to search the Black Canyon and they had around eight — 'around' because Edna was covering the ground between Glenaffric and the river in a Jeep, which couldn't really be called searching. They did have a helicopter, privately hired. The sheriff had been informed that Charlie was missing but, with no chopper at his disposal, he was relieved when Edna said she'd hire one herself. As for the ground search, the trail was being covered from Ballard to the hunting camp, even beyond, to the lake.

At first light Miss Pink and Sophie had ridden the section between the swing bridge and the town on the premise that Charlie, after a fall from his horse, could have been disorientated, or the horse, riderless, could have gone that way because it wouldn't cross the bridge. They'd found nothing, however, and were now riding over the grasslands above the canyon, making for the lake.

'This country is too big,' Miss Pink protested. 'Look at it. Eight people and a helicopter: what can they do?'

'You'd be surprised. People do go missing and are never found, but that's way back in the high country. The canyon's wild and dangerous but we know where he is, even if we can't pinpoint the place. We've only just started — and here's Bret Ryan. Now I wonder — ' A lone rider was approaching. 'If Jen's at Benefit she's keeping clear of the family,' she went on, 'except for Charlie.'

'We have to find her,' Miss Pink said. 'She could have been the last person — ' She stopped, appalled.

Sophie seemed not to notice any sinister significance in the words. 'Bret will tell us where she is,' she said firmly. 'He has to tell us. Val says both he and Sam are being cagey. I won't have that.'

His horse was tall but the man suited it; long and lanky himself, he appeared relaxed as he pushed through the sage but the eyes under the dark hat were intent. He sported a thick moustache, which gave him the air of an old-timer, accentuated by the buttoned-up, long-sleeved shirt and fringed chaps. He acknowledged Miss Pink with a nod, unsmiling, and shook hands.

'Is Jen coming?' Sophie asked.

He raised an eyebrow. 'Jen — Jardine, ma'am?'

'We know she's here.'

'I guess she's about somewhere.' He held her gaze but he was defiant rather than honest. 'Maybe she'll meet up with us.

How many people do you have and where are they?'

That, at least, was authoritative and Sophie had to back down, allowing the problem of Charlie to take precedence. She filled him in on the disposition of the searchers. Val and Clyde were concentrating on the area of the landslide, Clyde having driven back last night from Billings; Erik Byer was on his way to the hunting camp. He had been told to go there last night, she said, but he retreated from the landslide saying he was unable to see anything below the trail for the moon shadow. Actually, Miss Pink thought he would have had the last of the daylight when he reached the landslide but — a foreigner and a stranger to the canyon — she said nothing.

Sam Jardine would be joining them, Sophie told Ryan; as for himself, he was to do what he thought fit but they were all to rendezvous at Mazarine Lake and decide what to do if nothing had been discovered by that time.

He looked thoughtful. 'Where will you guys be?'

Sophie hesitated. 'If I have a choice,' Miss Pink put in, 'I'd prefer not to go over the landslide, nor down that steep bit we came up yesterday.'

'Someone should do it,' Sophie said. 'Bret,

would you? You know: the cut-off that goes down the escarpment upstream of the landslip?'

'If you came up it yesterday — '

'We weren't looking for sign. You take that section and we'll go along the top to the lake. I think I can remember the line. I was with Val when she got a moose up there one time.'

Ryan opened his mouth, caught Miss Pink's eye and thought better of it. He chewed his moustache. Miss Pink realised he was considerably younger than he appeared: late twenties, she hazarded; the clothes and his bearing disguised his youth.

Sophie stiffened. 'I can hear the helicopter. We'd better split or they could think we've found something, bunched together like this.'

They moved off, the horses alert as the helicopter flew up the canyon, hidden from view but noisy in that confined space. When the upper band of cliffs showed ahead Ryan left them, making for the precipitous drop into the canyon; the others stayed high, walking side by side where it was possible.

'Jen's with him,' Sophie said with finality. 'If she's not, he knows where she is.'

'Perhaps you should have told him that you know she met her grandfather at the cabin. That's important.'

'If she's with Bret, he knows already. If not — well, he isn't family.'

'What difference does that make — in the circumstances? Jen might know something about Charlie's movements after she left the cabin.'

'How could she? Listen, Melinda, it could be just an evil joke on Charlie's part. You don't know the man.' Which was not only a contradiction of her earlier statement but a curious choice of words. An *evil* joke?

They came to rocks and were forced into single file. Now the walls of the canyon were occasionally visible below on their right. They passed groups of antelope and there were bluebirds in the aspens — and still there was no real sense of urgency.

They rode slowly, working sideways to find the way across a draw or to turn an outcrop or a cluster of trees. This wasn't correct procedure on a search; they should be investigating obstacles, not avoiding them. Miss Pink felt distinctly uncomfortable.

They came to a slope leading to a ridge. 'This was where Val shot her moose that time,' Sophie said. 'You can see miles from the top.'

They crested the rise, emerging to a stiff breeze and a superb view. Way down in the south, in Wyoming, the Teton range sparkled on the horizon, while below them was Mazarine Lake where they'd lunched yesterday: a sapphire set in green enamel. Immediately below there was rock scree under the ragged escarpment. The upper slopes of the corrie held random clusters of fine conifers.

'They got here before us,' Sophie said, her eyes fixed. 'What are they doing over there?'

'Who? Where?'

'That *is* a horse, isn't it — under the scarp? Or is it a moose? It's not moving. Maybe it's a rock.'

'This is a horse, anyway.' Miss Pink, unable to see what was attracting her companion, had shifted her attention to the near side of the basin where a rider on a piebald had appeared.

'That's Byer,' Sophie said, 'he rides a pinto. Ah, there's Val — and Clyde. And there's Bret, know him anywhere, he sits so tall. We'd better get down there and — Wait a minute! Then who's — ' She turned back to the far side of the corrie. 'Could be Sam Jardine,' she muttered, raising her binoculars. Miss Pink had hers up already, trying to find the focus.

'It *is* a horse,' Sophie insisted. 'And it's a sorrel, but I can't see . . . there's a rock in the way, and juniper. It doesn't move. That's weird. It's standing up but it doesn't move.'

'I see it. The stallion's a sorrel, isn't it?'

They shouted to Val and started to descend obliquely, the others making their way up the slope to join them. 'It's probably a total stranger,' Sophie said. 'There'll be more people around somewhere, and horses. Sorrel's a common colour.'

The parties converged and everyone fell in behind Sophie. The others hadn't seen the solitary horse, which was invisible from below. Sophie repeated, diffidently, that there was most likely another party here, perhaps lunching, but everyone knew that with the pretty lake and meadows below no one was going to move up into rocks to picnic.

The horse neighed as they approached, to be answered by a high whinny from Val's mare. They couldn't see the sorrel until they came round a spread of junipers. It was the Glenaffric stallion.

He was facing away from them but his head was turned, his eyes rolling. He was bridled but the heavy Western saddle was under his belly. He was filthy with mud and sweat, and there was a nasty cut on a hind leg.

They dismounted. Leaving Miss Pink with

the horses, the others moved forward, Val first and talking quietly. The stallion's head drooped. Val said, 'There's a stirrup fast in the rocks. How long's he been here?'

No one responded. Miss Pink wondered where Charlie could be. And why had the stallion come this way instead of heading for home?

The animal was exhausted. Once the saddle had slipped he would have tried to kick it free and then wandered until the stirrup caught in a crevice among the boulders. Why he should have gone up to the rocks in the first place was a mystery — 'Unless he were being chased,' Bret Ryan said. 'Like a bear was after him.'

They freed him, removed the saddle and took him to the other horses. There was no spirit left in him; he was lame, he'd lost a shoe and there were more cuts on his legs and chest, but he could walk. Both reins had been snapped but the halter was still in place, the end knotted on his neck.

They mounted and fanned out, Miss Pink in the rear, leading the stallion, its saddle in place again, padded where the cinch had rubbed him sore. All eyes were on the ground, looking for his tracks as they tried to reverse his trail. Once, glancing up, Miss Pink caught a flicker of movement and glimpsed a rider on a pale horse turn on the skyline and disappear. Sam Jardine evidently, about to join them, looking for a way down.

The others pushed ahead, drifting lower. The stallion lagged, limping, not wanting to turn downhill, so Miss Pink started to contour the slope on a faint game trail. The sorrel was happier on the level; could he have come into the corrie by this route? She peered at the ground beyond her horse's head. There were prints of horseshoes in the dust but then she — or Sophie — could have trodden this path as they descended; neither had noticed minor features like a game trail.

Below her Val had stopped. 'Keep with us, Mel,' she called.

'He's too lame. He doesn't want to go downhill.'

The others conferred. Miss Pink felt chastened; she was a nuisance, she couldn't even lead a docile horse.

'Join us when you can,' Sophie shouted. 'If he won't lead, I'll come up and drive him.'

Miss Pink would have liked to ask why she couldn't take the stallion home by way of the easy ground on top, but the others were moving again.

After a few hundred yards the game trail

entered a belt of timber and the sorrel pulled back, almost dragging the halter rope from her hand. His feet were planted, his eyes fixed — not wildly, he was past being wild — but he didn't like those trees.

'Look,' she said, trying to soothe him with her voice, 'no bears are going to hang around with all these people about . . . ' His ears twitched and then she felt Jake's muscles harden. Surely this old horse wasn't going to bolt? She prayed she could hold the two of them. She called to the others but they were out of sight, below the trees. She turned downhill to catch them up and to her relief the sorrel followed, limping but trying to hurry. Bears lying up, she wondered, or lying in ambush?

She rounded the lowest trees. The others were waiting below. She stopped and waved. After a moment Sophie came towards her. 'There's something in the timber.' She pointed. 'The stud won't continue along the trail.'

'There's no trail except the one by the lake.'

'A game trail. A horse has come along it. I think he came that way.'

Sophie looked doubtful. 'There can't be a bear in the timber, we'd have frightened it off, but if it's Charlie in there it would explain why the chopper hasn't spotted him. I'll tell the others.'

It was unlikely that the chopper had come this far because apparently the crew hadn't spotted the stallion. Or if they had seen the horse they'd attached no significance to it. A fat lot of good it did to hire such an expensive machine . . . Miss Pink's nerves were jangling, backlash to her state of mind earlier when she'd complained that there was no sense of urgency.

The others arrived and they filed up the slope, Jake leading, Sophie crowding the sorrel from behind. They came to the game trail and turned along it. The sorrel stopped. Sophie flicked him with her reins but he wouldn't budge. Jake's ears were flat — and now Sophie's horse was trying to back away.

Bret Ryan stepped down, handed his reins to Byer and walked into the trees. They sat like statues watching him through the trunks. He stopped and looked down. Then he came back. 'He's there,' he said.

He'd lost colour under the tan. Sophie made an instinctive gesture towards Val who disregarded it. She was staring at Ryan. He shook his head.

They tied the horses and walked into the trees. Charlie was unrecognisable, but no one questioned the identity of the thing on the ground. He was naked and flayed. Not quite naked, he was still wearing a belt — with a sheath but no knife — and there was a sock on the left foot. He wasn't completely flayed either; the left leg below the knee was more or less intact although dislocated at the ankle. The sight was reminiscent of a carcass in an abattoir.

Sophie murmured something to Val. 'It doesn't *matter*!' Val exclaimed. 'It's only a shell.'

Clyde was leaning against a tree, his chest heaving. Miss Pink saw that Ryan was watching her as if wondering what she was doing there. They were all in shock. Someone had to say something. 'How did this happen?' she asked.

'He woulda been mounting,' Byer said doubtfully, not looking at anyone, 'and his horse spooked and drug him.'

Miss Pink frowned at the body and moved away, not without purpose, following a track that was now all too plain. The body would have been a terrifying encumbrance and the horse had blundered through the timber like a crazed elephant. A few yards away a boot lay on the ground: not greatly worn but the leather gouged like a wound at the ankle where it had been held by the stirrup.

Charlie's foot would have slipped as the stallion threw him and the weight of the suspended body had twisted the stirrup, trapping him until the leg slipped out of the boot. As Byer said, he'd been dragged to death. She shuddered. How long had it taken to die?

They returned to the horses and discussed what action to take, or rather Ryan and Sophie discussed, Miss Pink pondered, while Byer left decision-making to the others, presumably thinking that an employee's opinion carried no weight when the family was present. As for Val, she appeared to be trying to comfort Clyde. He stood on the far side of his horse, his hands and head on the saddle, the picture of grief — or shock, or both.

A stranger was riding along the trail by the lake. 'Who's that?' Miss Pink asked.

'Looks like Sam Jardine,' Sophie said.

'Jardine?' Miss Pink echoed. 'I thought — ' She looked towards the escarpment. That horse had been pale. Jardine was on a dark bay. She observed him curiously as he came up. He was a small, spare man with a grizzled beard and surprisingly delicate features for one who was a ranch hand, or had been until he ran off with Val. She watched with interest as he received the news. He dismounted and entered the trees. He came back visibly shaken — as who wouldn't be?

'Sorry about that,' came Sophie's voice, 'but Jake's the only horse will tolerate it. Is that all right with you, Melinda?'

'What was that? I was miles away. Do what?'

They had decided to take the body out themselves because they had no way of contacting the helicopter; in any event, there was nowhere for it to land except on top and once they'd put the body on a horse the easiest option was to continue to Benefit. They would avoid the canyon and go back by the route that Miss Pink and Sophie had followed this morning. Someone must go down to the cabin for blankets and to leave Charlie's saddle there. The stallion was too sore to carry it to Benefit.

Jake was the quietest animal so he was to be the pack-horse. Jardine and Ryan started to lash the spare saddle on top of Miss Pink's. Val said she would go down to the cabin as well, while the others were looking for Charlie's rifle.

'His rifle?' Miss Pink echoed. She had overlooked the fact that there was a scabbard on the saddle.

'Of course.' Sophie was impatient. 'He brought one. Had to, with bears about.

It'll be somewhere nearby.' She came closer. 'And his clothing,' she murmured. 'We can't leave that lying around.'

'But his clothes will be strung out for miles,' Miss Pink whispered.

'It gives us something to do while you're gone. And Lord knows, this track's easy enough to follow.'

'What about Clyde?' He had moved away to sit on a rock and stare at the lake.

'I'll look after him. You two get off now and fetch those blankets.'

Miss Pink walked, leading Jake. Val followed, keeping an eye on the ungainly load, so there was no opportunity to talk until they reached the cabin. When they arrived Val retrieved a key from a crack in the logs and unlocked the door. 'So he had locked up,' Miss Pink observed, stepping over the sill. There was no response from Val who had gone back to Jake for the saddle.

It was a one-room cabin with four windows, all shuttered. Either Charlie had put the shutters up as he was about to leave or he'd never taken them down. The light admitted by the open door showed a stove, bunk beds, a solid table and a number of folding chairs stacked against one wall. There was an armchair with its stuffing protruding, shelves with cans of food, saucepans, crockery and a large blue enamel coffee pot.

Val came in, dropped the saddle on the floor and picked up several neatly folded blankets. 'Do you need more?' Miss Pink asked.

'No, this is enough. Lock up, will you?'

She took one last look round. The term 'spick and span' came to mind and she wondered why. Such an old-fashioned phrase, almost archaic, inappropriate. But was it? It meant tidy, clean or cleaned up, and that was what this cabin was.

'Are you coming?' The tone was harsh. The woman was still in shock, of course; after all, she was Charlie's daughter.

'Was your father a domesticated man?' she asked as she untied Jake's halter. As if she'd not witnessed the man's behaviour at home, had heard no gossip from Sophie.

'God, no! Why?' It was barked out.

'Because he left the place like — well, like a woman would.'

Val snorted angrily. 'Wilderness manners; you have to leave a cabin clean for the next person to use it. *You* should know that, for heaven's sakes; you're a mountaineer.'

She was rigid with hostility, as if she'd reached the next stage of shock: determined to whitewash the image of Charlie, the ogre of Glenaffric. Odd, then, that she should seize on such a trivial feature, maintaining the old autocrat was house-trained. Such an obvious lie.

6

In the middle of the afternoon, the hottest part of the day, the cortège started back to Benefit. Miss Pink was still on foot, having ridiculed the suggestion that she might find the walk tiring. Jake plodded behind her, not bothered about his load once it was on his back. They'd tied a bandanna over his eyes as the blanketed form was heaved across the saddle, and boxed him in to prevent his moving. But Jake was no kicker; he'd had deer carcasses on his back, a corpse didn't make all that much difference. In addition he carried the remnants that had been found along the stallion's back-trail: a shirt that was no more than a bloody rag, a stained bandanna, Charlie's wallet: open but with credit cards in place, and some dollar bills. These, and the boot, had been crammed into a plastic bag from Safeway's supermarket, adding a bizarre trim to the gelding's load. The rifle had not been found, nor the other boot.

Val led the stallion, bringing up the rear with Clyde. Sophie was with Miss Pink. The rest rode ahead in a bunch, giving an impression of distancing themselves from the women and their burden. Close to Benefit Ryan broke away and cantered ahead. Watching him go, Miss Pink said, 'There was a rider on a pale horse, a buckskin probably, on the rim above the lake. D'you think that was Jen?'

'I guess.' Sophie sounded tired. 'Could be her on one of Bret's horses. Did you mention it to Val?'

'No, because I thought it could well be Jen, and we don't need any more complications today.'

'Thoughtful of you. Jen has to be with Bret. She'd have wanted to help search for her grand-daddy but she'd be bothered about meeting her mother at this time, not to speak of all the rest of us. I wonder if this' — she glanced at Jake's load — 'if it'll affect her . . . I mean, her relationship with her mother. Will it heal the breach?'

'It could depend on why she went in the first place — '

'But we know that. She went because — '

' — and what was said when they met.'

'When — they — met?'

'Jen and her grandfather. At the cabin two days ago.'

Sophie's horse stumbled and she pulled him up so jerkily that he jumped in surprise.

Miss Pink waited for him to settle, aware that the stumble could have been the result of a sudden tightening of the rider's muscles.

Sophie took her time, walking carefully round a sprawl of sage, coming back, looking ahead. 'Bret's away to telephone the chopper people,' she said. 'You can't take the body into town on the back of a pick-up.'

Miss Pink reflected that it was more likely Ryan had gone ahead to warn Jen of the approach of her mother. As if telepathic, Sophie said with sudden vehemence, 'It could be a total stranger you saw on the rim. Jen doesn't have to be in the area at all, she could be miles away. We know she called Charlie but she could have changed her mind about meeting him. You didn't find anything to show she'd been in the cabin, did you?'

'No. Have you asked Sam about her? Surely the first person she'd contact on her return would be her father, given that she hasn't been in touch with Val?'

'Well' — Sophie avoided Miss Pink's eye — 'I'm just the great-aunt, you know? And neither Sam nor Bret had anything to say about Jen when Val spoke to them last evening, only that she was around. We've been more concerned with Charlie, haven't we? Like now' — she glanced over her shoulder — 'I wouldn't have expected Clyde to take it so to heart, but he always was highly strung, even as a kid.'

Actually, Clyde was in better shape now, taking the stallion's rope from Val who trotted past the women to overtake Jardine and Byer. She didn't stop there but drew ahead with Jardine, leaving Byer on his own.

'Private business,' Sophie observed, and then, 'We have to think about Edna.'

'She has her family for support.' With the exception of her granddaughter. How soon would Jen appear? It was unlikely that the girl would be waiting at Benefit, at least to be visibly present. Having to face family and friends after ten years' absence would be bad enough; in the circumstances, escorting the body of her grandfather, the situation could be unbearable for her. 'Some good could come of it,' Miss Pink murmured, to be taken up by Sophie immediately.

'For whom?'

'Everyone. Jen will surely come to the funeral. Families draw together after a death and Charlie was the head of the family. I suppose it's possible' — Miss Pink seemed to be talking to herself — 'that he left his granddaughter well provided for.'

'Probably, I would think.'

'You mean you — that is, Edna — doesn't know?'

'Yes, I do know.' Subterfuge was difficult with Miss Pink, especially when one was tired. 'It's not a surprising will, if you know the background. The bulk of his fortune's left between members of the family, although most unfairly in my opinion. Jen gets the lion's share; she's going to be very rich indeed and she gets the horses — most of 'em. Edna is to live at Glenaffric for her lifetime, although the ranch is willed to Jen.'

'And Clyde and Val?'

'About half a million each, I believe. Enough so's folk won't talk but not much considering Charlie's — was — a multimillionaire. There are bequests to institutions and charities, the usual kind of thing. Like I said, it's not surprising, except in degree. It's hard on Edna but she gets to keep her home and presumably Jen will provide the upkeep since the house will belong to her.'

'Do the beneficiaries know the provisions?'

'How formal you are, Melinda. Yes, they know. Not from Charlie directly but by way of Edna. Jen won't know unless Charlie told her. I get five of Ali's colts, incidentally, and that's a sick joke. Charlie knew I didn't like Ali. However, the colts will fetch a tidy sum in a sale; no way am I going to ride any of

’em, let alone put anyone else up on ’em.’

‘So Jen has to appear in order to claim her inheritance,’ Miss Pink said absently and then, quickly, ‘I’m sorry, that was in bad taste.’

‘Not at all.’ Sophie was unperturbed. ‘I don’t give a damn what brings her back as long as she comes back. Val’s suffered too much over this business. I’m willing to bet that at this moment she’s far more concerned about Jen than about the load old Jake’s carrying.’

Miss Pink looked to make sure the load wasn’t slipping. ‘Does she know that Jen was pregnant when she left?’

‘Edna’s told her but it didn’t come as a surprise. Val and I had held so many post-mortems over the years that we’d considered it ourselves: that she could have left to have a baby.’ And now they knew that the girl had rejected her mother and gone to her grandfather for help. But they had only Charlie’s word for it that she’d been pregnant; if he was lying about that he was a monster. Charlie Gunn had a lot to answer for. Miss Pink smiled grimly. And, in a way, he’d answered for it.

‘Joke?’ Sophie asked.

‘He was a nasty piece of work, your brother-in-law.’

'Now he's gone I'd prefer to forget that we were related, even by marriage.'

The helicopter was at Benefit. It had landed on what would have been the main street when the mines were in production. Now it was no more than a stretch of dust bordered by the few houses left standing. Most structures had collapsed, probably under the weight of winter snows.

Miss Pink relinquished her horse and its burden to the men and moved back. Ostensibly she was keeping out of their way but in reality she was on the alert for a pale horse. She didn't expect to see its rider.

Bret Ryan's cabin was obvious: the only one with glass in its windows and a screen door. It stood a few yards back from the street, shaded by cottonwoods. The roof was shingled, the chimney stack built of bricks. A serviceable pick-up stood at the gate of a garden full of marigolds. There were corrals at the back, a barn, sheds and the usual collection of rusting trucks. The horses in a corral were dark; Miss Pink moved to see into the others when — 'You riding with me, ma'am?' Sam Jardine called, trudging through the dust to a pick-up and trailer. She started to say no, she'd go home on her horse and then she remembered that this was Jen's father. She beamed.

'That would save me five miles,' she admitted, 'and I'm saddle-sore. But isn't it out of your way?' He lived down the valley, towards Irving.

'I'm taking the stud to Val's place. Saves him the walk too. Val's gonna look after him. Can't expect Edna to be in a fit state to doctor him, 'specially when he starts to recover. He'll soon be hisself again, there's no bones broke.'

They loaded the horses in the trailer. The others rode away towards the swing bridge and, once all the animals were clear, the helicopter took off. There was no hurry, no urgency.

In the cab of Sam's pick-up Miss Pink stretched her legs and sighed deeply. He glanced at her, concerned. 'Nasty thing for you to see, ma'am.'

'Oh, that. I'm used to it, Mr Jardine. I'm just relieved to be sitting on a seat that doesn't move.'

'You're used to bodies? How's that?'

'I was in Search and Rescue.' The lie came easily. 'Falls down mountains can produce the most bizarre injuries, although I've never seen anything like this. How could it have happened?'

'Why, he were drug. You saw the ground: rocks and stuff; clothes would be scraped off of him first, then the skin.'

'I meant how could this happen to an expert rider? First he was thrown, then his boot was caught in the stirrup. Two coincidences: isn't that unlikely?'

'It happens.' But he was thinking. 'Third coincidence,' he said. 'Bear stands up from behind a rock: a she-bear with cubs. Up goes the stud, maybe falls over backwards, and Charlie's not ready for it — you see? He could have hit his head as he fell and was knocked unconscious. The weight of the body'd twist that stirrup and his foot would be locked in there. Then his horse bolts.'

She said nothing. The evening sun came streaming to light the ridges and deepen the shadows in the canyons. Timber was a folded green pelt, crags were rosy, water was silk set in emeralds. She saw none of it, she was seeing a body suspended, hurtling and bouncing over rocks.

'Does Jen ride a buckskin?' she asked at length.

'Jen — my girl? A buckskin? I wouldn't know.' He paused. 'Was there a buckskin at Benefit?'

'There was a rider on one above the lake, on the canyon rim.'

'And you thought it could be Jen.' He showed no surprise nor resentment that she should be privy to this family secret.

'I hoped it was her.'

He nodded. 'I were wondering if she was holed up with Bret Ryan. She'll be in touch shortly. Can't do nothing else now she's come this far. She'll be missing her mom. Bret will work on her, convince her she has to do the right thing. She's a good kid at heart. He'll make her see sense.'

She didn't pursue the subject; she was relieved to find him a sensible man and well-disposed towards his former wife.

They unloaded the horses at Val's ranch and he drove away, Miss Pink insisting that she could cope with the animals, it would be something to do while she waited for the riders. In fact, she'd scarcely finished brushing Jake when Sophie arrived. She had left Val and Clyde at the swing bridge and they'd gone straight to Glenaffric. 'They'll stay with Edna,' she said, 'so we'll tend to this animal' — eyeing Ali grimly — 'put some stuff on those cuts and then we'll head for home. What did Sam have to say? Any news of Jen?'

They talked as they worked: unsaddling Sophie's horse first, then Miss Pink held Ali while Sophie went over him carefully, cleaning and dressing the cuts. There was some swelling due to bruising; they'd have the veterinarian out tomorrow, give him a thorough check, make sure nothing had been missed. Val would be here in the morning, Sophie said, Clyde would stay at Glenaffric. She shook her head. 'Edna shouldn't go on living there, the place is far too big for a widow lady. Maybe I can convince her to come to the Rothbury.'

Miss Pink was scratching the stallion's skull, mumbling to him, her eyes glazed. Sophie straightened from a hind leg and stared. Slowly Miss Pink focused.

'You bonded!' Sophie was incredulous.

'It could be that his problem wasn't genetic after all. He had the wrong master. He could have been whipped.'

'I know he was.'

'I mean, back there: at hunting camp, when Charlie was thrown.'

They regarded the horse's dark eyes: clear but sleepy. Sophie said, 'Charlie was about to leave. He'd packed up, cleared the cabin, loaded the pack-horse.'

'Ye-es.' Now what was coming?

'Then he caught sight of a bear.'

'It would be hanging around?'

'Right. Only just in case the sheriff asks questions, I suggest we keep quiet about Jen. Val and Clyde agree. About that phone call, I mean, when Jen called Charlie. Edna needn't have overheard anything. Clyde will convince her to forget it.'

'I won't mention it.' Miss Pink was a bit stuffy. 'It's not my business.'

'Nor the sheriff's. There's no need to complicate matters by mentioning Jen.'

Fine. So the phone call was a coincidence, as was Jen's return at the same time — about the same time — that her grandfather died. As was the fact that Val and Clyde were only a few miles from hunting camp *where* he died. Coincidence, coincidence — and there was yet another, or two: Val and Clyde were each in line for half a million dollars and Jen was in for a whole lot more. Miss Pink shook herself mentally. My criminal mind again, she thought. How fortunate it was that Charlie's death was so obviously the result of an accident.

* * *

It was late by the time they reached the Rothbury. When they entered the apartment Sophie dropped her saddlebags on the floor and made for the drinks cabinet. 'First things first,' she announced, pouring whisky and bourbon with a generous hand. Miss Pink took only a token sip before excusing herself. On the drive home conversation was a monologue; Sophie, evidently anxious to avoid personalities, had concentrated on the disposal of Charlie's horses. Miss Pink had had as much of bloodlines as she could stand. She shut herself in her bathroom, turned on the taps and sat on a padded stool, sipping her drink and too exhausted even to undress.

There was a knock at the door but Sophie was only telling her not to dress, just to put on a robe and they'd eat in the apartment, they'd have dinner sent up from the kitchen.

⋆ ⋆ ⋆

It was another balmy evening. They sat at the window eating lobster Newburg, the food furnishing an excuse not to embark on distasteful topics of conversation. Wondering if Sophie would return to family problems with the conclusion of the meal, about to suggest another early night, Miss Pink was startled by the ringing of the doorbell.

They glanced at each other, then down at their robes. Sophie swallowed and stood up. She looked through the peephole, shrugged and opened the door. Russell Kramer stood there, diffident but solid. The time of evening, the absence of advance notice, indicated the diffidence was assumed.

‘Do I apologise and retreat?’ he asked. ‘Or shall I slip into something more comfortable and join you?’

‘Don’t be silly, Russell.’ Sophie drew him inside. ‘You know you’re always welcome. What will you drink?’

‘Talisker?’ He looked coy.

‘I keep it for him,’ Sophie told Miss Pink who was smiling weakly and wishing she’d combed out her hair after her shower.

Russell sat down with an air of purpose and glanced at the view. ‘Isn’t it a beautiful evening? If the Absarokas weren’t in the way you could see the Tetons.’

Miss Pink’s jaw dropped. She said faintly, ‘If it weren’t for the curve of the earth — ’

‘ — you could see the Colorado plateau,’ Sophie completed drily, placing a bottle, a shot glass and a tiny crystal jug of water in front of him.

‘How are they taking it?’ The sudden switch made him sound aggressive.

Sophie sat down and focused on Miss Pink’s glass. ‘Val is — contained, I’d guess you’d say’ — raising her eyebrows — ‘Clyde was upset, but then he shows his emotions more than her and — well, she talked to him, you know?’

‘It was an appalling shock for him. I mean, Charlie was his father after all.’

The women stared. He stared back, as if mesmerised. 'What I'm saying', he went on haltingly, 'is that when he heard Charlie was missing, he was very concerned. As anyone would be in the circumstances. Charlie is — was — an old man and Clyde said that horse is wild. He was worried that . . . What happened exactly?'

Sophie sipped her bourbon. 'He was thrown but his foot caught in the stirrup and he was dragged . . . It's not a common accident, Russell, but it's the sort of thing could happen to an old person, particularly with a nervous horse.'

'Poor Clyde. And Val — all of you. Terrible: finding the body.'

'How did you know?' Miss Pink asked.

'Clyde called me from Glenaffric. He didn't say much, I guess Edna was close by. No details — except Charlie was thrown from his horse, not even when it happened.' He wasn't asking a question but his eyes were.

'We hadn't really thought about that,' Sophie said. 'We all saw the pack-horse ready to go around noon, so it must have happened yesterday morning.' She frowned, her eyes met Miss Pink's and sheered away.

He left soon afterwards. 'Dear me,' Sophie said, closing the door behind him. 'He's very fond of Clyde.' She started to help Miss Pink who was clearing the coffee table. 'He had to make sure there was no way Clyde could be involved,' she went on. 'Silly boy.'

Miss Pink murmured non-committally. It was uncertain which 'boy' was meant: Clyde or Russell. She hesitated, but it had to be said. 'There's no way it could have been anything other than an accident.'

Sophie gasped. 'Of course it was an accident! What can you be thinking?'

'Not me. The police. There's no need to protect people: Russell trying to make sure Clyde isn't involved — your words. And not mentioning Jen's call to Charlie, or their meeting . . . It looks suspicious — '

'No way is there anything suspicious! Clyde was miles away, Jen was nowhere near the cabin. There's nothing to be suspicious about.'

'I meant that your not wanting to mention those facts looks suspicious in itself.'

'The reason why we're keeping quiet about Jen's phone call is that we're not going to have our family business gossiped about all over the country. Once the sheriff knows, he'll ask why Jen had to go to hunting camp in secret, why couldn't she meet her family in the open, instead of in the back country, and her grandfather on his own at that?

He'll want to know what's wrong with this family. You agreed you wouldn't mention it, Melinda.' She was pleading now.

'How are you going to silence Ryan? If Jen's with him then he knows about the arrangement to meet Charlie, and he's not bound by family loyalty.'

'We can work on him. I tell you, no one need know that she made that phone call. Edna can be persuaded to forget it. You do that too, Melinda. You said yourself: it had to be an accident.'

7

A night's rest and the security of a corral had revived the stallion. When Sophie pulled up outside Val's cabin he was still favouring one leg but his head was up and he'd watched the Cherokee's approach with interest.

'Doesn't he look good?' came Val's voice as she opened the screen door. 'The veterinarian was here and Ali stood like a lamb while he was being examined. Isn't that something? I tell you, this is a different horse.'

'There's no serious damage?' Sophie asked.

'Not physically. Just a sprain. 'Fact, he's more tractable now than he was before. Mind you, it could be a different story when we get up on him again.'

Sophie was disapproving. 'There's no need to ride him, Val, even if we do keep him. I don't know that I want to anyway. For heaven's sakes, who gets Ali? I have no idea.' They stared at each other.

Miss Pink marvelled how they could focus on trivial concerns when the previous owner had been virtually kicked to death by the animal. Her eyes strayed to the hoofs. No sign of blood there.

'Who's this?' Sophie asked. A pick-up and trailer were coming along the track, slowing for the entrance to the homestead.

'That trailer was at Benefit,' Miss Pink said. If this were Bret Ryan, Jen could be with him, which would explain the wary stance of the others. She was pleased, happy for them, then she tensed in her turn. It *was* Ryan and he was alone.

He parked with care, turning in the space between cabin and corral. The women hadn't moved. He walked towards them, stiff in the face of their united attention. 'Hi, Bret,' Val said, rather too loudly. She indicated the stallion. 'No harm done. The veterinarian says the leg's just a sprain.'

He nodded and regarded the horse without expression. Sophie was frowning at the trailer. No horse was visible through the slats. Val said neutrally, 'You'll stay for coffee, Bret?'

'I just come for the stud,' he said.

The women were immobile. A yellow butterfly flickered past the group, the horse lowered his head and plucked at a weed.

'We're not with you,' Sophie said.

He inhaled sharply and looked towards the creek. He said distantly, 'Charlie left the stud to Jen. She wants him there.' He swallowed. 'At Benefit.'

Val's eyes widened and she started to

shake. Sophie moved in front of her and said, not unpleasantly, 'If Jen has business with her family, Bret, she must come herself and discuss it. There's no way family property can be distributed like this, and so soon. You have no authority.'

'I do. She's my wife.'

Someone gasped. He went on hurriedly, 'She needs time to — to think things through. She just lost her grand-daddy' — he flicked a hostile glance at Val — 'so she's asked me to pick up the stud. He's valuable. She wants the care of him.'

'He's not hers yet.' Sophie was harsh but then her tone changed. 'Is that right: you two are married? When did this happen?'

'A few weeks since.' He looked sulky now: a long beanpole of a fellow, embarrassed in the presence of older women, two of whom were now his in-laws, if he was to be believed.

'Where did you marry?' Sophie asked.

'In Billings.' He returned her stare. 'I have the licence back home.'

'It doesn't make any difference.' Val was listless, as if she were past emotion. 'But she can't have the stud. It stays here.'

'He's hers!' His voice rose.

'No, he isn't,' Sophie said coldly. 'The will hasn't been read and it has to be probated.

You can't know the conditions.'

'She does. He told her. Charlie did.'

'My father was a liar,' Val said, without heat. 'He may have told her he'd left the stud to her and anything else he cared to name. That doesn't mean it's true.'

'Her dad says it's true.'

'Oh, my God! You're telling us she's seen her *dad*? He's always — '

'That's enough,' Sophie put in quickly. 'It doesn't matter who says what. This horse is staying here until the will's probated. Not just because it's a valuable animal, the same would apply if it were a dude horse. We have to observe the rules, Bret. You go back and tell Jen that. At the same time, since you're now family, you might suggest that it would have been more courteous for her to come here in person instead of sending a messenger, even if you are married to her.'

Miss Pink moved away, acutely embarrassed. Sophie was hard on the man but it was justified. He must have known he was out of order. The situation was awkward, fraught with difficulties.

Behind her, the pick-up started and moved slowly down the drive; his frustration wasn't apparent in his driving.

'It's monstrous!' Val exploded. 'I can't believe it of Sam.'

'Sam didn't send him,' Sophie pointed out.

'But they've been in touch! He's saying he has no idea where she is.' Val whirled on Miss Pink. 'You rode home with him yesterday; did he tell you he'd seen Jen?'

'No. He did say he'd wondered if she could be holed up with Ryan.'

'I'll kill the bastard!'

She strode towards the cabin. Sophie shook her head and sighed. 'What must you be thinking of us all?'

'Apart from his ignorance of business etiquette, Ryan doesn't seem a bad fellow,' Miss Pink said comfortably. 'He could make a good husband — and Jen has come back — almost.'

'Huh! 'Almost' is the operative word. Now this problem' — she gestured angrily at the stallion — 'could take us right back to square one.'

'It'll blow over. It's only a horse.'

'Only! That horse is worth thousands.'

'Even then it's not so important as the other problem: the one that drove Jen away originally.'

'But she came back — to Sam,' Sophie muttered. 'That's hit Val hard. She thought Sam was her friend. He's played her a shabby trick.' They could hear Val's voice raised inside the cabin. 'I wonder how he'll explain himself,' she said.

They turned to contemplate the stallion. After a while the screen door crashed open. 'He denies it!' Val shouted. 'He swears it isn't true! Who's lying around here? I'm going to Benefit and find Jen — '

'No, Val!' Sophie hurried after her as she made for her pick-up. Miss Pink leaned against the rails, an uneasy spectator, but not for long. After a few minutes during which Ali walked over to have his head scratched, the others approached. 'I'm going to Benefit,' Sophie told her, while Val looked mutinous. 'Val insists someone must go to Jen, her being so near, and if I don't, she will, and I think Jen is more likely to talk to me at this moment. The business about the horse gives us a handle — although why I should need an excuse to talk to my own kin I don't know. But it may work. D'you mind?'

Miss Pink was startled. 'No, no. I can amuse myself — '

'I mean, d'you mind coming with me?'

'Of — course not. Er — why?'

'I'm trusting your presence will keep things on an even keel.' Sophie peered at her doubtfully. 'Is it a presumption? I'm afraid things aren't exactly normal today. As you may have noticed.'

'I'll do what I can to help. Let's go. Might it be an idea to overtake Bret before he has a chance to phone her?'

'I'm going after Sam,' Val said grimly.

'No, you're not.' Sophie was firm. 'There's enough trouble around here without you going and making more with Sam. Besides,' she added slyly, 'someone needs to be here with Ali. Bret could come back and for all we know, Charlie changed his will and the horse is to come to you.'

Val looked at the stallion. 'You could be right. OK, I'll leave it to you — for the time being.' Implying that if anything went wrong at Benefit she would take over. Charlie's death was having wide repercussions.

* * *

As they drove down the Ballard road, Miss Pink said, 'Would it be possible to find out exactly who the horses were left to? You might cite the difficulty of making decisions regarding Ali's treatment: make his condition sound worse than it is. The lawyer who drew up the will mightn't know much about horses.'

'I've been thinking. I wonder if Edna has a copy of the will. I wouldn't say so in front of Bret. You know, I can't believe those two are married, can you?'

'I'm the outsider here. But why not? From what you've said, Jen's impulsive and he'd hardly say he had a marriage certificate if it's not true.'

'She's unpredictable, certainly. Volatile is how I'd describe Jen. She takes after her mother there. I don't know how I'm going to handle this meeting, but you may be sure that if it were Val had gone rushing over there, the state she's in, there'd be more than sparks flying, there'd be a conflagration. Jen's treating her mother like a neighbour who's cheated on her: trying to hang on to property that's rightfully hers.' Her tone hardened. 'And she won't face her mother, has to send someone else. I'll be interested to hear what this young lady's got to say about that. She's behaving outrageously.'

'Ryan's picked up speed.' Miss Pink was peering ahead. 'He's going to reach Benefit before us.'

'Not in that old truck; we'll overtake him on the highway.'

They came to the main road, skirted the southern fringe of Ballard and sped towards Irving. Down on their right the Thunder river belied its name, spread in braids between flats where weeds and willows formed a low jungle. The road was clear ahead and there was no sign of the trailer. 'He'll have stopped off at Ballard,' Sophie declared. 'So Jen won't be expecting us, long as he doesn't phone her.'

'Meaning she'd run if she knew you were coming?'

'Well, she's keeping clear, isn't she? Married for some weeks, he said.' She was bitterly resentful about that.

'Why should she be frightened of the family?'

'Frightened? She has no reason to be.' Sophie considered this. 'You're suggesting she's frightened of her mother?'

'Things point that way.'

They slowed for the turning to Benefit and slowed again where the tarmac ended. When Sophie resumed the conversation it was as if she were talking to herself. 'The truth is we're all scared of each other — except right now Val is furious, but before . . . She told me she doesn't know how to meet her own daughter, what to say. There's so much between them that's just blank: unknown territory. Val doesn't know where she stands. That's what makes her angry; she's so confused.'

'I can understand that.'

'Everything's so unpredictable. That's why I asked you to come along. The truth is I'm scared too. Like I said, you're — you're — '

'The plug in the volcano?'

'OK, I'm dramatising. Forget everything, we'll play it by ear. We're paying a call on my great-niece, is all.'

The little hills basked in the sunshine, deceptively smooth, sprinkled with juniper, a gentle world in contrast to the snow peaks in the background. Scattered ruins showed beyond a swelling in the grassy downs and they came round a curve to Benefit, trailing dust up its street to halt outside Ryan's cabin.

A woman stood in the doorway shielding her eyes. She was small and slim but with broad shoulders. Her eyes slanted a little and the eyebrows were like wings. Her hair was a rich brown, the colour of ripe chestnuts. 'She's lovely,' Miss Pink whispered, coming round the Cherokee to join Sophie.

'And she's not running,' Sophie whispered back.

She came through the marigolds, smiling. 'Aunt Sophie! Isn't this neat?'

They hugged, Sophie's eyes wide with astonishment. Miss Pink looked on benignly.

There were introductions. Jen acknowledged them politely, then turned back to Sophie with a look of inquiry. Sophie glanced at the cabin but left the suggestion of hospitality to her great-niece, who refused to pick up the cue. Her smile was fading. Appreciating that the welcome was over, that someone had to get down to business, Sophie said, 'Is it true you're married?'

'You've been talking to Bret. Yes, we're married.'

'Edna' — Sophie cleared her throat and started again — 'I'm disappointed. I would have liked to come to your wedding.'

Jen gave the faintest shrug.

'Edna too,' Sophie ploughed on, and then — desperately — 'not to speak of your mother.'

'She can go to hell,' Jen said.

Sophie gasped. Beaten, she appealed mutely to Miss Pink who, plunged into a weird fantasy land, all etiquette blown to the winds, said, reasonably enough, 'What can a person's mother have done that's bad enough for that?'

'Ask her,' Jen said. She addressed Sophie again. 'That is, if she'll tell you.' Her face crumpled like a child's. 'I'll tell you what she did: she ruined my life — for ever — you know that?'

'No!' Sophie cried. 'There's something terribly wrong here — '

'Isn't this Sam?' Miss Pink broke in urgently. 'How about letting him — asking him — ' She broke off, at a loss.

A pick-up skidded to a halt in a swirl of dust. Sam Jardine jumped down and strode towards them. Miss Pink and Sophie turned to him as if to a saviour, which he might have been but for the fact that when they looked back Jen had disappeared.

Sophie swore. 'Things were getting out of hand, Sam. Go in and talk some sense into her, for God's sake. She's saying Val ruined her life.'

Sam's genial face showed surprise, but not shock. However, he wasted no time asking for details but made for the cabin. He opened the screen door, called out and entered. Sophie turned away, sniffing angrily.

'Whatever's got into her? Ruined her life? Val can go to hell? What does the girl mean?'

'Come and stand in the shade.' Miss Pink was soothing. 'Let her father deal with it. This could be what's needed to clear the air: a confrontation.'

Sam came out of the cabin, glancing left and right, bewildered. 'Which way'd she go?' he shouted.

Miss Pink looked towards the hills. 'She must have gone out the back,' she called. 'She could have taken a horse.'

There was no point in going after her on

foot, she had a head start. They stood in the shade of the cottonwoods and Sophie filled Sam in on that heated exchange. After a while Miss Pink saw a pale form working through the junipers on a distant slope.

'You've been seeing her all along!' Sophie cried.

'I told Val. I've not seen Jen for ten years.'

'You came straight here.'

'Because Val said she was here and married to Bret. He never said nothing yesterday. I was riding with the guy! Why, he's coming to work for me but he never give me a hint he was married to her. I guess he'd have gotten around to it.'

There was a pause. 'There she goes,' Miss Pink said. 'Up that hill.'

They ignored her. 'So you're saying Bret Ryan's a liar,' Sophie grated.

'Well — no, if he says they're married — '

'Not that. He says they're in touch with you, that you say Ali is willed to Jen.'

'Then he *is* lying. He has to have some reason for saying that.' He sat down in the dust and put his head on his knees. They regarded him: Sophie bewildered, Miss Pink speculative. Someone was lying — but for what purpose? Something to do with Charlie's legacy, or his death, or both?

Sophie raised her eyes and looked towards the hills. 'Is that the horse you saw her on yesterday?' she asked dully.

'Presumably. It's pale, it could be a buckskin.'

'She left because you arrived,' Sophie told Sam and it was an accusation.

He raised his head. 'If she turned against Val, she's against me too,' he said and then, the picture of despair, '*Why*?'

'Ryan knows what's behind it all.' Sophie was vicious. She looked along the street as if willing him to appear but there was nothing to see beyond the sagging buildings other than the sage and rocks shimmering in the heat. 'I'm not waiting here for him,' she said and, remembering her manners, 'I mean, we're not waiting.' Adding fiercely, 'We have our own lives to lead.' It was by way of an apology, a declaration that family problems were not to be allowed to interfere with hospitality towards a guest, and it was spurious. Obviously family came first with all of them. 'I feel like a ball,' she went on, 'bounced backwards and forwards between other people.'

Sam was bleary-eyed. 'You don't believe me? If we was in contact why would she run when I arrived?'

'Because she didn't want us to know she

was seeing you? Oh hell!' Sophie shook her head as if trying to rid it of cobwebs. 'I don't know where I am any longer. What do we do now?' She glared at Miss Pink.

'We're doing nothing here. Shall we go home and eat?'

Sophie's jaw dropped. 'Life goes on,' Miss Pink pointed out. 'People get hungry.'

Sam giggled. Miss Pink looked for hysteria and saw none. 'I'll look around a bit,' he said. 'Maybe she'll be watching and if she sees you leave, she'll come down. I could go find a saddle' — he gave a wry smile — 'put it on one of my son-in-law's horses and follow her.'

'Well, he's old enough to take care of himself,' Sophie said as they drove away. 'Although why I should say that I've no idea, except that I don't like leaving him. Did we do right?'

'Heavens, he's not in any danger.'

'Someone's lying. I need to know what's going on. *We* have to know; it's affecting all of us.' She was speaking as if Miss Pink were family. 'If we meet Ryan on this road he's not going to pass without me finding out why he said Jen was seeing Sam when she wasn't.'

'Actually, Ryan didn't say Jen was meeting

her father. They could have been communicating by phone.'

'It's the same.' Sophie was grim. 'Sam maintains he hasn't been in touch with her at all. Do you think he's lying?'

'If he is, he's a very good actor.'

They reached the highway without meeting a vehicle. 'Ryan's still in town,' Sophie said. 'Or he went back to Val's place. Oh, I hope not. We have to see Edna, ask her about the will, find out who Ali is to go to — '

'There he is. Ryan — the trailer, see?'

They were heading west towards Ballard. A pick-up and trailer were approaching, coming east. Sophie slowed down. As it passed they saw that it was indeed Ryan but he gave no sign that he recognised the Cherokee. Sophie glanced behind her and performed a neat U-turn, but instead of overtaking she kept back until they left the highway. After they'd gone about half a mile on the dirt road she crept up and flashed her lights. Ryan plodded on for a short distance, then stopped.

Sophie climbed down without a word. Miss Pink stayed where she was. She wondered if Ryan carried a weapon. With the trailer blocking her view she couldn't see if there was a rifle on a rack as was often the case in Westerners' pick-ups. Her eyes widened;

this was a family at odds, not a confrontation with a gunman.

Sitting in the passenger seat she could see nothing of Sophie. She slid behind the steering wheel and looked along the side of the trailer. Sophie was standing back, stiff with some emotion — anger? Fear? Miss Pink switched off the ignition. Sophie was shouting.

'. . . ask anyone! . . . her grandmother . . . you could have asked *me*!'

Silence — he would be responding, but quietly.

Sophie's shoulders jerked. She gestured wildly. 'You're mad! It's impossible. Val never knew . . . Why should she lie about it?' She listened again, glaring, blinking. She spoke, but the words were inaudible. Her head was up, her face set; she seemed to be in command now, but as she continued to speak her body language was increasingly tense until she broke off . . . How theatrical people appeared when in the grip of strong emotion and you couldn't hear what was said. She came back to the Cherokee, treading lightly, carefully.

Miss Pink heaved herself over to the passenger side, the trailer drew away, Sophie climbed behind the wheel, turned the car and stopped. She switched off the ignition but kept her hands on the wheel. Miss Pink licked her lips nervously.

Sophie said to the windscreen: 'I'm not clear how I feel about this. I'm shell-shocked. He *is* in touch with Jen's father, as he thinks — because Jen told him her father is Paul Skinner.'

'Oh.' A long pause. 'Poor Sam,' Miss Pink said.

'Skinner isn't, of course.' Sophie was quick. She turned to her friend and smiled, but it was only her lips that moved, her eyes were cold and furious. 'And guess who told Jen that Paul Skinner was her father.'

Miss Pink could only shake her head helplessly.

'Charlie,' Sophie said, nodding. 'My son-of-a-bitch brother-in-law told his granddaughter that her daddy was that gross lump of grease who's never done an honest day's work in his life, who stuck to Val like a leech, living on her earnings, a parasite — for all we know, a thief, a poacher . . . What's got into you? Why are you looking at me like that?'

'No wonder the girl appears to hate her mother — '

'*Does* hate her.'

' — who she'll think kept her parentage from her. It's fortunate that Charlie's — '

' — that he's dead. You can say that

again.' Sophie switched on the ignition and started down the road. 'I put Bret right; I doubt he believed me but now we know what the problem is we can set to and sort it. Of course there's no way Paul Skinner could be her father; why, Val didn't even know Skinner when Jen was born . . . '

She continued in this vein while Miss Pink appeared to listen and all the time she was thinking about relationships and babies and abortions, and dreading the moment when Sophie — and others — would start to think along the same lines. Or had someone done that already?

* * *

'That stallion goes to Jen,' Edna told Sophie. 'She's to have all the horses except the five colts that come to you. And no, I don't have a copy of the will; Charlie would never have shown it to me, but I've seen a copy. He never knew.' She smiled slyly. 'I went to school with our lawyer,' she explained to Miss Pink.

They were in Edna's bedroom which, despite its four-poster, gave the impression of a room much lived in. They had come straight to Glenaffric to find her cleaning furiously. It was the Fourth of July and once again she was without domestic help. In the face of the family's problems no one had remarked that this was Independence Day. A halt was called for lunch and they took sandwiches and a pitcher of iced tea to this curiously intimate room with its old Chinese rugs and furniture upholstered in tarnished gold and threadbare crimson silk.

Sophie said crossly, 'I could do with a drink.'

Edna had shown no surprise at their appearance unannounced, nor at Sophie's blunt questions regarding the stallion and the will; now, without turning a hair, she moved to an elaborate corner cupboard and produced a bottle of Jack Daniel's and crystal glasses. She poured drinks with a steady hand and asked pleasantly, 'Did you want the stallion? I dare say Jen would do a trade.'

'We were at Benefit,' Sophie said, ignoring the question. 'She's there. We talked to her — and to Ryan. They're married. Oh, and there's no baby. There wouldn't be, of course. It'd be nine years old by now, but there never was one. Actually, we — I didn't ask, but there was no sign.'

'Just as well,' Edna said. 'She can start fresh.' She brightened. 'How is she? I've been expecting her.'

'She's fine: damning her mother to hell,

refusing to meet her father . . . Sam arrived while we were there.'

Edna was very still. 'What was that about her mother?'

'Jen says Val ruined her life. Bret Ryan told me Paul Skinner is Jen's father. One assumes the two things are connected, in their minds at least. Meaning Jen's got it in for her mother because she figures Val kept the truth from her about her parentage.'

Miss Pink stood up, muttering something about the bathroom. The others ignored her exit. 'Well?' she heard from behind her, Sophie throwing it out like a challenge. There was a murmur from Edna. 'These are your daughter and your grandchild!' Sophie stormed. 'You know it's not true! Sam's her father!'

Miss Pink blundered round a corner, nearly knocking Clyde down. 'What's going on?' he demanded, his eyes alert to the shouting. She pushed past him quite rudely.

★ ★ ★

Half an hour passed before Sophie came looking for her and found her leaning on a rail behind the corrals. Beyond the fence, mares with foals grazed unconcernedly, having already accosted the visitor for titbits and found her wanting.

'She knew all the time,' Sophie said without preamble, then thought better of it. 'OK, let's be fair; ten years ago Charlie hinted that he knew why Jen left, told Edna that the child should know that Skinner was her daddy. He said, he actually *said*, he'd told Jen himself. Edna's like Val: got no spirit left now, she's had too much of his lies, but back then I guess she reacted differently: horror, shock, whatever, and Charlie maybe, just maybe, realised he'd gone too far that time and he retracted. Said it was a joke, it wasn't true, he was only teasing Edna; he'd never told Jen anything. But you see, Jen didn't come back and there was never any contact, nothing to explain her going, and Edna says now she got to wondering was it true after all? Not that Skinner was Jen's father of course, but that Charlie had told the child so.'

Miss Pink's gaze was fixed on the horses. 'And Edna never said a word to any of you because she wasn't sure,' she murmured.

'That — and shame: for him. That he could be so cruel, so heartless.' Sophie paused. 'Clyde came in,' she added. 'We've been talking.'

'I gathered.'

After a long silence Sophie said, 'Has your brain made connections here?'

'You mean with the other alleged piece of information from Charlie: that Jen wanted money for an abortion, or was it that she wanted money to go away and you considered an abortion?'

'Go on.'

Miss Pink sighed. 'Yes, I do see a connection: that Jen was pregnant by the man she thought was her stepfather and who Charlie then told her was her father. That would account for the absence: hostility . . . guilt . . . towards Val. It can be put right now, of course.' Now that Charlie was dead.

'Try telling that to Edna and Clyde. They're obsessed with the difficulties. How do you tell a woman that she's wasted ten years of her life by exiling herself from a loving family (bar one monster) because she thinks she's been a party to incest?'

'It may not be that bad. She could suspect the truth already. That could be why she won't meet Sam: she's not *sure*.'

'Bret thinks Skinner is her father.'

'I wonder. Sam stayed behind when we left Benefit. Perhaps he went after her. In any case, she's come back to Montana, so she must be looking for a reconciliation. After all, even if Skinner were her father Jen was still responsible for her actions — unless he raped her.'

'Then she'd have told Val . . . No, maybe not. Children don't always, do they? Skinner's another one who should have been drowned at birth. Don't look so disapproving, Melinda. I mean it.'

'I'm not disapproving the sentiment, just your voicing it. It's not a good time to mention killing and members of your family in the same breath.'

'Skinner's not family. Oh, you mean Charlie. Yes, I'd have cheerfully killed him and that was before I knew about this last obscene joke of his. *Joke*? But that's how he'd have viewed it.' Her lips stretched in a grin. 'Poetic justice. He'd dragged the family through hell for ten years and in the end it was him was dragged to death. Neat, huh?'

8

'We've made no decisions,' Sophie confided as they drove away from Glenaffric. 'Every-one's exhausted. We think it's best to leave Jen to Sam. He may bring her here, to Edna, or she could come to me of her own free will.'

'Like a nervous animal,' Miss Pink said, 'let her make the running.'

'Exactly.' Neither saw anything fanciful in the comparison. 'I should drop by the ranch,' Sophie went on. 'I can't just pass. But what do I say? If Sam hasn't contacted Val she won't yet know that Jen thinks Skinner's her father. Someone has to tell her.' They were approaching the track to the homestead. 'I'll play it by ear,' she went on, 'stress the fact that whatever happened in the past, Jen's come back. Val will be furious when she learns the truth, but she can't take it out on Charlie now.' She gave a derisive snort. 'Fortunately,' she added.

But if there was any truth in the suggestion that Skinner had seduced his stepdaughter he was one live man who'd be well advised to keep out of Val's way. The fury she could no longer direct at her father could be deflected in Skinner's direction. Miss Pink didn't point this out. What she did say — and firmly — was that she would wait in the Cherokee.

'Shoot!' Sophie wasn't listening. 'There's Byer. What in hell's he doing here — and messing with my tack?'

She climbed down, threw a baleful glance at the fellow who was carrying a saddle into the barn and stamped up the steps to the cabin. The car windows were down and her voice carried clearly. 'What's Byer doing here?' she shouted over the slam of the screen door. The reply was inaudible.

'I'm not having — ' It was cut off like a switch.

Miss Pink left the Cherokee and strolled across to the rail where, on the other side of the corral, Ali was intent on a mare in another enclosure.

'He's doing fine.'

She turned. Byer approached and leaned on the rail, joining her in her study of the horse. 'Where did you ride today?' he asked, more ingratiating than friendly.

'I didn't. It's been a social day.'

'You shoulda rode out. These old horses need work, get some of the winter fat off of 'em. I'll have Ali out next week: just gentle work, get him used to a man on his back again.'

'I thought you worked at Glenaffric.'

'Wherever. At the moment she needs me here.'

There was no sound from the cabin. Miss Pink said innocently, 'You mean Mrs Jardine or Miss Hamilton?'

'Val. I'm giving her a hand. She's not long back from hunting camp.' Was he making conversation or did that remark have some special significance?

'What was she doing there?'

'Bringing the saddle down. Rode up there bareback, probably did some cleaning while she was there.'

'The cabin needed cleaning?'

'I don't know. You was there.'

'I have no idea how tidy a hunting cabin should be. Were you there, Mr Byer?'

'No. I went as far as the slide just. Light were failing even then.'

'That wasn't what I meant — ' Her quick ears had caught the sound of the screen door opening. She eyed him, demanding some reaction but his expression was bland, then he turned and went into the barn.

Sophie didn't speak until they were on the road. Even then all she said was, 'We'll talk back at the apartment. Have supper sent up again. How did Ali look to you?'

'Very well, considering. Fascinated by a mare.'

'Good.'

She wasn't thinking about the stallion, she was staring through the windscreen and, it would appear, practising deep breathing.

In the wing mirror Miss Pink caught sight of snowy peaks against a southern sky and was seized by the craving to be down there where the snows were melting round drifts of glacier lilies, a place where there were no people, no tangled relationships. She considered how she might approach the subject of her leaving without making Sophie feel that she was driving her guest away.

In the apartment Sophie closed the door and said bluntly, 'Don't shower. Not yet. Let's talk.' She fetched the Talisker and the bourbon. Miss Pink drifted to the sofa. Sophie went on, as if words had been dammed in the Cherokee, 'It's Byer. I told Val I wouldn't have him there. She begged me to leave it be. I swear she was virtually crying, beside herself. So I forced her to tell me why I shouldn't send him packing from my own property — my lease, anyway. That bugger's blackmailing her.'

Miss Pink sagged against the cushions. How bad could this get? She drank her malt rather than sipped it, put down the glass, longed for a cigarette. She had stopped smoking decades ago. 'How can he blackmail her?' she prompted.

Sophie stared out of the window and said coldly, 'Val visited Charlie at hunting camp and Byer knows she did.'

'What's wrong with — You mean, when she was out on the trail? She rode to the cabin — ' She hesitated. Sophie avoided her eyes. Miss Pink tried again, delicately, 'Why does she need to conceal the fact that she was at the cabin?'

'You shouldn't ask me that.'

'You're confiding in me.'

Sophie looked stricken. 'You're right. I don't know why she has to conceal it, at least not to want it publicised. He told her if she didn't let him help out at the homestead then he'd tell — ' She stopped.

'Tell whom? He must have known she'd tell you.'

'I'm family. He knows we're not about to talk . . . He'd have the newspapers in mind, the local rag.'

'Is he threatening her with the police?'

'Hell no! Whatever gives you that idea?'

Miss Pink was silent. Sophie went on, talking fast, 'All she'll say is that he has to be kept quiet, but Mel, she was at the cabin *before* Charlie had his accident' — the emphasis was marked — 'and that happened miles from the cabin — well, getting on for two miles. No way can there be any connection.'

'I didn't suggest one. It's Byer who seems to be doing that. And how does he know Val was there? He must have been there himself — surely? He was trying to pump me about the condition of the cabin. He says Val was up there today.'

'Of course she was; she went there to get Charlie's saddle.'

Unthinking, Miss Pink helped herself to whisky and poured a dram for her host. She said slowly, 'Why did she go to the cabin when Charlie was there?'

'That's simple.' Sophie was dismissive. 'She'd been worrying over Jen, what had brought her back, where she was, and she went to the cabin knowing Charlie was there on his own, determined on a showdown, make him tell her why Jen left and stayed away so long.'

'How did she know Charlie was concerned? When Jen phoned Glenaffric, Val was already out on the trail. Did she have a mobile with her and Edna called her?'

'No, no mobile.'

'Then did she run into Jen — '

Sophie shook her head vehemently. 'Jen never went to the cabin. Charlie admitted as much to Val although he couldn't help taunting her by telling her Jen had agreed to come. She must have thought better of the arrangement, or Ryan wouldn't let her go. Maybe what bothers Val is that she was the last person to see Charlie alive and if the sheriff were to know that and start asking questions he'd uncover all the scandal about Jen and Paul Skinner, and Charlie's crazy lies . . . No way can we allow that to happen. You do see, don't you?'

'Not really. See what, exactly?'

'Why, there's nothing to it, really. Storm in a teacup.'

'And yet Byer's blackmailing Val.'

'It's the family's dirty linen. Can't have it washed in public.'

Miss Pink got to her feet. 'I need a shower.'

She undressed slowly, torn between loyalty and a desire for untrammelled delights. She had been intending to introduce the subject of her leaving and now she was asking herself why that should be so difficult, why she should feel like a rat deserting a ship that was heading for rocks. She took her time in the shower, emerging from her room only when sounds indicated the arrival of supper.

Neither felt much like eating although it was salmon. Miss Pink said, 'You told Val about Charlie's misinformation: that Paul Skinner was Jen's father?'

'It didn't seem to affect her, just another of her father's nasty jokes.' Seeing the other's surprise, Sophie elaborated: 'Well, we've had so many shocks, one after the other, over the last few days, what's one more? We're drained. Actually, I was relieved to get the matter out of the way without hysterics from her. I was more concerned with that Byer. I mean, that's *immediate*.'

Miss Pink played with a lettuce leaf. 'I was considering driving south tomorrow.'

'No!' It was spontaneous and fierce. Sophie grimaced at her own reaction. 'Oh, no,' she repeated. 'You can't go.' Then, defiantly, 'Why should you?'

'I'm an embarrassment. I'm not family.'

'We're born with family. We choose our friends.'

'All the same, you're so concerned with Val . . . ' Miss Pink let it hang.

Sophie bit her lip. 'Of course. Wouldn't you be if she were your niece?'

'If she were being blackmailed, yes.'

'Are you suggesting it isn't true?'

'I accept that Byer is working some kind of scam, but I find it difficult to believe that

Val would give in to his demands — whatever they are — in order to protect a family secret. Charlie's behaviour was monstrous but it wasn't criminal and if Skinner slept with an under-age girl, that's his problem. Val wouldn't be protecting *him*.'

'Of course she wouldn't.' Sophie dismissed Skinner with contempt. 'What you're saying is, there's something else. What's on your mind, Melinda?'

'Didn't Val take you into her confidence?'

'I told you the truth. I trust you.'

'It's the truth as far as you know.'

Sophie dropped her eyes and fidgeted. 'That's what she told me,' she said stubbornly. She looked up and her expression was unreadable. 'Well?'

Miss Pink considered possible responses. In the circumstances . . . The police thinking might be . . . What she said was, 'Is there any way that Charlie's death could have been rigged to look like an accident?'

There was no reaction in the other's face. 'How long have you had that idea?'

'Since you told me Byer is blackmailing Val. And you? When did the possibility of murder occur to you?'

'For heaven's sakes!' Sophie's eyes slewed wildly from the door to the open window but Miss Pink's voice was pitched low. 'I agree Val's going to extraordinary lengths to protect reputations — Jen's and Charlie's — in any case, we'd all deny that Jen was pregnant — for God's sake, we don't know that she was! There's only Charlie's word for it' — she'd lost the thread — 'now what? You look as if you're waiting for something.'

'You didn't answer my question. Could the accident have been rigged?'

'No way.' But Sophie gave the matter thought, then jerked to attention. 'You're suggesting Byer is accusing Val of being involved in Charlie's death?'

'You see' — Miss Pink was calm but earnest — 'since he knows Val was at the cabin, it implies he was there too, or in the vicinity. So he could be setting her up for the fall guy. And Val, by giving in to him, is putting herself in the frame. Surely you see that.'

Sophie said sadly, 'She hasn't told me everything.'

'Where do you think she's not telling the truth?'

'Byer's got something on her. More than her being at the cabin, d'you think?'

'Could it have to do with Jen?'

'I guess. She's a woman would do anything for her daughter, but then any mother would. Yes, she could be covering for Jen. But you're assuming that there was something — not quite right about Charlie's accident.'

'There could have been a fight. He was an old man.'

'But powerful. Neither Val nor Jen could have — oh no! Listen to us! I can't believe we're talking this way.'

'And then the business with the stallion might have been rigged.'

'Never! Not by one person. You'd need someone to hold the horse, the other to put Charlie's foot through the stirrup.'

'So it could have been worked that way.'

'Only by two — oh!'

They were both thinking of Jen and Bret Ryan.

'They could have gone to the cabin together,' Miss Pink pointed out. 'And Ryan had a fight with him, knocked him down and he hit his head.'

'And Val's protecting them both by saying no one visited Charlie except herself?'

'It's odd, though,' Miss Pink mused. 'Why should Byer blackmail Val rather than Jen? It's Jen who's going to be rich.'

'He won't know the provisions of Charlie's will. And maybe he thinks Val's a softer touch without a man around. But he has me to reckon with there.' Sophie didn't smile, she bared her teeth.

'On the other hand' — Miss Pink wasn't listening — 'it could be that he knows Val was at the cabin but is unaware that Jen was. And Ryan? That is, if those two were there at all.' Her voice sank. 'This is all surmise. How can one find out?'

'Do we need to?'

'What? I was thinking aloud there. But Val needs help because blackmailers don't stop at one demand. He's got his foot in the door, he knows that whatever he has on her is solid; he might just have been fishing in the first place, trying it on. She's acceded to the first demand, if it was only to take him on as a hand, and he knows she's hooked. And she does inherit half a million dollars. That'll be a fortune to a ranch hand, if he does know about the will. He could bleed her dry. I wonder what he's got on her.'

'You could try to find out. She won't tell me.'

'What makes you think she'll tell me? What right do I have to ask questions anyway?'

'What right does Byer have to blackmail her? We can't go to the police. We daren't, we don't know what's going on.' Sophie smiled, this time engagingly. 'You can run away: drive south tomorrow and forget all about us, or you can stay. Charlie was the worst kind of louse; I'm not going to stand by and see any member of this family hanged because they put him down like a vicious hound. Whatever happened, he deserved it.'

Manslaughter didn't involve the death sentence, but that was only a scenario they'd dreamed up. The reality could have been murder. 'I'll have a talk with Byer,' Miss Pink said. 'And the others, if I get the opportunity,' she added grudgingly, knowing the alternative, as Sophie said, was to cut and run. That wasn't her style.

9

Byer was not at home. His pick-up was parked in front of the house, an old grey horse grazing close by, but there was no sign of the piebald. Miss Pink sat at the wheel of her hired Bronco and considered the house. Unscreened windows — there would be flies in hot weather, not to speak of mosquitoes so close to the water, but probably he didn't open his windows. Certainly he never washed them. Bachelors didn't need to be house-proud but they didn't have to be dirty.

She drove to the old homestead, rejoicing in the smooth running of this new car. Val was standing in the entrance to the barn, tense at the sight of the unfamiliar vehicle, but the hesitation was momentary. By the time Miss Pink had turned and come to a halt she was at the driver's door. 'My!' she exclaimed. 'You did yourself proud with this animal.'

'Good power-to-weight ratio.' Miss Pink was smug. 'Like a quarter horse. I brought a book from Sophie, something on equine medicine.'

'Right. She offered me the loan of it.'

Then, ostensibly casual, 'Where is she this morning?'

'She's visiting Sam.'

Val looked wary. Miss Pink went on, 'She wants to know if Jen talked' — beaming at the other's bewilderment — 'she says they have a good relationship: Jen and her father.' Still no response. She became flustered: the well-intentioned old lady pushing into ever deeper waters. 'Now that her grandfather's out of the way and the other problem's cleared up, it's all plain sailing, isn't it?' Eyebrows raised, the ingenuous expression demanding comment.

'What's she been saying to you?'

Miss Pink nodded as if the possibility of a snub, not to mention a furious reaction, had never crossed her mind. 'Gossip.' She shrugged. 'That ridiculous story of Charlie's: confusing your two marriages, implying Sam isn't Jen's father.'

'*Implying!* He told her Paul — my second husband — was her father. He told her as a fact.'

'Silly man.'

'He was evil.' Val was no longer bewildered, she was savage.

'How did you find out?' Miss Pink seemed to have shrunk to a harmless innocent and she asked the question in all innocence.

Val said, still angry, 'It was yesterday, when Ryan came for Ali. Remember? You were here.'

'Oh yes? And he said Paul was Jen's father?' Miss Pink turned to survey the corral where Ryan had accosted them, when he'd insisted he'd come to collect the stallion.

'No,' Val conceded. 'It was before that. Edna told me. She dropped hints. Not everything, but I got the gist of it.'

'Ah, now I understand. And you went to the hunting camp to confront your father.'

Val gasped. 'I told Sophie in confidence.'

'She's so worried. She needed to talk to someone. I'm a friend. She's an old lady, Val.'

The woman gave an angry laugh. 'And now the whole world's going to know.' She was struck by a thought. 'Why did you come here? The book was an excuse. You've been pumping me! What — '

'I'm looking for Byer.' It was cool and firm; the chameleon had changed colour again.

After a moment Val said warily, 'I don't know where he is.'

'Where is Ali?'

'That's the point! He's taken the stud out.'

'Riding him?' Miss Pink was shocked.

'No, no; leading him. Exercise, he said.'

'It seems rather soon, with his leg sprained.'

'He says it's all right.' Val looked wan.

Miss Pink hesitated. The next question was; What hold does he have over you? but that was going too fast. She had some kind of brief from Sophie to protect her niece and the question could be counter-productive. Why was that? Because Val didn't want to be helped. Why not?

Val said, confidentially, woman to woman, 'You see, Byer knows I went to the cabin to visit with Charlie that afternoon.'

Miss Pink swallowed. 'What's wrong with that?'

'If he spread it around everyone would know all our family problems.'

'What's more natural than your going to speak to your father when he was only a few miles away?'

Val regarded the older woman with what appeared to be speculation. 'He died shortly afterwards.'

'And you're assuming that the police, if they knew you were at the cabin, would think you had a hand in his death.'

'Of course.' Val smiled but the smile didn't reach her eyes. 'And I inherit a fortune.' She shrugged. 'Motive enough?'

'Byer would think so. You realise that he must have been there himself to know that you were.' Val's hand rose to her throat defensively. 'How does he know?' Miss Pink pressed.

'I have no idea.' Val considered this. 'Maybe he did go to the cabin — after me — ' Her eyes jumped. A pick-up was approaching. Her face stiffened into lines that betrayed her age.

The truck stopped and the man who got down struck a memory chord: an image against a background of a peeling mobile home, a large paunchy fellow with the vestiges of good looks in a fleshy face. Why was Paul Skinner visiting his former wife at a time when the rumour was current, at least in a limited circle, that he'd had a sexual relationship with his stepdaughter?

Val said quickly, 'My ex has come to see me on business.'

Miss Pink said nothing. Even had there been time to ask whether she should go she wouldn't have done so. She was here for information.

'Where's that sorrel stud of your dad's?' Skinner asked, ignoring Miss Pink, his eyes ranging the corrals.

'Gone.' Val was furious. 'What's it to you?'

'Is it over to Benefit?'

'It's nothing to do with you. My father's will is family business. Why would you think it was at Benefit anyway?'

'Byer said the stud goes to Jen.'

'So?'

Skinner seemed nonplussed. His eyes shifted to the visitor. Val said icily, 'This is my aunt's house guest, Miss Pink. Melinda: Paul Skinner. Now if you'll excuse us — ' She took Miss Pink's arm and shepherded her firmly across the yard. Her hand was trembling. The screen door banged behind them. 'I don't want those two to meet,' she whispered. 'Byer's up with the horse herd — the top pasture behind the house. Can you slip out the back and tell him to keep clear till I've got rid of Skinner?'

'Do I tell him why?'

Val stared, biting her lip. 'Tell him that — just say Skinner's breathing fire about — about Ali.' Miss Pink made to protest. 'Please don't ask questions,' Val was frantic, pushing her towards the back door. '*Please!* We have trouble enough without those two at each other's throats.'

Using the buildings as cover until she reached trees, Miss Pink plodded up the slope, so intent on puzzling over the reason for these two men to be at odds that she nearly blundered into Byer. He was riding the piebald and leading the stallion. She delivered the message, deadpan, and waited for him to ask why he should wait for Skinner to leave the homestead.

Byer was expressionless, looking past her. He was trying to work something out: a man who had difficulty thinking on his feet. A devious fellow but not a clever one. Miss Pink stepped aside and surveyed the stallion critically. As one expert to another she said, 'Even if the damage isn't reversible it won't affect his breeding capacity.' She nodded sagely. 'Yes, he could still hold his value. Have you put in an offer?'

He was dumbfounded, then gave a bark of amusement. 'She's selling?'

'Well, the price will be high . . . ' It was a discreet murmur.

He fingered his chin. 'I got the cash.'

'So you have put in an offer.'

'Of course. You need a man to handle this stud. Obvious he'd be sold when Charlie were gone. I put in the first offer.'

'When was that?'

'You're asking a lot of questions. What's it to you?'

'Oh, nothing.' Miss Pink was suddenly an embarrassed old soul. 'One forgets one's place — bad manners — not my business at all; it's between you and the owner of course. But she said nothing to us about selling Ali when we were there yesterday.'

'Who?'

'Why, Jen — Mrs Ryan as she is now. I had the distinct impression that she meant to keep the stud — '

'You got mixed up.' He eyed her speculatively. She was red-faced and sweating. 'I'm not sure about this horse,' he told her. 'If there's a problem of ownership — '

'You were told the stud was to come to Val?'

'Ah-h.' He spun it out. Blinking at him like a distressed owl, she imagined she could hear the brain working, the wrong cogs catching. 'What Charlie said was 'her'. I took him to mean Val. Maybe he meant Jen after all. Maybe he intended me to be confused. He loved his joke.'

Miss Pink gave a girlish giggle. 'As if it matters beside the money.' She glanced at Ali carelessly. 'He's worth a few thousand, certainly, but there are millions to be divided . . . '

He grinned and the piebald walked on. It was a few moments before she remembered that her mission had been to detain him until Skinner had left the homestead.

* * *

'No, they didn't meet,' Val assured her on her return. 'You kept him away long enough for me to get rid of Paul. Actually, I misjudged that guy' — she gave an odd little laugh and continued with a delicacy at variance with her usual manner — 'that old scandal was all Charlie's doing.'

'So I understood.'

'I mean, the suggestion that Paul had some kind of relationship with Jen. That's as wild as the lie that Paul's her father. Paul suspected something when he met Bret one time in Ballard and Bret said him and Jen were married. Paul wondered why Bret acted kind of familiar. He knows now, of course. Incidentally, it was Paul who confirmed that Ali was to come to Jen. Byer told him.'

* * *

'So how did it go?' Sophie asked, placing a bowl of clam chowder before her guest. 'Were you able to talk to Byer?'

Miss Pink described her morning. 'I didn't find out what Byer has on Val,' she admitted, 'but I'm certain Ali is the price he's asking to keep quiet: the stallion rather than cash. He tried to confuse me by pretending he wasn't sure who owned Ali now but he'd let slip that Charlie had told him the horse was to go to Jen. Val says Byer told Skinner, which makes those two rather friendly, doesn't it: Byer and Skinner?'

Sophie grimaced. 'Cronies rather than friends. Vultures more like: looking for pickings. What was Skinner doing at the homestead anyway? If Val didn't want those two to meet it wasn't because they'd fight but because she wanted Skinner on his own, find out something. Did she say anything about meeting Charlie at the hunting camp?'

'I put it to her that she went there to confront her father. She didn't deny it. She was insistent that Jen didn't go there. As for her needing to talk to Skinner alone, she says she's misjudged him, that there was no illicit relationship with Jen.'

'Well, he's not going to admit it, is he?'

'True.' Miss Pink reverted to the subject of the stallion. 'Byer said he'd put in an offer for Ali — '

'He's not for sale.'

'Calling it a sale would be the cover. Neither Byer nor Val could admit that the horse changed hands as blackmail payment. I was intrigued that Byer should be blackmailing Val instead of Jen, but I concluded that Byer's banking on Val buying

Ali from Jen, then turning the horse over to him, or — '

'Or what?'

'That Jen will give up the horse when Val tells her about the blackmail.'

'Jen would never — ' Sophie checked. 'You think Jen did go to meet Charlie, don't you?'

'I'd like to talk to Byer again. I think he was there, at the hunting cabin. What did Sam have to say?'

'Nothing. That is, he didn't go after Jen and she didn't come back to Benefit so he went home. He says he'll have a word with Bret when he starts work. You talk to Sam, you wouldn't think there was any urgency; things will work out, is his style.'

The telephone started to ring. Sophie picked up the receiver, listened, gasped, '*What?*' and the blood drained from her cheeks. Miss Pink moved quickly, pushing a chair towards her as the woman put out a hand to the sideboard.

The person at the end of the line clacked on, stopped, asked a question. 'She's here,' Sophie said in a small voice and held out the instrument to Miss Pink, but by the time she'd put it to her ear the line was dead. She frowned, shook the receiver and got the dialling tone. Sophie started to giggle on a rising note.

Miss Pink said coldly, 'This is where I slap your face and you collapse in tears. Don't make me do it. We're grown women.'

The giggling stopped. Sophie allowed herself to be steered to the sofa and pushed down on the cushions. Miss Pink found the brandy and brought stiff drinks for both of them.

'It was just that I didn't think Charlie had any shoulders left,' Sophie explained with terrible gravity. 'There's a bullet track in his shoulder, apparently, the pathologist says. I guess if you're used to gunshot wounds it would show even given the state he was in.'

'Drink your brandy.'

'Ah, Melinda: priorities in the right place as usual.'

'Who were you talking to?'

'Why, Val of course. The police are on their way.'

'On their way to where?'

'To see her. To arrest her?' The tone was mildly curious.

'No. If they connected her with foul play they wouldn't tell her in advance. They'll be thinking in terms of accident — as we've been doing all along, but now with the addition of a gun. He shot himself by accident.'

'Actually Val did say, 'They've warned me so I can't be a suspect.' The girl's realised they'd be thinking in terms of murder. We'll have to get our stories straight.'

Miss Pink opened her mouth and closed it again.

'There's Jen,' Sophie said. As if anyone needed reminding. She traced rings on the table with her glass. 'Jen doesn't shoot,' she went on, reddening under Miss Pink's stare. 'You know, I think Val said the police said it only *looks* like the track of a bullet, not that it is a track.'

'That makes more sense, given the condition of the remains. And no one's said they heard a shot.' Miss Pink sat up. 'This is ridiculous. The man was dragged to his death. Even if a shot had been heard there's nothing to say it wasn't a poacher. Or a hunter after coyotes. When are the police seeing Val?'

'Now — this afternoon. We'll be there, give her support. It's my ranch, they're not to know I don't spend all my time there. You'll have come with me for the ride.'

'Why did they contact Val? Edna's the next of kin.'

'That's easy. If the guy in charge doesn't know the family, he knows of us. Edna's old so Val's better suited to take the news. Probably tried Clyde but he'll be at Glenaffric. What the police have in mind, they'll be picking up Val on their way to see Edna.' It was a firm statement, spoiled by the qualification: 'Don't you think?'

10

There were no strange cars at the homestead, only one pick-up visible and no sign of the piebald or Byer, which could be significant. Val, looking haggard and breathing liquor fumes, saw Miss Pink looking around and said harshly, 'I didn't have to send him packing; all I did was mention the police and I couldn't see him for dust.'

'He could have a record.'

Val's eyes sharpened. 'I never thought of that.'

'We'd better be doing something,' Sophie broke in impatiently. 'Business as usual; we don't want them to see us in a huddle when they arrive.'

They came in an unmarked car. They were in plain clothes and they were both lieutenants. Tension was racked up a notch in view of their rank, although there was marginal reassurance in their appearance. A heavy older fellow in stained Stetson and shades, his jowly face flushed with the heat, and a younger man: sleek, with an expensive haircut and a carefully tended moustache. They both wore Levis but where the boots of the older man were worn and scuffed, the younger sported a dashing pair in grey snakeskin.

The older man, Hilton — no Christian names were offered — steered Val to the porch where they were visible but their conversation was inaudible. The youngster, Cole, stayed to chat to the older women. He talked ranching in an amateur fashion, concentrating on Sophie but occasionally including the English visitor with a warm smile. Miss Pink returned the smile. He confessed that he hadn't been riding long and confided his ambition to take the trail through the Black Canyon.

'That's no place for beginners,' Sophie said sternly. 'You have to gain experience elsewhere, like on the Bobcat Hills. And you'll need a steady horse for that trail; there are some nasty steep places above the Thunder river.'

'But you take the dudes in there, ma'am.'

'Not me. My niece does, but her clients aren't beginners and our horses are carefully selected. I'd never put a dude up on a horse I didn't know was steady as a rock.' Sophie's eyes strayed to Ali, grazing in a paddock beyond the corrals. Miss Pink saw that the police had talked to other people before they came to the homestead; someone had told them that dudes were taken through the canyon. On the other hand it could well be public knowledge.

'So you must be an expert rider, ma'am.' Cole favoured Miss Pink with his boyish charm.

'You flatter me, Mr Cole.'

'You were there when Charlie Gunn's horse spooked, right?'

'Who've you been talking to?' Sophie was furious.

'Not *when* he spooked,' Miss Pink put in smoothly. 'Some time afterwards. Although we'd seen the pack-horse — ' She stopped.

'Yes, ma'am? You saw the pack-horse — when?'

The women exchanged glances. 'The day before the search,' Miss Pink said. 'And that would be the day after Mr Gunn went to the cabin.'

Cole turned to Sophie. 'So he'd have been dead when you saw the pack-horse?'

She blinked, bewildered by the changed tone of the interview, for interview it was and no longer idle chat about ranching and learning to ride. She looked away for relief and fastened on Ali in the paddock. 'It could have been there a while,' she admitted.

'This is the same horse?'

She was astonished. 'This is a stud! He

was my brother-in-law's saddle-horse, the one that threw and dragged him.'

'Really? He looks quiet enough now.'

'He's settling nicely.' She was grudging. 'He's a horse likes women better than men. Can't say I blame him.'

'He was badly knocked about and confused,' Miss Pink butted in, trying to keep the record straight. 'He'll be quiet for a while, till he recovers from the trauma.'

Sophie looked startled but she was silent as the message sank in. She should watch her words; she spoke her mind without considering the consequences, a trait that seemed to run in the family. Uneasily, and without glancing that way, Miss Pink wondered how Val was faring with the senior partner.

'How was it you didn't see the horse when you were having your picnic by the lake?' Cole asked. 'That was where you found him next day, wasn't it?'

Miss Pink's heart sank. Whom *could* they have been talking to? 'We were low down,' she said. 'The stallion was higher, and further on — if he was there at all when we were eating our lunch. He could have wandered about. But there's timber and boulders back there, the kind of country you could hide a herd of horses.'

'He didn't neigh when he saw your animals.' It was a statement, not a question.

'If you know, why ask?' Sophie was losing it but he was unperturbed.

'There's a lot we don't know — like the state of the cabin when you were in there. You'd have been the first people inside after Mr Gunn left. What sort of condition was it in?'

Sophie hesitated. Miss Pink tried to remember whom they'd talked to about the state of the cabin. Sophie was hesitating too long, transfixed by Cole's stare. 'Was it locked?' he prompted.

Sophie swallowed visibly. 'Yes,' Miss Pink said. 'Val — Mrs Jardine and I were the first people there after the body was found. We went down for blankets to wrap it in. The cabin was locked. We didn't see any significance in that. The pack-horse had been standing outside, ready to go. We assumed Mr Gunn had seen a bear at that moment and gone after it. What other explanation could there be? There were signs of bear about — in fact, that was why he went there in the first place: to repair the roof where a bear had tried to break in.'

He regarded her shrewdly, as if well aware that words could be used as a smokescreen. He might be ignorant where horses were concerned but this was no callow youngster. 'And inside?' he asked.

'There was nothing remarkable about it. Obviously he'd packed up ready to leave — and then the bear appeared.' Now she saw a flaw in that theory, moreover Cole had seen it too.

'But the horses, this horse' — he gestured towards Ali — 'he didn't spook.'

The women shook their heads mutely. Sophie had seen the flaw too. 'But he spooked the other time,' Cole pointed out, 'the time he threw his rider.'

Miss Pink said, 'Possibly on the second occasion the bear was very close, whereas he'd been in the distance when Mr Gunn started after him.'

'Of course. It must have been a shock when you ladies came on the body.'

'Not really,' Miss Pink said. 'We found the stallion first, the saddle under its belly, so we were forewarned. We knew then that Charlie — Mr Gunn — was unconscious at the very least, probably badly injured. The state the body was in was a shock, of course, although not when you come to think about it.'

'Easy enough done,' Sophie said. 'The foot slips through the stirrup when a guy is thrown.'

'Funny thing,' Cole mused. 'The bear

never came near the pack-horse and he couldn't run. How do you explain that?'

Sophie shrugged. 'He did eventually: broke his halter and ran home.'

'Where did you find his rifle?'

She blinked. 'Charlie's rifle? We didn't find it.'

Miss Pink asked chattily, as if overcome by curiosity, 'Who've you been talking to, Mr Cole? You know more about it than we do.'

'We have to speak to everyone; what one guy forgets the next one will remember, right?' Their eyes moved and he stiffened. 'Maybe I'll ride in those Bobcat Hills,' he said. 'Get some experience.'

Hilton was approaching. Behind him Val came down the steps and crossed to the barn.

Hilton looked benign, his flush subsided. He nodded at the stallion. 'So there's your killer,' he said cheerfully.

Shocking bad taste. A reproof trembled on her tongue but Miss Pink was forestalled by Sophie. 'It wasn't malice,' she said angrily. 'He was crazed with fear.'

'It happens.' Hilton looked at the younger man and from him to the sky. 'Weather's going to break,' he observed and grinned at their surprise. 'Oh yes, I'm the country boy, he's the townie' — dismissing Cole with affable contempt — 'he wants to ride your canyon. Me — you won't get me within a mile of it. You don't have a horse could carry me anyways — except that there stud.'

Sophie rose to the bait. 'No one's getting on him till I give the word.'

'He belongs to you, ma'am?'

She moistened her lips. His eyes were invisible behind the shades. 'He'll be mentioned in the will?'

'He goes to my great-niece,' she said tightly. 'We're looking after him till he's fit.'

'Why can't she take him?'

'It's just that he fetched up here after the accident and we have better facilities for nursing him.'

'He don't look as if there's anything wrong with him.'

'You didn't see him then. He's a lot better now. We'll be taking him over there shortly but we're going easy on him for the present: resting him. He had a hard time.'

He nodded. 'I seen ladies do wonders with a mean horse. Well, we got work to do . . . '

* * *

Val was in the tack room. 'He was asking me about the provisions of Charlie's will,' she told them. 'It was no good me saying I didn't know, because all the family knows, someone would have given the game away. So I told him. He didn't show any reaction, except to remark that Jen had been favoured. I said she'd always been his favourite. We both acted as if there was nothing remarkable about the will.'

'He didn't ask any questions about Jen and — the estrangement?' Sophie pressed.

'No.' Val looked from one to the other uncertainly. 'He never mentioned it. Would he know?'

'Cole — the other one — knew everything else,' Miss Pink said wryly. 'He implied they'd talked to other people before they came here. They had time. The pathologist had all day yesterday. He could have discovered the bullet track in the morning.'

'July Fourth,' Sophie reminded her. 'It was a holiday. He needn't have started the autopsy till this morning and it's only a preliminary report.'

'So they say, but they're very well informed, Sophie.'

'They haven't talked to anyone in the family, and Sam would have told us if they'd been on to him.' Her eyes widened.

'What about Bret and Jen?'

They were silent, perhaps wondering how much the police knew, but Miss Pink considering how much there was to know, certain that for her part she had only pieces of the picture.

Val said, 'He asked how close Clyde and I were to the place where the body was found. When we were out on the loop trail, I mean.' Miss Pink had wondered that herself but it had been too delicate a question to ask.

Sophie had no such reservations. 'How close were you?'

'How do I know? We covered around ten miles that day and no one knows what time the accident happened. Besides, clearing the trail: using an axe and saw, we'd never have heard a shot.'

'I didn't think you would.'

'So? *He* said that was why he'd asked the question — did we hear a shot? But you want to know did I leave Clyde and ride on and find Charlie in the meadows above Mazarine. Don't look at me like that! I have an alibi.'

'Did you tell Hilton that?' Miss Pink was horrified. 'That Clyde is your alibi?'

'Of course not. There was no need. Hilton wasn't accusing me of shooting Charlie, he was on a fishing trip. Actually, he was quite friendly; he asked about the trail rides: where we went, did I screen the dudes for competence, that kind of stuff. He's a local guy, he knows the canyon, he understood when I said we didn't stop at the cabin on our way home after clearing the trail; we saw the pack-horse outside, thought Charlie was around and pushed on because I didn't want Ali behind my string, spooking them. He was making conversation, not really interested. He looks on this business as a chore; he's close to retirement and he doesn't want anything getting in the way of a smooth exit. He said so. He's a dozy bugger, says he hates wilderness deaths; if you can't land a chopper the only way in is on a horse and he doesn't like to ride. Ask me, he's too bone idle to go in the back country.'

'Cole isn't,' Miss Pink said. 'He's young, enthusiastic and has bags of energy, I'll be bound. He could be ambitious. And Hilton's not as idle as he makes out, otherwise how did he make lieutenant? They know more than they disclosed and I'm afraid they know more now than when they arrived. Did you tell Hilton Jen was at Benefit?'

'No. Jen wasn't mentioned except that she's the chief beneficiary in the will.'

'I think he knows she's there — '

'Why did he want to know about Ali?'

Sophie burst in. 'Why didn't he ask Val if he wanted to know?'

'Know what?' Val was at a loss.

'He wanted to know who owned the stud now. I told him, said we were taking him over to Jen soon as he was fit. I didn't give anything away, did I?' Sophie appealed to Miss Pink.

'You told the truth.'

They drifted to the door of the barn and looked out at Ali, his fine neck arched as he nibbled at a foreleg. 'Scab's itching,' Sophie said absently.

Miss Pink was frowning. If Val had it right Hilton hadn't been much impressed by the cash that Jen stood to inherit, and yet Cole had shown interest in the ownership of the horse. Sophie maintained that no one in the family had talked to the police — but Byer knew the contents of the will. And so did Skinner — 'Why would they do that?' came Sophie's voice.

'I'm sorry, I was thinking — about Ali. Why would they do what?'

'They've gone to see Edna — on her own — '

'She's Charlie's widow,' Val said. 'Of course they have to see her. Clyde's there, he'll make sure they don't bully her. Anyway, what can she tell them?'

'Why would they need to talk to Edna at all?' Sophie turned to Miss Pink.

'As Val says, she is the widow and she was the last person to see — ' She stopped just in time. 'They'll want to see all the members of the family, naturally.' She appeared to be stating the obvious but she was thinking: why *detectives*? Unless they *knew* it was a bullet track in Charlie's shoulder and therefore he had been shot. It could still have been an accident, but when the value of his estate was taken into account then the question was answered. What it came down to in police thinking was that other question: Who benefits? No doubt about the answer to that one.

The police didn't stay long at Glenaffric. Miss Pink assumed that Edna would phone Val as soon as they left but Val wasn't leaving that to chance. She posted herself in the paddock from where, ostensibly cutting down thistles, she could keep the start of the Glenaffric track in view. The others sat on the porch, watching and waiting. 'We should be with her,' Sophie said, her eyes on Val, glimpsed intermittently beyond the corrals.

'It would look suspicious: three of us chopping at weeds.'

'I meant Edna. She's my sister. She should have support at this moment.'

'She has Clyde.'

There was no response to this. Miss Pink stared fixedly as Ali came into sight, plodding after Val. 'You're thinking Clyde doesn't have the resources to cope,' she said.

'He could panic. Those two are a formidable team.' There was no need for her to identify which two, certainly she wasn't referring to Edna and Clyde. 'If they bully — hell, if they even hint that everything isn't as it should be, Clyde will go to pieces. He's nervy.'

'It's you who are panicking. Just because Clyde inherits half a million — '

'And you're forgetting how close they were to the hunting cabin that day,' Sophie pointed out.

'You're suggesting Val and Clyde — *together* — that they went to the cabin — '

'Police thinking. You know how their minds work.'

Miss Pink was silent. A gate clanged. Val was coming through the corrals. 'Now we'll know,' Sophie said, getting to her feet. 'Come along, you're with us. We could need you.'

Needed for what? To protect Clyde? Val and Clyde? Ridiculous, the police weren't even sure that it was a bullet track.

* * *

'They've taken Byer away,' Edna said when Val asked why his pick-up had followed the police car towards Ballard. 'They want him to take them to the place where the accident happened.'

Val grinned. 'Not today, he won't. The cloud's dropping; it'll be raining by nightfall.'

'Is that so, dear?' Edna fussed with paper napkins although they were in the kitchen, drinking coffee from mugs.

Clyde looked genuinely amused. Far from being in a panic, he appeared excited and eager. Miss Pink remembered his head bowed on his saddle and Val trying to comfort him after they found his father's body. He was the type who went quiet in a panic. 'What do they hope to find up there?' she asked, not expecting an answer.

'His rifle,' Clyde told her. 'And tracks.' His eyes shone.

Looking round the circle she saw that, without actually smiling, they all had this air of quiet amusement, except for Edna, struggling to open a packet of cookies. And Miss Pink, the countrywoman, knew why they were amused. It was going to rain and rain washed out tracks. 'Is that what they came for?' she asked ingenuously. 'To find Byer to act as guide?'

'They wanted to know about Charlie's will,' Edna said, sitting down, glancing at their mugs, concerned to be hospitable. 'I told them as much as I knew, bearing in mind Charlie could have drawn up another. We'll know tomorrow, after the funeral.'

Miss Pink had forgotten the funeral. 'So that's why they're taking Byer,' she said. 'Everyone else who was on the search will be at the funeral.'

'No,' Clyde said. 'They took him because he's the only guy who isn't family. There's yourself, ma'am, but he'll be classing you with us.'

'Possibly, but surely, with the cloud down, Hilton knows they can't go in today, not with a chopper, and it'll soon be dark. They'll go tomorrow. Why take Byer this afternoon?'

'They took him because they want information.' Edna's eyes went to her daughter. 'The fellow's been talking.'

Val licked her lips and looked dubious.

'What has he said?' Miss Pink asked.

'You don't have to ask,' Sophie cut in harshly. 'You said yourself: the police know everything, someone must have talked. It's obvious. It was Byer.'

'And now he's to take them to the site of the accident.' Miss Pink put no emphasis on the word 'accident'. She turned to Val. 'And the night before, when you sent him through the canyon to find out what was keeping your father, he turned back at the landslide, or so he said. Would he have had time to reach the cabin?'

Val said slowly, 'I have to think about that one . . . He didn't report back to me in person, he called from his house — quite late as I remember. But we were in such a state that evening, times and sequences just passed me by.'

Clyde was frowning. 'You're suggesting Byer could have had a hand — ' He glanced at his mother, then back to Miss Pink. There was no need for him to complete the sentence. 'What would his motive be?' he asked.

'I can think of one.' She smiled. 'It springs to mind, however far-fetched. If Byer were a petty criminal, an opportunist, he could never have made any money out of Charlie, who had a reputation for being — thrifty with his employees. On the other hand, the family, Charlie's beneficiaries, would appear to be a soft touch. And everyone has secrets they'd prefer not to be publicised.'

'Call him a blackmailer and be done with

it,' Sophie said. 'But in that case he'd want to steer clear of the police. Val said he was off like a shot this morning — ' She bit her lip. Unfortunate choice of words. 'Now he's working with them.'

The next move was for Edna to say she would fire him and for Sophie to follow suit, stating she wouldn't have him at the homestead. Val looked uncomfortable. Edna said, 'I shall be sorry to lose him. I'll advertise, maybe outside the state.' She nodded at her son. 'Someone has to be here when you're helping Val with the trail rides.'

'Jen and Bret will run the ranch, Mom.' He was gentle with her.

'I guess I'm jumping the gun, the will not probated yet an' all.' She made an apologetic gesture towards Miss Pink. 'We're going to make some changes around here,' she explained superfluously. 'Going to have our hands full for a while. We have to think where Jen and Bret are going to live. I can't picture them here, not as it is; I've been wondering how we could make the place into apartments: for Jen, Clyde, me; that is, if that's what they would like.' She sparkled happily at them.

'My sister's lost it,' Sophie said viciously as they drove away, leaving Val at Glenaffric.

'She's blocked out Charlie's death *and* the significance of detectives coming here; all she can think about is plumbing and extra bathrooms.'

'Displacement activity,' Miss Pink murmured.

11

The weather broke in a fierce summer storm. Through the evening and for much of the night thunder crashed above the town, raged away through the mountains and came rolling back, heralded by lightning flashes that were momentarily blinding. When the onslaughts were at their most sensational, sleep was impossible. Miss Pink stood at her window, amazed that the town lighting should still be working. With the rain at its heaviest, it was like being on the inside of a waterfall, but fascinating so long as you were safe indoors. They were to learn that three calves had been killed by hail the size of golf balls.

By dawn the rain had stopped and everything steamed: water, trees, the roofs of Ballard. Long wraiths of cloud layered the slopes and the Thunder river came roaring through its narrows with a force that threatened to bring down rock.

Asked out of courtesy if she would care to attend the funeral, Miss Pink had declined. She was putting the finishing touches to Sophie's outfit — a stunning suit in black and rose — when the doorbell rang.

'Russell?' Sophie murmured in surprise. But it was Hilton, dressed, like yesterday, as if his horse were waiting downstairs, which was almost literally so. He apologised for the untimely intrusion, his eyes absorbing Sophie's appearance with frank admiration, looking past her to Miss Pink, in slacks and shirt. Would she accompany him on a little trip?

Anticipating that she was being asked to assist them in their inquiries (a phrase as loaded as 'the usual suspects') she was wary. 'Tell me more,' she commanded.

Sophie was hesitating at the door, reluctant to leave without knowing the reason for this call.

Hilton said, 'You'll be away to the funeral, ma'am.' It was a hint.

Her nostrils flared. 'Miss Pink is my guest.'

He looked abashed. 'I know, and she's not used to our ways but' — turning to the visitor — 'you've ridden in the back country. D'you think you could go in there again, start from Benefit? Someone has to show us where the body was found.'

'What happened to Byer?' It was jerked out of Sophie. Miss Pink closed her eyes in despair.

A smile touched Hilton's lips — but he'd

know that the family would discuss every new development, every nuance; they'd all know that Byer was to have guided the police to the site of the accident. 'He's gone missing,' he said.

Miss Pink wasn't surprised; the news confirmed her belief that Byer had a lot to hide, possibly more than blackmail — 'There's only yourself, ma'am,' Hilton was saying, 'everyone else who was on the search will be at the funeral.'

He was right. Someone had to go. After all, with a mountain rescue, investigators have to be shown the site of the accident — incident, whatever — and that by one of the rescue team. 'Of course I'll come,' she said. 'What do I do about a horse?'

Hilton supplied the horse. He had arranged everything. He had a trailer waiting outside the sheriff's office, four horses already loaded, Cole and an elderly man called Breslow completing the party. Breslow was introduced as a former policeman. Blandly regarding the lean body, the worn chaps and thick shirt, Miss Pink thought: hunter, horseman, tracker; Hilton wasn't leaving anything to chance.

They drove to Benefit where the Ryans' cabin was closed and their pick-up absent. They unloaded and Miss Pink was mounted on a chunky grey with black points, whose movement was as neat as his appearance. Cole, she noted, looked a trifle strained but he should be all right on the relatively easy ground. It was fortunate they weren't going to ride through the canyon.

By the time they came out on the rim above the lake all the long cloud wraiths had evaporated and the world sparkled. New flowers had appeared after the rain: the big pale stars of bitter-root leafless on the drying soil, prickly pear with blooms of yellow tissue and always the haze of lupins drifted with Indian paintbrush. They halted on the lip of the escarpment and the lake below was gentian-blue, junipers deep green. A wren trilled bravely among the rocks.

They turned to her. At least, Hilton and Breslow turned, Cole seemed fascinated by the steep slope below their feet.

'Further on,' she said, and checked. 'No, it was the horse that was to the south, the body was below here, a little way back perhaps, in trees. We didn't see the body from this point, only the horse.'

'We'll start with the horse,' Hilton said.

They descended, Miss Pink now in the lead, the grey happy on steep ground, hopping neatly down rocky steps. The older men followed closely but Cole trailed behind, both hands clutching the horn, unable to straighten out his mount's lazy zigzags.

The night's torrential rain had removed nearly all signs of tracks; they had to look closely to see that horses had been here before today, particularly since the ground had been so dry that hoofs had made only shallow prints, now washed away. In fact, Miss Pink couldn't be sure at which cluster of boulders they'd found the stallion.

'So we'll leave the stud,' Hilton said comfortably after she'd described how they'd found the animal, with the saddle under his belly. 'And no rifle?' he prompted. No, there had been no sign of a rifle.

'Then where did you go?'

That was easy because she'd been leading Ali who was lame and didn't want to go downhill so they'd contoured the slope, staying on a thin game trail. That showed clear enough, marked by deer who had passed along it this morning while it was muddy.

The fresh tracks brought them to the trees and a scatter of sodden horse droppings where the party had waited for Miss Pink and Val to return from the cabin with the blankets. They dismounted and walked the few yards to the place where the body had been found, the location obvious from the trampled vegetation.

Hilton looked further into the trees. 'Now what?' he asked Miss Pink.

'This is as far as I came. It was the others who looked for his clothing while Val and I went to the cabin.'

'And the rifle. They looked for the rifle.'

She nodded. He knew it all, he was verifying accounts, looking for discrepancies. How much had Byer told him, *what* had he told him?

They continued on foot. Now Breslow took over and Miss Pink — who thought that the storm would have erased all trace of the stallion's passage — was astounded at the ease with which the man followed an apparently invisible trail over pine needles.

The belt of trees was thin and within a couple of hundred yards they emerged to open ground again. Above them was the escarpment, while steep slopes dropped away to meadows below. The ground was rougher here: bedrock on the trail, rocks jutting beside it, scree chutes below the scarp. This was where so much damage had been done to the body.

Here and there they found scraps of rag. Miss Pink came on a dime washed clean and shining. As she stood up, easing her back, she saw that the hunting camp had come in sight way below them, the pale thread of the main trail passing the cabin on a higher level. Ahead of them now was the start of the forest proper and, above, a break in the cliffs where a scatter of conifers climbed to the skyline. The slopes this side of the trees were covered with huckleberries and the trunk of a fir was raked with long claw marks: bear country.

They found his rifle in a patch where brambles hadn't recovered from being squashed by a heavy body, as if the stallion had reared and fallen over. There was a hat too, a Stetson clearly indented by a horseshoe.

The rifle was loaded. Charlie hadn't shot himself.

Breslow started to scramble upwards towards the escarpment. The men watched him but Miss Pink turned away, thinking that if there had been a bullet track in the body then there must be a bullet and, given the rest of the pointers, this would be the place to look for it. She considered the brambles and winced. No way was she going to search for it. She became aware that Hilton had turned to her.

'What did you do last Saturday, ma'am?'

Of course, everyone would be a suspect — well, everyone who was in the vicinity when Charlie died, everyone close to the family. She blinked but it was no good playing the doddery old lady; from her ability to cope with the country they knew she was a tough nut. What they didn't know was how devious she could be, although on that score she had the feeling Hilton might have suspicions, as she had of him. It took one to know one. 'I went to Irving,' she said, reflecting that at least she had an alibi, then, wryly, that the only person for whom she could vouch was Russell Kramer.

'Where was Miss Hamilton?'

'With her sister at Glenaffric.'

'So she left her house guest alone all day?'

'No. I was with Kramer from the hotel. I went back to meet her in the apartment for lunch.' Only a marginal lie.

'And Val Jardine and her brother?'

She couldn't resist a glance across the line of the river. 'They were clearing the trail, out there somewhere.' She gestured vaguely, aware once again that he would know all this already.

Breslow came sliding down through the trees. He looked at Hilton. 'A horse come down there,' he said.

Hilton looked at Miss Pink. 'That would be you, ma'am?'

'I didn't even know there was a way down

there. When we came here on the search we came the same way as today: to come out on the rim towards where the stallion was trapped.'

He wasn't listening. He was staring up the slope, and now Cole had caught on and his eyes were shining. Benefit lay over the top and a man on a sure-footed horse could drop down this slope and return the same way as quick and quiet as a deer. Of course he would have to know that Charlie would be at the cabin. Jen Ryan had known. Miss Pink tried to ease her facial muscles. She said inanely, 'We haven't found his other boot.'

Hilton's mind returned to her. 'It's not important.'

No, they didn't need the other boot, they had enough. Hilton had his motive: a multimillion-dollar fortune, and he was focusing on the suspect who would receive the lion's share, and her husband.

With suspect courtesy he suggested that she might like to go back to the horses and rest a while, maybe eat a sandwich — he had brought food for all of them. The others were going to climb the cliff. By that he meant the break in the cliffs. She suggested it might be safer if she remained with the party since this was bear country. He said blandly that she was quite safe, any old bear would steer clear if she made plenty of noise as she walked. He wanted her out of the way. She wanted to point out that a horse's tracks could have been made at any time: by poachers, hunters, day trippers, all could come down this slope from Benefit, thus avoiding the dangers of the lower canyon. She said nothing, aware of the risk of protesting too much.

On her return she found the missing boot. It lay below the path, drifted with silt. It told her nothing. She looked back and down the slope, and saw that the cabin was still in view, appearing curiously abandoned in its wild setting. Her eye travelled up the fringe of the forest to the break where presumably the men were now conferring, speculating on the identity of the rider whose track they were following. But if he — or she — had come this way to meet Charlie with the intention of killing him, wouldn't he have been more careful about leaving tracks? Not necessarily; in a place such as this, horse tracks were the flimsiest of circumstantial evidence, the courts would need something considerably more substantial on which to convict a suspect. And Byer came to mind; did he possess the kind of evidence needed, was that the nature of his hold over Val?

A movement caught her eye. Figures were emerging from the timber. Two of them started down the slope in the direction of the cabin while the third moved towards her — Hilton to judge by his heavy walk.

He arrived, sweating profusely. 'I'm not built for this kinda country,' he complained.

'You could have ridden.' She was tart.

'You're right, ma'am; I made a mistake there. But I figured the going could get tough for a horse.'

Her eyes went to the timbered skyline. 'Someone managed it.'

'Oh, yes. You can't miss the tracks. It's the shoes: they make scratches on the rock, easy enough for an old hunter like Breslow to see.' She was looking meaningly at the figures moving down the slope. 'He reckons they went to the cabin.'

'They?'

'The tracks, ma'am.'

'Why didn't you go with them?'

'I'm far too old for that slope. I come back for my horse — and to let you know what's happening, ease your mind.'

She took that at face value. 'I'm quite happy since you're sure there are no bears around.'

'Good, good. So tell me how you come to be here, in the wilds of Montana. The Black Canyon's not on the tourist route. Yellowstone, yes, but what brings you to Ballard?'

He was in no hurry to reach the horses. He appeared to be engrossed in the progress of his men but she knew that this exchange hadn't come about by chance. His purpose was to pump her, although the first question could have been innocent, the kind any curious native might ask of a visitor. She told him how she'd met Sophie, that her staying at the Rothbury was no more than return for hospitality she'd extended in Cornwall.

'It's the best way to do it.' He nodded approval. 'Visit with folk in their own homes: the best way to get to know a new country. Do they strike you as very different from folk at home? I guess you have lots of houses like Glenaffric in England.'

She was amused. Nice day, nice man — now sitting down, herself following suit: nice man sitting on a bank fishing, herself the big fish and well aware of the hook inside the bait. 'You mean Scotland,' she said. 'Glenaffric is in the Highlands, where Charlie Gunn's people came from originally. Actually, Scottish houses of similar size would be very different.'

'Not so much money around, maybe. Charlie was a multi-millionaire. Did you — '

'Oh, just as much money,' she exclaimed, blocking his question by rushing to the defence of Victorian entrepreneurs. 'But darker, you know? Glenaffric, at least on the outside, is bright, quite dazzling, in fact. A large house in Scotland would be built of granite, not whitewashed, very dull, with dark slate roofs and shrubberies. A little brighter inside: no blinds but cluttered. There it would be like Glenaffric: full of ornaments and stuffed heads.'

'You didn't like Charlie.'

A slight pause. 'What makes you say that?'

'You'd have said 'trophies' if you admired his den.'

'And by extension, him? His den? Sounds like a bear. Actually I didn't know him.'

'You met him, ma'am.' A statement, not a question.

'Once. We were invited to supper when Miss Hamilton was buying some horses.'

'A family meal?'

'Quite.'

'I mean, you met the whole family there?'

'Just his wife.'

'Not the son?'

'No, Clyde has his own house, down by the bridge over Bear Creek.'

'Ah. And he doesn't eat with the family?' Miss Pink refused to hear that as a question. There was a trace of impatience in his voice now, but it was a hot day, the sun climbing.

‘So he was eating at home,’ he said.

‘Presumably.’ She considered. ‘I forgot; that was the first day of their trip to clear the trail. He was in the mountains with his sister.’

‘Where exactly?’

It wasn’t a stupid question to ask of this particular stranger to the area. From here they could see a vast distance, not so much on the near side of the river because the forest and a great spur blocked the lower canyon from view but opposite, west of the river, they could see from the Bobcat Hills to the peaks this side of Yellowstone. He’d done his homework, discovered she was a mountaineer; he guessed that, given times and distances, she’d have a rough idea of the route taken by Val and Clyde even though she didn’t know the ground. But in asking the question he’d shown his hand. He’d been checking up on her.

‘Three days,’ she murmured, playing for time. ‘I have no idea where they camped for the two nights. We saw them leave and we passed them on the third day in the canyon. The stretch between is an unknown quantity.’ They looked upriver and she waited for him to push it, to probe further, expecting him to ask how far away they’d been on their second day out, the day Charlie was at the cabin.

'When you were looking for Charlie,' he said, 'where was Paul Skinner?'

She frowned. 'Skinner? He wasn't with us.'

'Jen Ryan? Where was she?'

Her eyes flickered. 'She wasn't on the search either.'

'Where was Ryan?'

'We met him on top and I think he went down by way of that very steep drop this side of the landslip. You know the canyon? Yes, well, that would be the only way down except above the lake.' She looked back to the timbered break. 'And there, in the trees. No doubt there are more places.'

'What did you do after you met him?'

'We came down close to where we did today.'

'So if Ryan came down this way' — he nodded towards the break — 'he'd have been travelling close to you, virtually with you, in fact.' She said nothing. He was saying that if Ryan descended close to the landslide on the day of the search, as she maintained, then he used the timbered break on another occasion: the crucial one. His next question would concern Ryan's reaction when they found the body — but he had found it first, no one had seen his immediate reaction.

'He had a visitor,' he said flatly, focused on the cabin.

She stared blankly, reorientating. Hilton was back with Charlie. 'It crossed my mind,' she admitted. 'But if so, it had nothing to do with his death. He died over a mile from the cabin.'

'The guy who visited Charlie down there coulda been the same one as shot him up here.'

Motive, she thought; now he's going to mention motive.

'Means, motive and opportunity,' he said and beamed at her. 'You all had 'em. Now what we have to do is find which one dunnit. You read detective stories, ma'am? Just my little joke.'

Dangerous ground; Charlie Gunn had liked his little jokes too and look what happened to him. 'What could be *my* motive?' she asked lightly. 'Viewed as a joke, of course.'

'Motives aren't necessary; if you got the evidence you don't need motive.'

'Granted. And the means?'

'Easy. You had a pistol, you shot him, you disposed of the weapon, threw it off of a bridge.'

'Imaginative. What about opportunity? I'd have had to use a horse. And — ' She stopped. This was getting too close to the bone.

'— And if you'd come in by the loop trail you'd need to pass Val and Clyde, and if you come in the middle way, like we did, you'd have to pass Bret and Jen's cabin at Benefit, and if you come the bottom way, through the canyon, you'd have to go by Erik Byer's place. There you are: collusion. Only way it coulda been done. I won't read you your rights, ma'am, we're only joking. That's his boot you found? Let me relieve you of it.'

She relinquished it and he started along the path. She followed, staring sightlessly at the ground, negotiating boulders on automatic pilot. Only her own role in his scenario was a joke; everyone else was family, any or all could have acted in collusion; all had means, motive and opportunity, all had kin as alibis, all bar one.

* * *

'Everything comes back to Byer,' she said, adding lemon to her China tea. 'He knows something, or he found something . . . ' She trailed off deliberately.

Sophie filled her own cup and replaced the teapot on its stand. She selected a slice of lemon and squeezed it with silver tongs. 'I'll ask Val,' she said, as if she would request the loan of a book. 'Did you learn anything new? I find it difficult to picture Hilton and Cole on that kind of ground. They managed to stay on their horses?'

'Hilton was more unhappy on his own feet.' Miss Pink was snappy. Horsemanship wasn't what the day had been about. 'In fact, Breslow and Hilton returned by that ghastly steep stretch where we came out after my first trip to the canyon.'

'It's only bad the first time.'

Miss Pink's lips thinned. 'Cole could never have ridden up there. Hilton sent him back with me, up the easy climb from the lake: the way we'd gone in.'

'What made him split the party?'

'He didn't give me explanations. Anyway, you can't believe a word the man says; when he isn't fobbing you off, he's being facetious. I'd hazard a guess that he split the party because he wanted to investigate another approach to the cabin from Benefit. He needed Breslow because the man has an eye for tracks. Cole couldn't cope with that route but Hilton couldn't send a novice back on his own so I was sent with him.'

'Did Hilton say if he discovered anything on that route?'

'Only that horses had been there. I

reminded him that we had gone up that way, Ryan had gone down, probably others.'

'More tea? Another slice of cake?' It was the American version of a pound cake: redolent of brandy and spiced fruits. Sophie was the perfect hostess. 'What did he have to say about the cabin?' she asked politely.

'Nothing. Just to ask was that how we found it, Val and I, when we went down for the blankets. It was, of course. No one's been there apart from Val when she went up for Charlie's saddle.'

'So really you learned nothing.' She meant about police thinking.

'Only this pig-headed emphasis on Bret Ryan and the proximity of Benefit. The part about us all being suspects is technically correct and I'm sure Hilton knows I'm aware of that. He elaborated on it as a joke in my case — his idea of a joke.' Miss Pink paused, then resumed, very English and ladylike, 'And how did the funeral go?'

Sophie smiled broadly. 'Marvellous. Oh, my appalling bad taste!' But she was still smiling. 'Afterwards, I mean: back at Glenaffric. We were all there: *all* of us, Jen and Ryan too. She's come home again.'

'I'm so glad.' Miss Pink was circumspect. 'There was no embarrassment?'

Sophie shrugged. 'Obviously — after so

long away.' Her smile faded. 'Not with Edna and Clyde; I guess it wasn't the first time she'd seen them since she came back. The same goes for Sam; he was at the ranch after the interment. But Val' — her eyebrows lifted at the memory — 'shy and stiff, you know, but fighting hard to appear natural. No hugs, of course; well, you wouldn't expect that, would you? They actually said — this was at the church: 'You're looking well' and 'You look great!' as if Jen had been on a few weeks' vacation. At the house they talked horses, would you believe, and every now and again when Jen would start about the ranch or the homestead — once I even heard something about money — one of the others would hush her. Of course, there were lots of people at the ranch and the maids. Jen's as indiscreet as ever.'

'Was Paul Skinner there?'

'Heavens no! He's not on those kind of terms — Why d'you ask?'

'I'm puzzled about him. Hilton mentioned him. When we went down to join the others at the cabin he was obviously on to something: looking round the interior carefully, not casually. He went to the door and looked up the slope to the escarpment. He'd already suggested that Charlie had a visitor. He'd asked about Skinner: where was he on the search? I said he wasn't there at all. He didn't comment on that but it left me thinking about Skinner: him and Byer.'

'Hilton thinks Paul's involved?'

'No. That is, he's pretty blatant about the family, implying all the members are suspect, but he's going for the money motive. However, Skinner doesn't benefit.'

'Of course he doesn't!' Sophie was vehement, but then she wouldn't want Skinner to be a suspect because if Hilton went after him, that can of worms would be opened which the family was so concerned to keep shut. But if he were ruled out through absence of one motive, he had another: he had been the butt of Charlie's last joke.

12

The telephone calls began: Val, Clyde, even Jen, all exchanging chit-chat about the reception after the funeral, all asking after Sophie's guest. She said that Miss Pink had had an uneventful day with the police: the ride to Mazarine Lake, a diversion to hunting camp.

At six thirty Val arrived, straight from riding. Miss Pink appreciated that she would have wanted to go round the horses after a day's absence, but it seemed perverse to call on her aunt still smelling of horse. She did apologise for not having changed, she was bushed after a hard day. 'Social life is so exhausting,' she told Miss Pink, bright-eyed and jumpy. 'Meeting people you haven't seen for years, some of 'em, having to be polite, putting on an act for my mother's sake. Family solidarity, right, Sophie?'

Her aunt brought her a stiff bourbon. 'Sit down,' she ordered. 'Take the load off your feet.'

Miss Pink sat opposite, blandly observing the younger woman. Sophie placed herself on the sofa beside Val; the arrangement had the effect of suggesting aunt and niece were ranged against her.

When the others remained silent, drinking rather than sipping, Miss Pink opened proceedings. 'My day was less tiring,' she told Val. 'A pleasant ride over the tops and down to Mazarine. I could have done without the police version of a packed lunch, however: cold sausage and squashed buns.'

Val giggled wildly and Miss Pink realised that 'buns' might have a different meaning here from what she'd intended. Val caught herself and asked shakily, 'Why did they take you along?'

'I was the only person on the search who was available. Everyone else was at the funeral.'

'Except Byer,' Sophie put in.

'Hilton said he was missing,' Miss Pink said.

'He was at Glenaffric.' Val sounded sullen.

Sophie was suddenly irate. 'With Clyde and your mother at the funeral? He could have made off with anything he fancied from the house.'

'No. The maids were around. They never let him go beyond the kitchen.'

'He has a reputation as a thief?' Miss Pink asked. 'In that case he may well have a record.'

'Did Hilton mention Byer?' Sophie asked of her. Questions and answers were loaded. 'Byer wasn't mentioned,' Miss Pink said. 'Paul Skinner was.'

'How?' Val asked. 'In what respect?'

'Hilton was interested because Paul wasn't on the search.'

'He wouldn't be.'

Sophie cut in quickly: 'That's what I said.'

'Did he mention anyone else?' Val asked delicately.

'Bret Ryan. Hilton was intrigued by the proximity of Benefit to the cabin and the lines of approach down the escarpment. And, of course' — Miss Pink was dismissive — 'he wanted to know how close you and Clyde were to the hunting camp that day.'

'He would.' Val was dry. 'What did you tell him?'

'Nothing. I don't know the area. All I did was show him where we found the stallion and your father's body. He did want to know the state of the cabin when we went down for the blankets. Actually, it looked just the same, but it would if no one's been there other than yourself.'

'When was I there?'

'Didn't you go back to fetch Charlie's saddle?'

'Of course. I'd forgotten.' There was a pause. 'Did he say anything else?'

'He did say Charlie had a visitor.'

Val gasped. Sophie said, 'He was guessing, Val: fishing. He can't know.'

The younger woman was rigid with hostility, glaring at Miss Pink. 'She was never there. The phone call means nothing, she changed her mind. I'm telling you she had nothing — '

'I never mentioned Jen or the phone call.' Miss Pink was firm. 'I gave them no information other than what I've told you — except I did say that when we were searching for Charlie, Bret had gone down that steep descent — '

'Upstream of the landslip,' Sophie supplied. 'But Hilton found another way down. Tell her, Mel.'

'There's a break in the escarpment above the cabin. It's timbered — '

'I know it.' Val was harsh. 'Why was Hilton interested?'

'They found horse tracks there.' Miss Pink took the plunge. 'It seems obvious that Hilton has his eye on Bret.'

Val was silent. Sophie said, 'But not Jen? He didn't mention her?'

'Not a word.'

'He does know they're married?'

Miss Pink thought about that. 'He did mention her,' she amended. 'He asked where she was on the search and when I said she wasn't out — with us — that was when he asked about Bret. He must know they're married and he's considering Bret because his wife is now a rich woman. He talked about collusion, said it was the only way it could have been done — and then he said he was joking.'

'Was he?' Val was tense.

'No. He wasn't actually accusing anyone, rather he was looking for my reactions, but he wasn't joking.'

'You said Jen wasn't on the search: 'not with us', you said. Did you see her somewhere?'

'There was a rider on a buckskin who showed for a moment when we were down below. Why not ask Jen if it was her?'

'I'll do that. It would have been the natural thing to do. She was shy about meeting us but she couldn't keep away. Charlie was her grandfather, after all. She'd have been keeping an eye on things: wanting to know what was happening. Maybe she was searching too, on top.'

'That would be it.' Miss Pink was equable. 'Incidentally, why would Byer agree to guide the police and then back down?'

'He couldn't refuse if Hilton asked him face to face, but he'd make himself scarce when the time came. Maybe there was some reason he didn't want to go near the cabin . . . Did they fingerprint it?'

'No. Why should they?'

'You said Hilton mentioned a visitor.'

'You think it was Byer.'

Val licked her lips. 'I wouldn't know.'

Sophie and Miss Pink exchanged glances. Sophie said, 'If your visit to the cabin was innocent, what does Byer have on you?'

'One hell of a lot — ' Val's voice climbed alarmingly, then stopped in mid-flight, her eyes frantic.

'Charlie died over a mile from the cabin,' Miss Pink reminded her. 'But think back: where was Byer that day? Could he have gone up there?'

'I sent him, when Charlie didn't come home. He said he turned back at the landslide.'

'That was Sunday and Charlie was probably dead by then. Suppose he'd mended the roof and decided to come home Saturday? Where was Byer that day?'

'Clyde was in the mountains,' Sophie said. 'Byer would have to do chores at Glenaffric, then he'd have the rest of the day to himself.'

He would have had heaps of time to reach the cabin. Miss Pink began to see that his hold over Val could relate to some specific feature of the cabin. She hesitated, caught Val's eye and knew that another question would be a bludgeon where what was needed was a fine probe. She said nothing.

* * *

'I know what you're thinking,' Sophie said. 'And you're wrong. I would have said so in front of Val but you can see she's keeping up the pretence that Jen isn't involved.'

Miss Pink was amazed. It was late, Val had left, Sophie had drunk a lot and was now being appallingly indiscreet — or trailing a red herring. 'You're saying Jen *is* involved?'

'Of course not. But Hilton thinks so, making believe he's focused on Bret when it's obvious Jen's millions are the motive. He maintains it was collusion. There's your answer: Val's fighting for Jen. Naturally. It's her child's life that's threatened.'

'The police are blinded by those millions. There isn't a shred of evidence to suggest either Jen or Bret was near the cabin.'

'Is that so?' Sophie brightened. 'Why didn't you tell Val that?'

'There was no need. When . . . if Hilton

were to pull Bret in for questioning, then we might reconsider. What did you assume I was thinking — and where was I wrong?'

'Oh, that! You figure Jen told Bret she was going to see Charlie at hunting camp and Bret wouldn't let her. He went in her place.'

'Actually I was thinking about Byer — '

'What's his motive?' Quick as a flash.

'So you'd considered him too.' Miss Pink pondered the question. 'Is it too far-fetched to speculate that he would kill Charlie in the expectation that he could blackmail a legatee — or legatees?'

'But that's exactly what he is doing!'

'I think in Val's case it's opportunism. He seized his chance. What I've seen of the fellow, and the way people speak of him, suggests a petty criminal, a thief, opportunist — all of those, not a murderer, not one who can plan. That takes strength of character.'

'You have someone in mind?'

'I'm not trying to squeeze someone into the frame. I'm saying Byer doesn't fit the role, unless there's something we don't know.'

'What we don't know is the hold he has over Val.'

Miss Pink went to bed grateful that Sophie was virtually stupefied by fatigue and bourbon. If she'd had her wits about her she would have realised that if you ruled out Byer for Charlie's death — and Skinner? — the spotlight came back to the family. But Hilton had shown an interest in Skinner. It was her last thought as she drifted to sleep. And her first in the morning.

'Tell me about Paul Skinner,' she demanded, coming into the kitchen. 'Skinner and Byer are friendly, if not friends, and Charlie said Skinner was a thief and responsible for the death of his second wife?'

Sophie handed her a mug of coffee the colour of molasses. 'Skinner had an alibi,' she said. 'He was in Ballard when his wife was drinking in Irving. Or so it was said. He was never charged, you know. You figure he'd have what you call the strength of character for murder?'

'With Charlie he has a motive.'

'No. He has no claim on the family, no bond. Unlike Sam. Hilton might suggest Sam has a motive because he's the father of an heiress.'

'I wasn't thinking in terms of money but hate: revenge for the slander that he murdered his wife and made Jen pregnant, was even her father. We considered a fight between Bret and Charlie, why not between Paul and Charlie? A fight, a shooting and the 'accident' rigged with the stallion.'

'Impossible. How could you hoist a corpse on to Ali's back? Remember how spooky he was. And then you have to twist Charlie's foot in the stirrup so it wouldn't come out and Ali would be standing still all this time, allowing you to do it? Come on, Mel!'

Miss Pink was unperturbed. 'Suppose Byer and Skinner acted in collusion. Hilton never saw Ali before. The horse is as quiet as a lamb now, he remarked on it; I had the feeling he didn't believe your insistence that Ali was wild before Charlie's death.'

Sophie breathed hard. 'It removes suspicion from the family.'

'It brings two more people into the frame,' Miss Pink corrected.

They soon learned how Hilton was thinking. They were sitting over French toast and Cooper's Oxford when Clyde rang to say that Bret Ryan had been taken in for questioning.

13

Hilton worked out of Irving and that was where Bret had been taken. Jen was frantic and had called Val to ask about securing the services of the family's lawyer. Val had dissuaded her, dismissing any suggestion that Bret could be in trouble. She did say she was going to Irving this morning and would have a word with the lawyer herself. Val had called Clyde to inform him of this latest development and he rang Sophie. It appeared that Val viewed the matter with more urgency than she'd intimated to her daughter because when Sophie phoned the homestead there was no answer. 'Left for Irving already,' she told Miss Pink. 'Now what do we do? If they suspect Bret, they have to be thinking Jen's in there with him. Collusion, Hilton told you. But it's impossible. Bret's a plain, simple guy and Jen would never — ' She shook her head, unable to finish it.

'An accident,' Miss Pink said, adding quickly, 'at the worst.'

'You suggested a quarrel. Maybe Charlie did shoot himself — during a fight.' Sophie's face lit up.

'His rifle wasn't discharged.'

'A pistol then. He drew a pistol — they were quarrelling, Charlie threatened Bret, both of them shouting — Ali reared, Charlie was thrown and shot himself, and Ali bolted. There! It could have happened that way.'

It wasn't a good moment to point out that no pistol had been found.

* * *

Glenaffric's kitchen was full of bustle, two large women in overalls at the sinks, Edna setting down a tray of glasses — 'How nice to see you again, Melinda. Did you come for a ride? Sorry about the mess; we're going to buy a dishwasher. Isn't that neat?' A vacuum whined and growled in the passage.

'Coffee?' Sophie said meaningly.

They took it to Edna's bedroom. She was full of chatter, raising the blinds, smoothing the bedspread. 'The women have finished in here,' she told Miss Pink. 'Nancy — she's the one doing the vacuuming — she's persuaded me to take it easy; why, she wouldn't let me make my bed. She did it. They're very thoughtful.'

Miss Pink murmured agreement. Sophie said harshly, 'We have to talk. Where's Clyde?'

'He's down with your horses, dear. Didn't you see him?'

'We didn't stop, and the herd's up the back. Is that where Val is?'

'No, she went to Irving. She asked Clyde to check on Ali and the others.'

'For heaven's sakes, Edna, couldn't you stop her dashing off like that? How does it look to the police?'

Edna smiled sweetly. 'She hasn't gone to the police; she has to fetch some feed and she's going to look in on Mr Seaborg.' She turned to Miss Pink. 'That's our lawyer. There's so much business to attend to at a time like this; not that anything's settled as yet but my daughter is bothered about taxes and stuff. I don't understand any — '

'Edna!' Sophie was beside herself. 'She's not seeing Seaborg about taxes, she's consulting him about Bret.'

'Bret?' Edna looked surprised. 'What does he have to do with Mr Seaborg? Nice manners,' she resumed to Miss Pink. 'He was here yesterday — Bret, I mean, not Mr Seaborg, although he was here too, of course, he came to read the will and stayed for champagne. I had the will right, Charlie hadn't changed it. We brought the Veuve Clicquot up from the cellar, Sophie — oh, but you were here! Stupid of me.

Nicely dressed, too, and he takes his hat off indoors.' She nodded happily. 'I'm pleased. Jen's gotten herself a good man there.'

'Bret', Sophie said, 'is being questioned as a suspect in Charlie's death. *Now* did I get through to you?'

'You always have to dramatise everything.' Again that sweet smile and, turning back to Miss Pink: 'Bret and Jen live at Benefit. That's an old ghost town at the back of the canyon rim.' She must have been told that Miss Pink had been at or near Benefit several times. 'And that's one of the trail-heads for our hunting camp,' she went on. 'Anyone going into the back country has to leave his rig at Benefit and ride from there. So the police need to ask Bret who passed that day, or maybe in the days before the accident, because they could have gone in and set up camp some place.'

'Did Clyde tell you this?' Sophie asked. 'Or did you make it up yourself?'

'She always treated me like the kid sister,' Edna told Miss Pink. 'She's five years older than me. Actually, Byer told me.'

'You're getting worse.' Sophie shook her head in despair. 'Tell me, how do you feel in yourself?'

'Free,' Edna said, and looked pleased with the word. 'The atmosphere's less strained.

Nancy was remarking on it: 'You got no one to consider now except yourself,' she said. And Kay's a good cook, I should let her fix me some fancy meals for a change. 'What's the use of having maids if you're going to work yourself,' Nancy said. So kind, treating me like an invalid. I've told them to go home at noon, make a long weekend of it; they worked so hard yesterday: all the baking and then waiting on the company.'

'So you'll be alone over the weekend,' Sophie said.

'No. Clyde will be here, and Byer.'

'Byer has weekends off. Clyde won't be here at night. Come to my place for a few days.'

'This is my home,' Edna said with dignity. 'It wouldn't be right to abandon it so soon — '

'I'm not suggesting — '

'Homes are like people. They demand loyalty. I'll come later, dear. Besides' — her eyes shone — 'the house belongs to Jen now; I'm a kind of custodian.'

* * *

'It hasn't penetrated,' Sophie said. They had stopped on their way to the car to watch a leggy foal skip jerkily round its mother.

'It could be shock. It's less than a week since Charlie died — and violently at that. Violence always intensifies the shock of bereavement.'

'I don't see any signs of shock in her.'

'That kind doesn't show. It goes too deep.'

'I hear what you're saying but — hello, here's Byer. So he's working up here and Clyde's down at the homestead. Everything's at sixes and sevens today. Now what?'

Byer was approaching with deliberation. He nodded casually to Miss Pink. 'Any news?' he asked Sophie.

Miss Pink turned towards the brood mares, ostensibly excluding herself from the exchange.

'News of what?' Sophie asked, hedging.

'Have they charged Ryan?'

'With what? He's helping the police just.'

'He don't have nothing to do with it.'

Miss Pink stiffened but they were too intent on each other to notice. After a long pause Sophie asked, 'So who has?'

'It weren't Ryan. Nor Jen. Nor Val.' He seemed to be enjoying himself.

Miss Pink turned. 'It was Clyde,' she said flatly.

'No!' He was startled at the intervention but behind the surprise she sensed something else. Fear? 'It weren't family at all,' he blurted. 'I know. Charlie talked to me.'

'Of course he did — and he told you someone was gunning for him, right?'

Sophie was gaping, looking from her to Byer. 'Right,' he said. 'It were some property developer — ' He stopped.

'A land sale,' Miss Pink stated. 'It went wrong.'

He nodded eagerly. 'Worth millions. The guy figured he had a raw deal. Lost everything — he were bankrupt. Said he was gonna get Charlie.'

'He put out a contract on Charlie?'

'I'm sure of it.'

'Have you told the police this?'

He shuffled his feet. 'I don't want to get involved. I've been in trouble: just cars, no insurance and stuff. I keep my head down.'

'It can't be true,' Sophie said as they drove towards the homestead. 'Charlie'd never talk to him about an important land deal.'

'No, but he might have spun him a tale about someone gunning for him. Alternatively, Byer could have fabricated the story to relieve the pressure on Bret — and, by association, on Jen.'

'You're saying Byer's suffered a sea change towards the family, or it's just that he doesn't want to lose his job?'

'Neither. It's that he can't employ blackmail if Bret or Jen, or both, are charged with homicide. He wants Bret off Hilton's hook and back on his own. Byer's out for Number One as usual.'

'He wasn't blackmailing Jen or Bret. It was Val.'

'So it was.' Miss Pink became thoughtful. 'Will he go to the police about this so-called property deal?'

'No, he'll expect you to do that. He knows you'll leap at any opportunity to keep Jen and Bret in the clear. Are you stopping at the homestead?'

'You bet. I want to hear some sense after listening to my kid sister's maunderings. 'Homes demand loyalty' indeed!'

* * *

Clyde was cagey at first. They'd come on him leading Ali across the yard towards a saddled horse. 'Val wants him taken to Glenaffric,' he told them, eyeing Miss Pink warily.

Sophie frowned. 'Why? He's better off here. Why does Val want to be rid of him?'

'She said she may be away some time.'

Sophie turned to Miss Pink in alarm. 'She meant overnight?' Miss Pink asked.

'Yes, ma'am.' He was tense.

'She's giving herself up!' Sophie said wildly.

'Heh! I didn't say that! She meant — ' Again that cautious glance at the visitor. He turned back to his aunt and took a deep breath. 'She never left me all the time we were clearing the trail,' he stated. 'Not once; no more'n five minutes, I mean.' He looked from one to the other, defiant as a small boy.

Sophie appealed to Miss Pink who said calmly, 'I'm not sure about the law here, but Hilton would probably view that testimony in the same light as he would that of a spouse.'

'Like Jen giving Bret an alibi,' Sophie explained, in case he didn't get it.

Ali was nuzzling Clyde's shoulder. He put up a hand to the soft lips. The defiance faded and the lines in his face relaxed. They made an impressive picture: the ageing Adonis and the sorrel with the shining eyes — much more alert today — back to normal? What was in Val's mind, handing the animal over to Edna? 'You could be right,' Miss Pink said. 'She may be expecting to be away a long time. She could have gone to the police.'

'There's bail,' Sophie pointed out. 'That will be why — '

‘*Bail!*’ Clyde was enraged. ‘I told you! She was with me all — ’

‘You’re as bad as your mother,’ his aunt told him, ‘refusing to face the facts. You figure your word stands for proof where the police are concerned — and now there’s Byer saying a developer put out a contract on Charlie. You’re all crazy.’

‘Byer said *what*?’

Sophie gestured impatiently. ‘It was just a story to get Hilton off Bret’s back.’

He pushed up his hat and wiped his forehead. ‘Byer never said anything to me.’

‘It’s a lie, Clyde.’

‘I’d have thought he’d want Bret jailed. They never hit it off. I’d never expect him to try and keep the guy out of jail. Why would he do that?’

‘He was blackmailing Val.’

‘He was?’ He looked stunned. ‘She never told me.’ They allowed him to think about it and they saw the moment the next question surfaced in his mind. ‘What — how could he blackmail her? What for?’

Another dead loss, Miss Pink thought; he was an ingenuous fellow, he really didn’t know the answer. Val had taken no one into her confidence. She listened distractedly as Sophie protested that she had no idea what kind of knowledge Byer held. She observed Clyde's efforts to recall distant events — a week old, anyway — and she was convinced of his sincerity. She wondered if Byer could be broken — and dismissed the idea; blackmailers didn't reveal the nature of their hold, even to their victims . . . Her brain faltered, checked and diverged. Did Val know herself? What kind of information was capable of disabling the victim without her knowing its exact nature? This called for lateral thinking. 'He could have planted something,' she said aloud.

They turned to her in astonishment. 'What?' Sophie asked, and 'Who?' came from Clyde.

'I'm thinking of the blackmail. Suppose Byer had stolen something of Val's and dropped it at hunting camp?' Or Jen, she thought: placing something of Jen's in the cabin. 'Not a good theory,' she went on, backtracking. 'Val's been to the cabin twice since Charlie was there. Anything of hers could have been dropped subsequently.'

'But Charlie didn't die in the cabin.' Clyde was mystified.

Miss Pink turned to Sophie. 'Let's go to Irving. We need to talk to Val.'

'You said it looks bad to go rushing off — and anyway, what excuse do you have to barge in there — if she's with the police? I mean, does Hilton know you've investigated murders before?'

Clyde's jaw dropped. Miss Pink said, 'Not investigated; I've just been there when they happened, or someone asked me to find out — I don't have to go to the police. You do that: find Val and try to get her away from them.'

'What do I say to her?'

'We'll work it out as we drive. The first question could be crucial. If it doesn't succeed she could throw up defences — more defences. We'll stop at the Rothbury, I'm going to need my car.'

* * *

After dropping Miss Pink at the hotel, Sophie went ahead, having given directions to the Riverside Restaurant where they would meet, providing she could find Val.

Miss Pink located the restaurant without trouble and sat in the shade of an umbrella on a deck overlooking the water. Here, in the city, the river had been dredged and deepened, and the water slid by with sluggish power. The occasional log floated past and once a pallet with an egret perched on the slats.

As the egret faded in the distance Miss

Pink became aware of Val approaching, with Sophie so close behind that she gave the impression of herding the younger woman, of giving her no chance to run. Val looked drawn, at the end of her tether.

'Found her parked outside the sheriff's department,' Sophie explained. 'Seaborg told me she'd gone there to wait, give Bret a ride home. But they're keeping Bret a while.'

Val sat down opposite Miss Pink. A waitress came and Sophie ordered coffee all round. Miss Pink asked curiously, as if in the middle of a conversation, 'How did Byer know it related to yourself and not to Jen?'

Val stared as if she hadn't understood the question. After a pause she shook her head in the faintest gesture of denial. 'It didn't matter.'

Sophie's mouth opened, and closed as Miss Pink's glasses flashed a warning. 'Either would do,' she mused. 'You'd fight even harder for Jen than for yourself. How does Bret come into it?'

'I don't know till I've talked to him. He hasn't — ' The waitress brought the coffee. They made small movements in their seats, looking automatically for spoons and sugar. 'How did you find out?' Val asked.

'It was obvious as soon as one realised

that Byer need not have turned back at the landslide that evening, that he went all the way to the cabin.' Miss Pink switched her attention to a sachet of Sweet and Low. 'If only you'd stopped off as you were passing next morning,' she murmured, and left it hanging.

'I didn't *know*! Besides — ' She stopped and glowered. 'I mean I didn't know I'd dropped anything when I visited with Charlie the — the day before. Anyway, Clyde was with me when we passed and no way would I have him implicated.'

'You *what*!' This was too much for Sophie. 'You really did visit with Charlie? For God's sake, girl!'

'I told you I did.'

'Yes, but we never believed — we thought — ' Sophie turned on Miss Pink, dumbfounded.

Miss Pink asked pleasantly, 'What was it that you left behind?'

Val's hand went to her ear and a tiny gold hoop. 'An ear-ring like this. Byer found it. He had a flashlight.'

'He wasn't to know it was yours.'

'It didn't matter. All he had to say was that Charlie had a lady visitor.'

'And the fact that you were intimidated by that told him he'd guessed correctly. But how does your visit to the cabin relate to Charlie's accident over a mile away, up by the escarpment?'

Val shrugged. 'I'm tired. We went up there. Charlie was trying to shake me off. I knew what he'd done, you see: coming between me and Jen; I lost ten years of my daughter's life. Can you understand that? I could have killed him. I would have killed him and he knew it, and he threatened to shoot me — well, my horse — he said he'd kill my horse if I didn't leave him alone. And I shouted at him, I flipped, and Ali spooked and reared, and Charlie'd drawn his pistol and it went off and Ali bolted.' She stopped and her ravaged face broke into a ghastly grin.

'What did you do with the pistol?' Miss Pink asked.

'I threw it away of course.'

'You're going to tell Hilton this?'

Val studied her. 'I'll see if he charges Bret. Are *you* going to tell him?'

'Of course not. It's your business and I'm Sophie's guest. And I'm tired too.' Miss Pink looked apologetically towards her host. 'I think I'll go back to the apartment and sleep for a while. I have the spare key. You'll stay with Val, of course.'

Sophie nodded distractedly. It was obvious

that neither cared what Miss Pink did at this moment; Sophie was intent on extracting more information from Val, and Val — Miss Pink nodded to herself as she went out to her Bronco — Val was too intent on incriminating herself to bother about anything else.

14

Meadow larks were singing on the road to Benefit, their breasts bright sulphur in the sun. Showers of little blue butterflies rose from drying puddles and overhead the vultures wheeled, alert for rodents washed out of flooded holes. The storm had left the world noisy and colourful, with a bonus of easy pickings for the opportunists.

Jen had company. Sam Jardine sat beside her on a bench outside the cabin and, seeing them like that, their expressions expectant, a little wary at the sight of the Bronco, Miss Pink wondered how anyone could have thought that Sam was not the girl's father. There were the same delicate features and wiry build; both had the aquiline nose and chiselled nostrils hinting at Indian ancestry. No one could think Jen the daughter of the blond and beefy Skinner.

Sam was standing. 'Nice morning, ma'am. Take a seat, enjoy the sunshine. I'll fix some coffee.' He stepped indoors.

Jen was eyeing the Bronco, uncertain how to react to this visit.

'I've been to Irving,' Miss Pink said.

'Talking to your mother.'

'Bret?' It was a whisper. She cleared her throat. 'Did you see Bret?'

'No. I didn't go there to see him. The first person to clear was Val.' Miss Pink smiled pleasantly and didn't turn, although she hadn't missed the other's glance at the doorway. 'She didn't go to the hunting camp,' she went on, 'although she's fighting like mad to convince Sophie and me that she did.'

Jen grinned and then was serious again. 'How do you know she wasn't there?'

Sam stepped out of the doorway and stood beside the bench, waiting for the answer.

'Because she has no idea what was left behind,' Miss Pink said. 'What it was that Byer found.'

'What was it?' Sam asked, looking down at his daughter. Jen was shaking her head. He put a hand on her shoulder and regarded Miss Pink. She hadn't sat down and they confronted each other like adversaries. 'Jen didn't go to the cabin,' he said firmly. 'So you can tell us what was left there.'

Her mind raced. Sam? This would add a new dimension, she had never seriously considered Sam.

The pause had been momentary. 'Bret will have told them the truth,' she said.

Jen stared into the distance. She nodded as if in agreement. Sam's hand tightened on her shoulder. She looked up quickly. 'Charlie was fine when Bret left,' she assured Miss Pink. 'He figures that it was a bear frightened Ali and Charlie's gun went off by accident. No one else was involved.'

Miss Pink glanced at Sam to see if he knew that Charlie's rifle hadn't been fired, that no pistol had been found, but he was deadpan, observing her own reactions. 'Why did Bret go to the cabin?' she asked.

'To see what Charlie wanted.'

'Charlie made the arrangement with you.'

'Bret wouldn't let me go.'

'What did Charlie have to say?'

'Nothing really.'

Miss Pink moved impatiently. Sam said, 'Bret told Charlie that him and Jen were married but Charlie didn't have much to say about that. Bret felt it wasn't the right moment to say anything about — what Charlie had told Jen — ' He stopped in confusion.

'I didn't know then!' Jen protested. 'It was only afterwards . . . why, it was you told me only a few days back. How *could* I have known?'

'You'd told Bret.'

'Not all of it and not the worst part. That's

the point, Sam. I'd told Bret I'd gone away because I was having a baby but I never told a soul who was responsible.' She pondered a moment and then: 'I told him Paul was my father because that was what I thought myself, but Bret didn't make the connection: that Paul was the baby's daddy as well.' Her eyes widened madly. 'Who would? It's wild, horrible!' She inhaled sharply, let the breath go and went on, 'I got used to it, though: the horror, blocked it out, I guess, over the years' — she was addressing Miss Pink — 'but imagine a guy like Bret learning that . . . He loves me, you know.' She smiled shyly and the next moment she was grim again. 'He'd have killed Paul. But I blamed my mom. There was no way I could take the blame myself, I'm too much of a coward.'

'She couldn't,' Sam told Miss Pink earnestly. 'It were too great a burden. She were only a kid.'

'And as for Paul' — Jen shrugged — 'he wasn't worth blaming; you have to be big to take a load like that on your shoulders. I mean, Paul wouldn't be *worthy*. Now my mom was a good person to hate. I'm telling you how it was for me all those years away. I blamed Mom for letting me think that Sam was my daddy when really it was Paul, so I figured it was all her fault that he — that we — the baby, I mean; she was to blame for everything. I was so angry, I coulda killed her. My God, I was a mess! I guess it was guilt, right?'

'You had to turn the rage against someone,' Miss Pink said calmly. Alone in Texas and pregnant (and through incest, as she had been led to think) if she had turned the rage inwards she might have killed herself. As it was, she had killed . . . there had been an abortion, presumably. More guilt.

Sam was watching Miss Pink. 'It was Charlie told her Paul was her daddy,' he said heavily.

'So when you came home,' Miss Pink said, 'you meant to confront your grandfather — '

'No! I told you: I didn't know then! I still thought Paul was my father. I came back because — because — '

'She was lonely,' Sam put in. 'She wanted to be with her folks again.'

Miss Pink couldn't hide her scepticism as she turned to the younger woman.

'I'd found out I couldn't have babies.' Jen's face was set. 'Something about internal damage. The abortion was botched, they say. Actually, I don't know why I came back. To confront Mom? Someone anyway, make them pay for everything. How I felt, it was the old ghastly mess back again, only worse, and one moment I wanted to be with my family, like Dad says, the next I was full of hate again.'

'I see.' Miss Pink did. She saw more. Jen was to discover that the person at fault was her grandfather — but she hadn't found that out until after Charlie died. Fortunate timing for her, but Hilton would never believe the sequence of it. 'When did your mother learn the truth?' she asked.

'I never told her. I wouldn't dare.'

Sam said, 'Now she's scared of Val because she misjudged her so. She don't know how to make it up to her.'

'She was sweet to me yesterday, though.' Jen's tone was soft. 'After the funeral, but then she doesn't know what a bitch I've been.'

'She knows,' Miss Pink said. 'And she thinks you killed Charlie.' And after this demonstration of her feelings Jen had motive enough.

'She'll get over it.' She was unperturbed. 'Bret will tell the truth. He went to the cabin, told Charlie he'd seen a bear on the way down, in the rocks there above the cabin. Charlie was all set to leave, the pack-horse loaded, having a last coffee, when Bret arrived. That's why they didn't say much; Charlie — '

'Wait a minute.' Miss Pink stirred impatiently. 'Charlie was expecting you to visit; why would he be leaving if you hadn't come?'

'Just that: I hadn't come. He told Bret he'd given up on me, wanted to get through the canyon before dark. He said he'd ride out to Benefit only he had the pack-horse — and then there was the bear. I guess at that the bear had priority. If it wasn't shot it would try to break into the cabin again. So Bret just had some coffee and they both took off: Charlie up through the meadows, Bret coming down the canyon because he didn't want to be close by with Charlie out shooting bear.' Jen stopped, considered and added, 'He thought someone else was about.'

'You didn't tell me that,' Sam exclaimed.

'I forgot till now.'

'Where was this?' Miss Pink asked.

'Upstream of the landslip, before he headed up that steep climb to home. But it couldn't have been anyone, not really. How could you tell among all those tree trunks? Most likely it was a moose.'

'It coulda been a poacher,' Sam said. 'He wouldn't want to be seen.'

'Then he'd have to leave his rig here and there was no one left a trailer that weekend.'

'Unless he rode in from Ballard.' Sam's eyes gleamed. 'Or from Byer's place. It was a Saturday. Where was Byer?'

'His day off,' Miss Pink supplied, thinking that Skinner could have ridden in from Ballard.

* * *

'If you eliminate the family — as, of course, one does — you come down to Byer and Skinner.' Miss Pink added aubergine to the pilaf.

'What makes you so sure the family can be eliminated?' Sophie leaned against the wall, looking tired after the long day. 'Devil's advocate,' she added, 'but I did feel that Val was protesting too much when we were at the Riverside.'

'Oh, undoubtedly, but it can't be Val or Bret; their stories are too thin.'

'Everyone is speaking the truth — '

'Some of them are, a framework of truth, perhaps, but much embroidered. The weft but not the warp? Byer admits he was in the canyon but stops short of saying how far he went. Val, of course, is lying; she was never at the cabin the day Charlie died — '

'She's protecting Jen.'

' — and she hasn't thought her story

through. If Charlie shot himself with a pistol, where is it?'

'She said she threw it away. What's wrong with that?'

'You're taking devil's advocacy too far. What is wrong with Charlie having a pistol is that he wasn't wearing a gun belt. It couldn't have come unbuckled any more than his pants belt did. Clothing gets ripped off when a rider's dragged, but no way can a belt come undone. Besides, if Val had been at the cabin, Bret would have seen her.'

'He wouldn't say so.'

'Hilton would get it out of him.'

'Bret doesn't have to have seen her anyway; they could have been at the cabin at different times.'

'Unless she was hanging about, waiting . . . ' Miss Pink checked and frowned. 'Someone was hanging about,' she resumed thoughtfully.

'Bret saw someone. He told the police. He figured Hilton didn't believe him. Is that where you say his story's thin?'

'It couldn't have been Val.' Miss Pink was on her own tack. 'She had to come from the opposite direction: down through the meadows, but Jen says Bret saw someone between the cabin and the landslide. It comes back to Byer — again. And Skinner?

Byer preferably. Skinner has no motive . . . well . . . '

'He hated Charlie: spreading all those stories about him; you pointed that out yourself.' Miss Pink was silent, staring at her friend. 'They're still not saying for certain it's a bullet track,' Sophie went on. 'How can anyone be sure, all the damage that was done to him?'

'If he was shot, someone took a gun in there with them and that would make it premeditated.'

'Not necessarily. Val carries — I mean, loads of guys carry pistols — much more convenient than a rifle. You can scare off a bear, kill a rattler . . . Not that I would — carry a gun, I mean, or kill snakes — but there are men would never leave camp without a gun, they wouldn't feel dressed.'

She was talking too much and Miss Pink hadn't missed that reference, so quickly stifled, to Val carrying a pistol in the back country. She sighed heavily. 'But how many people knew about Charlie?' she mused.

Sophie chose to misunderstand. She looked sullen. 'All of us. It was an open secret. Edna had seen a copy of the will. And then Charlie had told Byer, who told Skinner.'

'No, no.' Miss Pink dismissed the will out of hand. 'How many people knew that Jen had been pregnant and that Charlie told her Paul was her father?'

'Nobody . . . ' Sophie thought back and went on slowly: 'We didn't know until Bret arrived that day at the homestead and demanded we hand Ali over because her father — and he meant Paul — said the stud came to Jen in Charlie's will.'

'But when did you know she left home because she was pregnant?'

'Why, not until the morning Charlie left for hunting camp. You remember: he told Edna and she called me. We'd had suspicions, Val and me, but that was all it was: suspicion.'

'But you didn't tie the two threads together — Jen being pregnant and Paul being, supposedly, her father — until later, did you?'

'You're right.' Gradually the significance dawned on Sophie and she was elated. 'No one knew the whole truth until Charlie was dead.'

Miss Pink shook water from sprigs of parsley. 'Hilton would suggest they did.'

'Oh Hilton! He can go to hell. *We* know we were all in the dark. In any case, he's not going to find out about that business unless someone tells him and you're not about to do that.'

'Of course not.' Miss Pink started to

chop the parsley. 'Actually, he has enough motivation with the money angle, he doesn't need another motive. It's odd', she mused, pushing parsley round the chopping board, 'how the motives accumulate: family members might equally well have murdered Charlie out of revenge as for the money. An *embarras de richesses.* I still can't understand how Hilton came to release Bret.'

'He was never arrested, Mel. I told you: they wanted to question him just.'

'At home that would be synonymous with his being a suspect. Assisting the police with their inquiries, it's called.'

'They had nothing to charge him with. No bullet track even — not for definite — although apparently there are guys out there looking for the bullet.'

'Did Hilton ask for Bret's rifle?'

'No. To test-fire it, you mean? Can they do that?'

'I wouldn't think so, without a charge. You know, you could be right and they don't suspect him — well, not to head the list.' Miss Pink hesitated. 'I take it he told them the whole truth: about going to the cabin, telling Charlie about the bear and so on?'

'Yes, only he said he happened to be riding that way looking to locate the elk herd and first he glimpsed a bear, then he saw the cabin chimney was smoking so he went down to see who was there.'

'Why did Charlie have a fire when he was just about to leave?'

'He wouldn't put his stove out till the last minute, it's the only way to brew coffee when — '

'Wait! Did Bret say that Charlie washed up?'

'You mean did he *wash*?'

'Did he rinse the coffee mugs? Jen said Charlie gave Bret coffee. And there'd be the pot . . . That's it! That's how Byer knew Charlie had a visitor: he *did* go to the cabin Sunday evening: he found a dirty coffee pot and two mugs, thought nothing of it until — ' Miss Pink stopped, staring at the chopping board.

'Until what?' Sophie prompted.

'Until he reached the cabin the following morning — when we were searching — and he found the mugs and pot had been put away. I'll bet Val got there ahead of him and rinsed them, and wouldn't say anything because she thought Jen was the visitor. *That's* Byer's hold over her. The point is,' she went on slowly, 'how did she know on the morning of the search that it was imperative she remove any trace of Charlie's visitor?'

'Edna had told her about Jen's phone call.' Sophie's mind was working, trying to keep up with Miss Pink's. 'But Byer had to know something was very wrong the previous evening if he reached the cabin. He wouldn't think anything of two mugs and a coffee pot on the table but you forgot the pack-horse standing outside. He knew something had happened to Charlie, but he came back, called Val from his house, said he'd gone only as far as the landslip. If that's what happened, it's gruesome, Mel.'

'He may not have the guts to kill but that doesn't mean he wouldn't be pleased if Charlie died. Look how he's taken advantage of it. Perhaps he even went further than the cabin; after all, he had all day Saturday — '

The doorbell rang. Sophie crossed the floor to admit Russell Kramer, as usual beaming good nature, as usual apologetic for calling without advance notice. He proffered a plastic bag heavy with fish but his face fell as he took in Miss Pink's activity at the stove.

'I'm too late but these will do for your breakfast.' He turned to Sophie. 'We were up to the Finger Lakes, caught us enough rainbow for Edna too. Clyde and me,' he explained to Miss Pink.

Sophie was puzzled. 'Clyde went fishing

today? That's not like him, leaving his mother on her own. I mean, we only buried Charlie yesterday.'

'She insisted he go. There was nothing to do at Glenaffric and she said he was getting under her feet. When I called to say I was going fishing, he was off like a rocket. Now tell me, how was your day?' He looked eagerly from one to the other.

'You know the police questioned Bret?' Sophie asked.

He nodded happily. 'Another kinda fishing trip. They'd think the poor guy was the weak link: he'd spill the beans on the family, except there are no beans to spill.'

'How right you are. Yes, the police let him go. Val was waiting and gave him a ride back to Benefit. There's no news really.' She glanced at Miss Pink who turned to the pilaf and stirred it with concentration. Regarding her back Sophie said casually, 'Bret told them it was him visited Charlie at hunting camp.'

Russell gave the ghost of a sigh. He was no longer amused. 'And?'

'He left Charlie fit and well, and riding up to the rocks where he — Bret — had just seen a bear. Then Bret thought he glimpsed someone in the trees off the trail as he rode down the canyon.' He stared at her. 'Clyde was *upstream* of the cabin,' she said with careful emphasis.

'So who — Bret *thought* he saw someone?'

'It could have been a moose.'

His mouth twitched. 'Where does Hilton stand now? Does he still suspect foul play?'

'Did he ever?' They drifted into the living area, Miss Pink absently cradling the Tio Pepe she'd been using in the pilaf. Sophie took it from her and filled three glasses. Russell accepted a drink without thanks, his eyes on the traffic below the window, his expression vacant.

'Clyde and Val were together all the time,' Sophie said, as if he didn't know that. 'Bret had no call to say he was at the cabin, he volunteered the information. He's too simple to play a game of double bluff. Besides, if he had followed Charlie up to the rocks, he'd know he'd leave horse tracks?' It turned into a question and it was directed to Miss Pink.

'The slope was covered with tracks after the search,' she pointed out. 'And then it rained.'

'What are you saying?' Russell had emerged from his reverie. 'That Bret could have shot Charlie, or that he's covering for Jen?'

'Jen had no motive,' Sophie said. They

stared at her. 'She didn't know,' she reminded Miss Pink.

'Everyone knew,' Russell protested. 'Even I knew. Clyde — ' He stopped.

'I'm not talking about the money.' Sophie was impatient. 'OK, so Jen knew about that, but it wouldn't mean anything to her.'

It would mean something, thought Miss Pink, recalling the evidence of straitened circumstances at Benefit, but Sophie continued. 'I meant the other — factor: that she didn't know about her parentage until after Charlie's death. That is, she was unaware exactly how depraved her grand-daddy had been. Why' — her voice rose — 'she couldn't have been more abused by that old monster if he'd done it physically.'

'Keep it down.' Russell was quick and firm, startling Miss Pink. Hidden depths were not revealed by three words and yet occasionally she'd had a glimpse of something powerful behind the clown's mask. He had turned to her. 'This family is volatile,' he informed her. 'They wear their hearts on their sleeves. Operatic, that's what they are.' He put an arm round Sophie's shoulders. 'We must learn to practise a little subterfuge, dear, if we're not to arouse Hilton's suspicions.'

'He's right,' Miss Pink said when he'd

gone and they had sat down to supper. 'You are inclined to speak first and think afterwards.'

'Only in my own home. In fact, I wasn't speaking my mind to Russell. I'm annoyed that Clyde should have gone off and left Edna on her own.'

'She had the maids.' Miss Pink frowned and added, 'And there was Byer.'

'That's what I'm thinking — and you forgot: she told the maids to leave at noon. She can't cope with Byer in her condition — and I never asked Russell if Clyde was going back to Glenaffric or to his own place.' Sophie put down her fork. 'I'm going up there, tell her about this morning. She'll be worried about Bret.'

Not if Edna was convinced Charlie had died in a fall from his horse; it was more likely that Sophie was worried about Edna . . . 'I'll come with you,' Miss Pink said.

* * *

Sophie need not have been concerned. At Glenaffric they were met by Clyde who told them that his mother was lying down. Miss Pink didn't miss the exchange of looks between aunt and nephew. 'You can go up,' he said. 'She'll be pleased to see you.'

There was no feeling in the statement but Sophie chose to take it at face value. 'I'll just look in on her,' she told Miss Pink. 'You stay here.'

Seeming a trifle embarrassed, Clyde poured coffee and set himself to entertain the guest, but she forestalled him.

'Russell brought us some fine trout,' she said brightly.

He nodded. 'There were plenty. Those lakes back of the Bobcats swarm with rainbow. Cut-throat too. Do you fish?'

She confessed that she was the rawest of amateurs and without a change of tone told him he must have heard about the outcome of Bret's interview with the police that morning.

'Val called,' he admitted. 'She's over to Benefit. Kind of a reunion. Sam's there too. I'm so glad.' And he did look happy for them.

'Hilton's given no indication that he wants to speak to you?'

'No-o. Why should he?'

'Jen is the principal beneficiary in your father's will. Val would do anything to protect her. Now that Bret's admitted he was one of Charlie's visitors at the hunting camp, Hilton will be wondering if Val was the other. And you are Val's alibi.'

He'd listened intently: an incredibly handsome man, like a ravaged hawk. 'He isn't thinking that way,' he told her. 'If he was, he'd have pulled me in. Who was the other visitor Charlie had?' He smiled. 'Seeing as it wasn't my sister.'

'Bret saw someone below the hunting camp.'

'No, ma'am, he thought he did but all he saw was its legs. At a distance you can easily mistake a moose for a horse.'

'It could have been a poacher.'

'What's that?' came Sophie's voice as she entered from the passage. 'What was a poacher?'

'That Bret saw below the hunting camp.'

Sophie shrugged. 'Could be.' She addressed Clyde: 'No wonder she gave the maids the afternoon off! I should have guessed.' She glanced at Miss Pink and mimed lifting a glass to her lips. 'Are you staying?' she asked Clyde.

'Yes, I'll stay the night.'

'I will if you want to go out. Melinda can take the car back.'

'No, I'll stay. She should be all right by tomorrow.'

'She shouldn't be — '

There was movement behind Miss Pink. Clyde leaped to his feet and plunged round the table. 'Now, Mom — '

' 'Don' fuss, son, you shoulda told me we had company, shoulda offered her something — oh, you have coffee . . . '

Miss Pink was aghast at the appearance of Edna: hair like old hay, bleary-eyed, in a gaping pyjama top that exposed a greyish brassière: staggering and drunkenly resisting Clyde's efforts to turn her back to the passage. He gave up and lowered her to a chair where she succeeded in placing one elbow on the table. She tried to turn towards Miss Pink who had sunk into a chair at her side, but it appeared that arthritis prevented her from twisting her spine. This annoyed her. 'Shoot!' she mumbled. 'I can't see you.'

Miss Pink stood up and walked round the table but Edna was still making the effort to turn to the empty chair.

'Come on,' Sophie urged Miss Pink. 'Let's go.'

'I'm sorry.' Clyde grimaced at them.

'Not your fault,' Sophie said roughly. 'But you should have guessed; it was why she wanted you out of the way. And the maids. She does it,' she told Miss Pink, 'not often, she's not an alcoholic.'

'Who said I'm an alcoholic?' Edna shouted, her hearing functioning if her vision was temporarily impaired. 'Don't you go saying I'm an alcoholic. I don't drink at all — really, do I Clyde? Clyde! Where's Clyde?'

'Mom, how about a Scotch? There's a bottle in your bedroom, let's go and have a nice big Scotch, how's that?'

'I'm out of here,' Sophie grunted. 'You too, come on.' And she grabbed Miss Pink's arm and hustled her out of the kitchen.

15

Over the grilled trout at breakfast time they discussed what they should do this day, each avoiding mention of that embarrassing scene at Glenaffric, but Miss Pink thinking that Sophie would want to visit Edna on her own. 'Delicious fish,' she observed, although, with the exception of kippers, fish wouldn't be her preferred choice at breakfast. 'Where are these Finger Lakes?'

'On the west slope of the Bobcats. You're thinking of going fishing?'

'Oh, no, I'd never have the patience. I was thinking in terms of a ride. Barb could do with the exercise.'

'That's an excellent idea. Will you feel comfortable on your own? There are things to do . . . You see, the problem is the stock. The money doesn't matter' — she gave a light laugh — 'it will be ages before the will's probated and they're not in urgent need, any of them; besides, I'm sure Seaborg would give the go-ahead and there's always credit . . . ' Miss Pink was buttering toast with care, as if she had nothing else to do but wait for this flow of words to run its course. ' . . . Although there's the interest,' Sophie gabbled on. 'Charlie would turn in his grave . . . But there, you're not interested in us discussing which animals are to go where. And to whom. Funny thing, us all being family it's more complicated, not simplified as you'd expect. I mean, the brood mares at Glenaffric, the stallions, Val and her business . . . I guess she'll be wanting to buy me out now.'

Miss Pink chewed stolidly, listening with only the surface of her mind, but vibrations must have been apparent. 'Boring old stuff,' Sophie announced, now with an edge in her tone. 'A nuisance for you.'

'Bad timing,' Miss Pink observed. 'Charlie's death, Edna hitting the bottle. I'll be fine on Barb. You'll know where I am.'

Sophie was tight-lipped. 'I'm scared stiff,' she confessed, coming clean, as so many people did under Miss Pink's bland eye and shock tactics.

'I don't see why you should be. Admittedly Val thought Jen was involved, but she wasn't — '

'Jen thought it was Val.'

'Really? How do you know?'

'Jen told Sam.'

'Ah yes, he's Jen's obvious confidant now she's returned to the fold. And Val is Clyde's alibi and vice versa — and there's Edna convinced that Ali was the perpetrator. I take it you rule out Bret; he didn't have to tell Hilton he went to the cabin. Which leaves Sam — '

'Oh, no. You might just as well cite Russell — '

'No. He doesn't ride.'

'Melinda! You're serious!'

'Police thinking. And I've taken over the devil's advocate role from you.'

'You really think the police would consider Sam?'

'They'll consider everyone in the family, or connected with it. Now I wonder: do they know about Byer? That's a thought; we don't *know* that Val washed the coffee mugs, it was guesswork on my part. You should ask her. There's no point in her lying now that we know Charlie's visitor was Bret.'

'You pointed out that there could have been another visitor at hunting camp.'

'Bret's apparition? That had to be a moose.' Miss Pink was too casual and Sophie's eyes narrowed.

'You're thinking of Byer. Are you meaning to go to his place?' Miss Pink said nothing. 'No way!' Sophie was adamant. 'If you have any suspicion — and you have, I know you have — then I'm coming with you. For

God's sake, Mel, if there's a chance he was involved in Charlie's death I'm not about to let you go to that house on your own.'

Miss Pink protested but Sophie refused to budge. In the event, protests and argument were superfluous; when the Cherokee nosed down the track to Bear Creek, Byer's horses were in their pasture but there was no sign of his pick-up.

'Saturday,' Sophie said, without expression. 'He could have taken off last night.' She turned in the yard and started out again.

'Stop!'

'Why?'

'I want to go inside.'

'Mel! You can't!'

'*You* can't, you're his employer's sister. I have no connection.'

'Suppose he comes back?'

'We'll think of something. He can't kill us.'

The words hung in the air. Otherwise there was only the sound of the creek, still running high after the rain, and a group of redwings talking in a reedy slough.

Sophie advanced to a dirty window. Miss Pink went to the door and turned the old-fashioned knob. The door opened obligingly. Sophie stared in alarm, but Miss Pink entered as if it were her own property.

It was a shabby little house: two up, two down, of no character other than that lent to it by a horseman. One room was given over to his saddle and tack, a slicker, chaps, old boots and spurs, tins and bottles on the dusty windowsill containing salves and thick brown liquids.

The other ground-floor room was furnished after a rough fashion with two ancient armchairs, a formica-topped table with tarnished gilt legs, kitchen chairs, cupboards, a sideboard and a telephone. There was a television set and a radio, tattered copies of *Western Horseman* and a stack of magazines on guns and hunting.

At the back there was a slip of a kitchen and a sink, but cooking would have been done on the wood stove in the living-room.

They went up the uncarpeted stairs. There were two bedrooms containing four single beds, only one of which was in use. The sheets were neither dirty nor clean, the blankets looked as if they were military surplus stock and dust swirled in sunbeams at every move they made.

There were clothes in a dark wood closet: mostly the usual possessions of a ranch hand, a few bright Western shirts but an unexpectedly smart fringed jacket in cinnamon suede. There was a new beaver

Stetson with a turquoise and horsehair braid, stiff new Levis and a pair of lizard skin boots.

'That hat will have set him back a few hundred bucks,' Sophie observed. 'He had to have stolen it — and look at that jacket! No way could he buy that on a hand's pay. Curious, you'd expect him to wear his good gear on a weekend trip.'

Miss Pink mumbled something from the depths of the closet. She backed out, studying an object in her hand.

'Broken cup,' Sophie said. 'What's it doing in the closet?'

'It's Wedgwood.'

'It can't be. You mean genuine Wedgwood? Something from Glenaffric?'

They stared at each other. 'I wonder,' Sophie breathed. 'Edna has this gorgeous vase — that colour — '

'Blue jasper. I saw it when she showed me over the house.'

Sophie gasped as the significance dawned on her. 'He stole it and *broke* it? The bugger. It had to be worth a small fortune. Where would the rest of it be?'

'In the creek I would think.'

They moved to the window and looked out at the water beyond the cottonwoods. 'I wonder what else he took,' Sophie said.

'And where he disposed of it? Billings?'

'Too close. He'd have to go to an antiques dealer and anyone who recognised its value would be suspicious. What's a cowboy doing with an eighteenth-century Wedgwood vase? He couldn't fence this one but there were probably others. He'd hardly stop at stealing one piece — and would Edna notice?'

'So he stashed them somewhere till he had the chance to go to a big city? He's probably got a buddy — ' It hit them both at the same time. 'Skinner!' they exclaimed.

* * *

Edna stared at the three fragments of jasper on the kitchen table. She looked fresher this morning but after a moment it was obvious that she was on a different wavelength from the visitors. She touched one of the blue chips with a finger. 'A lovely colour,' she observed. 'Like my pretty vase in the English room.'

'Show us,' Sophie ordered.

They trooped through passages to a shady bedroom where the colour scheme was blue and gold, the spindly chairs poor imitations of the type found in the corridors of great English houses. A flock of Meissen swans floated across the surface of a marquetry dressing-table that even in this dim light looked anything but fake.

'It's French,' Edna said, seeing Miss Pink's interest. 'Lewis something.'

'Louis Quinze,' Sophie corrected. 'Where's the Wedgwood vase?'

'Wedgwood, dear?'

'The blue vase. You said those broken bits were like your pretty vase.'

'The same colour, yes.'

'Edna! *Where's the vase*?'

'There, you see' — pointing — 'the swans swam — no, they're walking, you can see their little black feet. Aren't they neat? They arranged themselves round the vase, like they made a setting for it.'

'The vase isn't there, Edna.'

There was a long pause. 'No.' Edna stared at an empty space in the centre of the white swans. 'It's gone.'

'Have you missed anything else?' Miss Pink asked.

Edna peered up at her. She really was a tiny ball of a woman. And exasperating. 'Such as?' she asked, trying to be helpful.

'She wouldn't know,' Sophie said. 'Look at all this junk.' Her gesture took in the whole house. 'She's no idea what she has.'

'I do so.' Edna was indignant. 'And it's not junk.'

'Some is. Not this table, I grant you, nor the swans. I always admired those swans.'

'Take them, dear — '

'How about looking around?' Miss Pink suggested. 'See if you can spot any more gaps. Among the valuable pieces,' she added, raising an eyebrow at Sophie.

They toured the house, Edna able to recall which items had stood where but displaying no emotion regarding disappearances except in one instance. A missing stein didn't bother her — 'A German tankard.' Sophie was contemptuous. 'An ugly thing, but it was gilded and with one of those European hunting scenes on it, worth a bit, I guess.'

A bracket clock had gone, a collection of porcelain snuff boxes, a silver tray. 'And the scent bottles,' Edna said sadly. 'That'll break Clyde's heart. I was about to ask Jen could he have them.'

'Not those little bottles with the painted peacocks?' Miss Pink was incensed.

'Who's taken them?' At last Edna was back in the real world. 'It can't be any of the maids.'

Back in the kitchen Sophie said, commanding her attention: 'Edna! You have to report this, or' — she glanced at Miss Pink — 'I'll do it.' Edna stared at her, blinking confusedly. 'Byer has been stealing from you,' Sophie said clearly, as if she were addressing a child. 'Those pieces' — she indicated the jasper fragments. 'We found one in the bottom of his closet, the other two were at the edge of the water. He broke your vase and threw the pieces in the creek, except these bits that he missed.'

'Where are the little scent bottles?'

'He'll have sold them — but we'll get them back, don't worry.' There was small chance of that but neither she nor Miss Pink was comfortable in the face of Edna's bewilderment. 'I'll call Hilton,' Sophie went on. 'He'll know what to do.'

'Where is Byer today?' Miss Pink asked gently.

Edna made an obvious effort to orientate herself. 'He'll be at home, dear; he has a house on Bear Creek — '

'He's not there,' Sophie cut in. 'His pick-up's gone. Where does he go weekends?'

Edna thought about that. The question seemed to demand excessive concentration. 'With Paul?' she ventured.

'How close are they?' Miss Pink asked as Sophie, disgusted, turned to the outer door.

'Paul and Erik? They're very close.' Edna considered. 'They're buddies, partners — hunter-poachers, Daddy called them. Thieves, he said; you name it, Paul and

Erik did it. Isn't that so?' She appealed to Sophie. 'Daddy said Paul killed Carol. That was Paul's first wife,' she told Miss Pink.

'Second wife,' Sophie said, resigned, as if she'd heard this a hundred times. 'And Charlie was not your daddy, for Christ's sake!'

'What's going on?' Clyde opened the screen. 'You sound like you're bullying Mom.' But he was grinning as he entered, nodding affably to Miss Pink, removing his hat.

'She's started referring to Charlie as 'daddy',' Sophie protested.

'She does that. She did when we were kids. It's natural as she — gets older, nothing to bother about.'

'Clyde, there are a lot of valuable things missing from this house.'

'Oh, no, don't — ' Edna cried and lapsed into silence as they turned to her, fingering her lips, her eyes on her son.

'Don't what?' He put an arm round her shoulders. 'It's all right, Mom, don't be scared. What's wrong?'

'The perfume bottles you liked,' Sophie said, 'they're missing, and the German tankard and stuff — and that's all that's left of the blue Wedgwood vase.' She pointed.

He started at the fragments. 'Where'd you find those?'

'One piece in Byer's closet, the other two at the edge of the creek by his house. The rest will have been swept away by the water.'

'He broke Mom's vase?'

'By accident probably,' Miss Pink said. 'He'd have intended to sell it — and the rest of the stuff he stole — in some big city.'

'How long's this been going on? Mom, why didn't you *say*?'

'She didn't know, Clyde.' Sophie rushed to Edna's defence. 'Where's Byer now? He's not at home.'

He shook his head. 'How would I know? He'll be back Monday. My God, I'll — I'll — '

'You'll leave it to the police,' Sophie told him firmly. 'I'm going to call Hilton — ' She stopped and stared at Miss Pink, aghast at a thought.

'Let's go outside,' Miss Pink said. Her eyes slid meaningly to Edna. It would be highly imprudent to discuss matters in her presence: no knowing what she might repeat to the wrong person.

Clyde followed them out. In the yard Sophie clutched Miss Pink's arm. 'We can't report it. If we accuse Byer, he's going to open the whole can of worms.'

'Does he know?' Clyde asked.

'He knows Val was at the cabin — '

'But she wasn't — '

'Right, she didn't visit Charlie, but Bret did.' She told him how they'd come to the conclusion that Byer was blackmailing Val on the strength of the washed coffee mugs and pot. 'If Byer tells Hilton,' she said, 'Hilton's going to ask Val why she washed up and never said a word to anyone. Once he tumbles to it that she thought she was protecting Jen, it puts Jen in the frame, see?'

'Why shouldn't she wash up? It's an innocent action. But if Byer was at the cabin the night before, and said he wasn't, now *that*'s not innocent.'

'Nice one, Clyde. We have to go down there, talk to Val before Hilton does.'

'No one's phoned Hilton yet,' Miss Pink reminded them, her brain racing. 'Val never said she'd washed those mugs. Make sure you find out about that.'

Aunt and nephew were moving to the Cherokee. 'You stay with Edna,' Sophie called back. 'Don't let her use the phone, or go out, or anything. We won't be long.'

Miss Pink returned to the kitchen, thinking about Byer.

'Where did they go?' Edna asked.

'To talk to Val.'

Edna sighed, stood up from the table and walked to the refrigerator. From the freezer compartment she selected a large parcel. She placed it in the sink and turned the hot tap on. Miss Pink followed, switched off the water and read the label: Saddle of Elk. She hoisted the parcel to the draining board, calculating it weighed all of ten pounds. 'You're expecting company?' she asked.

Edna looked confused. 'Are we, dear? You're good company.'

'Tonight? The family's coming to dinner?'

'That will be nice.'

Miss Pink replaced the venison in the freezer. 'We'll all help with the cooking,' she said. 'Not such a large joint, perhaps, this would take too long to thaw. Tell me, what plans have you made about where you're going to live?'

Edna blinked. 'This is my home.'

'Isn't it a little inconvenient for one person?'

'Jen and Bret will be here.' Edna beamed happily. 'And there will be children.'

Not if Jen was telling the truth. 'When did you find out Jen was pregnant?'

If Edna was happy before, now she was radiant. 'She is? Isn't that neat? I must think about a nursery. How about we go and — '

'She's not pregnant,' Miss Pink said kindly. 'She was, ten years ago. Your husband knew.'

'You could never believe Charlie.' Her mind switched channels without any appearance of emotional transition. 'He was a great joker,' she assured Miss Pink.

'So I understand. Like telling Jen that Paul Skinner is her father.'

Edna started to fidget with the broken Wedgwood. She hadn't been asked a question and she didn't respond.

'Did Skinner murder his second wife?' Miss Pink mused, seeming to commune with herself.

Edna was trying to fit the jasper fragments together like a jigsaw. She looked petulant. 'Carol? He couldn't unless he used Erik — ' She regarded Miss Pink doubtfully. 'As the hit man?' she hazarded.

'Was that Charlie's opinion?'

'I don't remember. He said they were two of a kind. He was about to fire Erik.'

Miss Pink was very still. The refrigerator was quiet and from outside there came the cry of the red-tailed hawk. 'But he liked Erik,' she said. 'He confided in him, told him the contents of his will.'

'He changed after Abdullah was stolen. He was Ali's sire.'

'Erik stole a *horse*?'

'His statue. Solid silver it was. Didn't you notice the gap above the fireplace in the den? No, I moved the others along so the gap wouldn't show. But Daddy saw. He always knew Erik was a thief but he said he'd never dare steal from Glenaffric. It was why he wouldn't have live-in help; he said servants were all thieves.'

'Had he told Erik he was fired?'

Edna shrugged and looked blank. Then something snagged in her mind. 'Daddy didn't like them being buddies.' She nodded emphatically. 'He was frightened of AIDS.'

Miss Pink's mind did a backwards somersault. 'Buddies,' she repeated slowly. 'Paul and Erik?' Edna had gone rigid, staring at her. 'A gay couple,' Miss Pink went on, looking out of the window as if bored, making polite conversation.

'I shouldn't have said that,' Edna muttered. 'Daddy loved his little joke.' She paused. 'They went to Seattle.' She frowned. 'But they couldn't . . . '

Miss Pink said clearly, 'Paul and Erik went to Seattle at the same time?'

Edna shook her head irritably. 'That's what I'm saying: they had to go separately or people would talk — '

'Wait a minute. Seattle's what — five hundred miles away? One day to drive there' — Miss Pink's eyes glazed — 'a day to return, a day there? Charlie gave Erik three days off at a time?'

'No, dear. Erik leaves after he's done chores on Saturday morning — that is, when Clyde doesn't do chores. If he does, then Erik leaves Friday evening. Clyde did chores today because Erik didn't come in.'

'He should have done?'

'Oh yes.'

'So Erik has only two days off at the most. How could he drive to Seattle and back, and attend to business . . . He doesn't go, Edna.'

'Doesn't he, dear?'

'No.' Miss Pink was grim. 'Byer does the stealing, Skinner takes the loot to a fence in Seattle.'

Edna smiled. Miss Pink sighed and stood up. The woman seemed happy enough and now that there was plenty of money available the family could run to nurse-companions round the clock. It was comfortable to think that here was one old soul who wouldn't have to be incarcerated in an institution.

16

'Let's get this straight,' Cole said. 'You say Byer stole this silver statue before Charlie Gunn died, but all the rest he took afterwards?'

He'd arrived at Bear Creek to find Sophie and Miss Pink waiting for him. Hilton was engaged on another case, he told them; Miss Pink thought it more likely that Hilton was concerned with another aspect of the investigation into Charlie's death, but she wasn't about to question the statement.

She had telephoned the others from Glenaffric, bringing them back to hear her suggestion on how the thefts could be reported without touching on the family scandal. Cole had been run to earth in Irving and a message delivered for Hilton. Cole came back with the request that a member of the family should meet him at Byer's place.

While they waited at Bear Creek, Sophie told Miss Pink that Val had come clean. On the morning of the search she had been the first person to reach the cabin. She had left Byer with Clyde to look for signs of Charlie in the vicinity of the landslide. And yes, she had rinsed the mugs and the coffee pot and replaced them.

'It's as well to know for certain,' Miss Pink said. 'Now we know what to avoid and how to skirt round it. Byer won't say a word; no way is he going to admit that he reached the cabin the previous evening when he's always maintained he turned back at the slide.'

'But if you're thinking that Byer shot Charlie on the Saturday why would he go back to the cabin Sunday evening?'

'Because he left something — ' It was at that point that Cole arrived.

They showed him over the house, gave him the piece of Wedgwood found in the closet and took him to the creek bank, where they looked for more fragments without success. Sophie handed over a list of the missing items.

'How would he expect to get rid of this stuff?' he asked. 'These porcelain boxes: eighteenth century? What would they fetch?'

'I've no idea,' Sophie confessed. 'It could be hundreds, maybe thousands. They have to be insured, there'll be a record.'

'Thousands? Where would he find a dealer who wouldn't be suspicious?'

Which was when Miss Pink told him about Skinner and his trips to Seattle.

'Byer may have gone there himself this

time,' Sophie said. 'He'd guess that an inventory is going to be made of the more valuable contents of the house. I figure Byer isn't coming back.'

'He left that buckskin jacket and his good boots.'

'Maybe he went in a hurry; he didn't lock the door. He could have known you were getting close.'

'Ma'am! You only just reported it. How could we be getting close?'

'She means Charlie's death,' Miss Pink said. 'You might ask Byer what he was doing on the Saturday that Charlie was at hunting camp.'

Cole couldn't hide his amazement. He stared at the shabby little house. 'Charlie didn't die in the cabin,' he said weakly.

'Just a thought,' Miss Pink said, adding, as if it were an afterthought, 'Charlie was about to fire him; he'd spotted the silver horse had disappeared.'

Cole gulped and took refuge in the list of missing articles. 'How could he get this stuff out of the house? A silver tray? What size would that be?'

'The maids don't live in,' Sophie told him. 'Byer's there all hours, tending the stock, and my sister is — er — confused. And she likes her drop of Scotch . . . '

He took a deep breath; he was feeling his position keenly. 'I have to be getting back. Thank you for your help . . . ' They knew he was dying to get to his mobile; Miss Pink could hear the gears meshing as he prepared to tell Hilton that there was another suspect for Charlie's violent end. Or suspects. Skinner was in for a big surprise; however, if he was disposing of the stolen items it was unlikely that he'd kept any in his trailer.

A feature of this case was that, although it would seem that a lot was known about the movements of most family members and people connected with them, nothing was known of Skinner. Sam had appeared on the search, at Benefit, at the funeral; even Russell — connected through Clyde — could be placed: he went fishing, he drove to Irving for supplies; but Paul Skinner was an unknown quantity. Living in his tacky mobile home he had two horses and, presumably, a pick-up and trailer at his disposal. What did *he* do all day — and night? Had he been to Seattle since Charlie's death and the latest thefts? Was he there now? Was Byer with him?

'Useless to speculate,' she said aloud, as the dust rose behind Cole's car. 'Except,' she added, with a glint of amusement, 'one wonders whether he should have put a seal on Byer's door.'

'A seal?'

'To prohibit entrance. He should do that if Byer's a murder suspect.'

'So since he hasn't — '

'He may come back. Cole, I mean. I don't think Byer will. Cole will be reporting to Hilton and I'd guess that he's going to be sent to speak to Skinner — unless Hilton comes himself.'

'Now you are speculating.'

'*Touché.*' Miss Pink looked up at the slopes of the Bobcat Hills. 'We've done our part here. I think I'll go and ride.'

Sophie blinked at what looked like a declaration of withdrawal from the action. She said coldly, 'Like I said, you take Barb. I have to check my stock and the Glenaffric animals. There's a lot to do. I doubt if Val and Clyde are putting in much time today.'

'I need to clear my head.' Miss Pink was apologetic. She wanted to empty her mind of theories and times and alibis, and the niggling suggestion that it would be a great relief if it turned out that Byer had been the one to shoot Charlie. And yet there was the possibility that Charlie had not been shot. Still there appeared to be no confirmation of a bullet track. How could that be proved in the circumstances? Would there be traces of metal if the bullet had scraped bone?

* * *

'You see,' she said to Barb as they plodded up the long slopes, 'my mind is going round in circles. I need to clear the cobwebs and perhaps there'll be a flash of light that will illuminate one corner.' Barb's ears had twitched at the first words but as her rider rambled on the mare lost interest and settled to the job in hand.

They were following an old wagon road that climbed the Bobcats, steering well clear of the old mines and steep gradients. The going was excellent although the outlook was a trifle dull: a few low flowers, the odd woodpecker in a juniper, no view until they reached the top, which turned out to be a false summit.

The ways divided. Below, in a shallow basin that was scattered with statuesque firs, several small lakes formed the shape of a hand with three fingers, their water reflecting the bright sky. The wagon road dipped to a turning circle, its dust marked by tyre tracks, presumably those of Russell and Clyde on their fishing trip yesterday.

The basin had an abandoned air and, as if to deepen the feel of wilderness, a large ungainly shape was motionless on the far side of a tarn, watching them.

Miss Pink's lips tightened. Barb's head was up, her ears pointing. 'He can never run as fast as an Arab,' Miss Pink murmured soothingly.

The bear dropped on all fours and ambled away. Barb turned with alacrity and resumed the plod to the summit ridge. They came to the top and the ridge continued southwards, heading for the high country where the grizzlies hung out. The snow peaks were dazzling, white as the puffy clouds that appeared motionless in the cerulean sky. Below, seemingly close in that crystal atmosphere, the Black Canyon was marked by its bottle-green timber, rimmed on the far side by the pearly crags.

A pair of red-tailed hawks were rising on a thermal, calling shrilly. Miss Pink remembered the red-tail she'd heard when in Glenaffric's kitchen. The house must be quite close below.

The breeze was from the south-east. Very faintly through the bird calls, she caught the sound of an engine.

She dismounted, knotting the reins and slipping them over her arm. She raised the binoculars and, tracing the far rim of the canyon southwards, the glasses swept past a helicopter in the air to focus on the stretch of meadows about Mazarine Lake. She glimpsed a sliver of water but the distance was too great to distinguish figures. She imagined she could see movement among the rocks of the escarpment but she didn't need to see people. It was enough to have seen the helicopter; either it had brought men in or was taking them out, or they were working a shift system. Hilton was looking for the bullet. She wondered what he was doing about the gun — but there was nothing he could do until he found a bullet.

On the return, Barb elected to take the direct route of descent rather than the long way round by the Finger Lakes. Miss Pink struggled with her for a few moments, then gave in, rationalising that since she didn't want to go down past the mines because it was steep, then she should face her fear. They started down.

The descent was frustrating: shuffling gaily along innocuous-seeming spurs that ended in impossible drops, backtracking to the first reasonable gully, hopping down rock steps, dreading a broken leg, coming out on grass to another ridge, another false cast.

By the time they reached the mines

Miss Pink was worn out and the thought of wandering through the workings, never knowing when the ground might give way, filled her with horror. She held the mare in as they walked through the area, her attention on the ground in front of the horse, alert for signs of subsidence. Once, passing a shed without a door or windows, there was a scuffle inside which sent Barb leaping sideways. Only the fact that Miss Pink was already gripping hard saved her from a fall. Dragged to death, she thought grimly, and saw how easy it could be — staring at the next drunken ruin, recognising it for the one Sophie had pointed out: the entrance to a shaft, the roof supported by one baulk of timber, and even that was leaning. It looked as if the vibration of a passing horse would bring the lot crashing down.

The mines ended and they picked up a worn trail which entered the forest to drop in wide zigzags towards the valley. With all the dangers behind them they descended quickly and easily, and after a while the trees stopped at a break left by an old rockfall. Below and less than a mile away a vehicle was speeding along a road trailing dust. No houses were visible and if the Black Canyon was in view it was lost in the vastness of the forest. From higher up the trail meadows would have been visible but there were only the conifers and that stretch of road which appeared totally alien. She hadn't come this way with Sophie last week.

Common sense kicked in, saying that the mare knew she was going home, but when the animal started off again with her fast, shuffling gait and the trees closed in Miss Pink realised that, judging from the position of the sun, they were heading for the high country. And that road was disturbing — a dirt road, certainly, given the dust cloud — with nothing on this side of the canyon other than the track to Glenaffric and no one would take its potholes at the speed that pick-up had been driven. Pick-up? *Byer*?

They came to a series of short, sharp zigzags and then the trail swung round an elbow, straightened out and the trees ended. There were railed pastures on each side containing horses and, at the end of the trail, which ran like a drove road between the fences, Glenaffric basked in the sun under its angled roofs.

The loose horses ranged along the fence, keeping pace skittishly as Barb broke into a canter. At the corrals she skidded to a halt, nose to nose with Ali, as excited as only a stallion could be. Miss Pink dismounted, dragged the reluctant mare to the big horse barn and pushed her inside a loose box.

There were two pick-ups in the yard. As she passed it she glanced in the one closest to the back door. He'd been to the supermarket. Two full paper sacks were on the seat — and no rifle on the rack.

In the kitchen a man raised his voice. Frightened? Threatening? He was answered by a murmur. Miss Pink walked in without knocking.

Edna smiled at her and continued with what she was saying: ' — for a number of reasons. You could say it was a lady you visited. I'm sure you know lots — '

Paul Skinner, red-faced, his eyes bulging, ignored her and glared at the newcomer. 'Who the hell are you? Oh, Jeez, yeah, you're the one was with Val when I come . . . They're saying you found the bits.'

The remaining Wedgwood fragments were still on the kitchen table. 'That's right.' Miss Pink, breathless after struggling with her horse, tried to sound neutral. 'They were in Byer's house.'

'Byer!' He spat it out. 'It's him they should go after, not me. I didn't know nothing about it. She says I was in with him.' He jerked his head at Edna.

'You go to Seattle,' Edna said.

He licked his lips and his eyes looked

as if they would burst from their sockets. Prudence warred with rage.

'What does Seattle have to do with it?' Miss Pink was all innocence. Edna looked at her and smiled.

'That Cole,' he hissed. 'He says that stuff — all the stuff stole from *her*' — a venomous glance at Edna — 'it couldn't be sold around here. It goes to Seattle. Where was the last lot, he wanted to know. I said he could search my trailer. He didn't have no warrant, I didn't have to let him but I did. That shows I got nothing to hide, don't it?'

'You go to Seattle,' Edna repeated.

'So I go to fucking Seattle — and you know why I go — don't you? *Don't you?*'

He took a step towards her. Miss Pink said quickly, 'You touch her and you have to kill me — '

'Kill? *Kill?* Listen, you — ' He caught himself just in time, dropping his voice but sounding the more menacing for that. 'Don't you start about me killing,' he grated. 'You and her, and that Cole. I go to Seattle to sell deer meat. I never stole nothing from this house in my life. I'm no thief — '

'You're a poacher,' Edna said calmly.

'So? I take a deer now and again but them never belonged to Charlie. Them's wild beasts. I'm no thief, I tell you, and here you are: all of you, trying to pin murder on me.'

'I didn't say that.' Edna looked shocked.

He gaped at her, then turned to Miss Pink. 'She lost her mind. I'm outa here.'

'Daddy said — '

He checked on his way to the door. '*Daddy* said I pushed my wife in the river,' he told Miss Pink in grotesque mimicry. '*Daddy* said I was Jen's father and I give her a baby. Daddy's roasting in hell right now and I bet he's telling the devil I shot him and hung him up in the stirrup so's Ali drug him to his death.'

'You *did*?' Edna asked, surprised.

* * *

'Where was everybody?' Miss Pink asked. 'There was no one at Glenaffric except — '

'We had a problem here,' Sophie said, running her eye critically over Barb. 'This animal's sweating too much. We had a mare dropping her foal early, had to send for the veterinarian. We saved her and the foal but it was touch and go there for a while.'

'You'll have to keep better records. Barb's in season. She came down to Glenaffric rather than here, just to find Ali.'

'Did they — ?'

'Not yet. She's all yours. Skinner was at Glenaffric.'

'He was? Why?'

'Logical when you think about it. Cole must have gone to him and implied his collusion in the thefts — that is, if he didn't actually accuse him. Evidently Cole said too much, threw in something about Charlie; Skinner rushed up to Edna to — well, I'm not sure exactly why he went, you know the state she's in now. He didn't hurt her, just railed against the family. I arrived and he treated me to a tirade about being accused of theft and murder, and all he did was take deer meat to Seattle. Maintains he's no more than a poacher. Oh, he did say that if Byer was the thief then he was in it on his own.'

'Typical,' Sophie grunted, pulling off the steaming saddle. 'Thieves falling out.'

17

Spiro Blair was in the process of seducing his new secretary, the first move being to buy her an expensive lunch at the Riverside Restaurant. Spiro owned and managed the Lonesome Cloud Guest Ranch and Resort, and he went through secretaries as fast as his wife discovered his affairs, which was easy since she looked after the accounts of the business and Spiro's ladies didn't come cheap.

Tami Ford was pleased with life. Not euphoric — she would have preferred her host to be young and muscular, but she was enough of a realist to know that in this town a girl was unlikely to find a hunk with money. Tami was the youngest of a family of six: junk food and big sisters' hand-me-down clothes. At eighteen and with ravishing looks she was revelling in the attentions of a wealthy man.

Beautiful, Spiro thought smugly, observing her profile softened by the umbrella's shade but illumined by the reflection from the water. The river slid past, smooth as oil with only the occasional dip and swirl of a lazy whirlpool. A pallet drifted by, residual debris of the storm.

'Isn't there a leash law in this town?' Tami asked idly. She was a country girl.

'What?' He tore his gaze away from her face. 'Leash law?' A German Shepherd and some kind of hound showed on the far bank of the river, slipping through the willows, approaching the water as if they would take to it, retreating, running along the bank.

'I see,' Tami said. 'It's that log they're interested in. You don't think there could be a puppy caught up . . . ?'

It wasn't a log but a small tree complete with roots now washed clean, but tangled with a raft of sticks and the odd plank, with plastic litter and something that rolled as it came level with the restaurant.

'It's a dead cow,' Spiro said. 'Drowned in the storm.' At that moment, out of the wrack an arm appeared and a hand. The hand waved to them.

Tami's screams heralded a period of frenetic confusion and put paid to Spiro's peace of mind. For some time he was the only person available for interview and the Press made a meal of him, in lieu of the police. The sheriff was concerned to catch up with the body, although he wasn't convinced that the couple had seen a hand; stripped twigs could produce the effect, and as for the waving — they'd said it had rolled at that moment, this object that they said was a man. And why did it have to be a man? Given some of the teens that hustled in local bars it might as well be a woman. So by the time his deputy had got around to deciding that some action had to be taken and he'd reported back to the Sheriff's Department, the body had passed Irving and was among the braided channels and the swamplands below the town. And no way was the sheriff going to call in a chopper because a couple who'd had a skinful of margaritas thought they'd seen a hand. The body floated on, nestled in its raft of debris. It was the dogs that finally revealed its position.

* * *

At Glenaffric and the homestead they were short-handed at a time when the tourist season was about to start and, as luck would have it, two animals demanded expert attention. Tomorrow Val and Clyde were scheduled to take the first pack-trip into the back country so there was all the sorting and packing to do for that, and now they had a newly foaled mare who must be watched for a while and a decision had to be made regarding Barb. And there was Edna who shouldn't be left on her own. Fortunately, on the Monday the maids would return after their weekend off.

On Sunday Jen and Bret drove to Glenaffric to confer with Sophie on the ever-present problems of breeding, then Sophie left for Irving and a business lunch with Mr Seaborg, the lawyer. At the homestead Val and her brother worked frantically to cram days of preparation into a few hours, Miss Pink being pressed into service to fetch food and last-minute essentials from Ballard. She arrived back at the homestead as Jen emerged from the barn, carrying a bucket. The woman looked quite at home, as if the years of estrangement had never existed. Had Charlie's death and the revelation of his lies been the ultimate catharsis that reunited mother and daughter?

'Mom's bringing in the herd with Uncle Clyde,' Jen said. 'Did you see the foal yet?'

Miss Pink went across to inspect the new arrival. 'I hadn't realised your mother was breeding horses,' she observed, smiling as the creature stopped suckling and collapsed in a tangle of legs.

'If you have a good mare, you breed. No sense in wasting the opportunity. It means that Val has one less animal for the pack-trips but of course she can have her pick of the others.'

'The others?'

'Mine. I find it difficult to come to terms with: that all Glenaffric's stock belongs to me, barring the colts Sophie chooses. Ali is worth a fortune on his own.'

'And the animals are only a part of it,' Miss Pink murmured as the foal's mother stepped delicately across the loose box to nuzzle her shoulder. 'How does it feel: being fabulously rich?'

'It's a hassle, deciding what to do now that we can do anything. I mean, what do we do about Glenaffric — and this place?' She gestured at the old cabin. 'I'll give Mom the land but she has to let me build her a proper house. She's being awkward.'

'She inherits too,' Miss Pink pointed out.

'I shall have far more — and I owe her.'

'I imagine she thinks it's enough to have you back.'

'That's what Sam says.'

'What does *she* say?'

'We don't talk about that. We carry on as if none of it happened. I guess we're both embarrassed. Do you think there's any harm in it . . . not talking about the past?'

'Not in the circumstances. You both have confidants, you see; you can talk to Bret and

Sam, she can talk to Sophie' — Miss Pink's eyebrows rose — 'and to Sam, of course, so your feelings will permeate as it were.'

Jen looked puzzled. 'Neither of you is hiding anything,' Miss Pink insisted. 'And you're both fond of each other, right?'

'I'd die for her,' Jen said, and her eyes widened as they did when she was startled, or she startled herself. She turned jerkily and Miss Pink followed her over the dusty floor to the head of the ramp.

They looked down the track towards the canyon. 'Hilton's a drag,' Jen said, sounding curiously petulant. 'He keeps badgering us about Erik Byer. How would we know where the guy is?'

'It's because of the new development.'

'*What?* What development?'

'The theft of your grandmother's antiques.'

'Oh, that. Yes, they told me. Byer always was a pain . . . ' She seemed to be waiting for more.

'And he could have been involved in your grandfather's death,' Miss Pink said calmly. 'If he was shot. Perhaps he wasn't.'

Jen swallowed. 'Are you saying he wasn't shot? So what do the police think happened?'

Miss Pink looked vacuous. 'A murder rigged to look like an accident? One person to hold Ali, the other to lift an unconscious man and fix his leg in the stirrup?'

'You're mad.'

Miss Pink appeared not to have heard. There was no retraction, no apology; there was denial, then deep thought, visualising possibilities. 'Byer?' Jen ventured. 'But then who — oh, Skinner!' More thought. 'What would the motive be?'

'Charlie had discovered the thefts, but there would be revenge as well in the case of Skinner: for the lie about your parentage.'

The colour drained from the younger woman's face. She took a step and leaned against the door jamb.

Miss Pink glanced at her. 'All in the past now,' she said comfortably. 'You're reconciled with your mother — '

'She didn't know. *I* didn't know until after he was dead. How could she have known? I told you a couple of days ago: Sam told me part of it, Edna told me the rest — but only *afterwards*. There's no way it could have been rigged: even with one of them holding his head, even Mom couldn't have made him stand while Uncle Clyde worked the foot into the stirrup, and Mom can do anything with a horse. I know it couldn't have been like that, anyone would know. If Hilton's saying that he's got some ulterior motive.'

'No one's saying it. I was presenting an

hypothesis: considering how Byer and Skinner might have worked it. Your mother's in the clear, Jen. She was trying to incriminate herself but that was only to protect you.'

Jen grinned. 'Actually I'm the obvious choice — all that money I inherit. That'll be why Hilton pulled Bret in. The only reason he hasn't questioned me is that he's frightened of the money. Wild, isn't it: Charlie's money protecting me against an accusation of Charlie's murder? But Hilton has to be careful; he's not going to come up against the kind of heavyweight lawyer I can afford — for myself or anyone else.' She sounded vicious now, looking past Miss Pink, focused on something beyond the corrals.

Sounds became audible: the drumming of hoofs, people's cries; in the barn the mare neighed.

They moved down the ramp as the horse herd jostled through an open gate into a corral. Behind them Val stared at Miss Pink, slid down from her horse and slammed the gate shut. She strode towards them, pulling her mount, glowering from Jen to Miss Pink. 'What's going on?' she barked.

'I'm just back from the store,' Miss Pink said, with only a trace of surprise. 'We've been looking at the new foal.'

'What have you — ' Val began, turning on Jen.

'Where's Uncle Clyde?' the girl asked wildly.

Val stared at her and blinked. 'He's fixing a fence,' she said distractedly. 'The horses got into the woods. It's why we took so long . . . ' She was trying to smooth out her expression. 'Who's with Grandma?'

'Bret. I gave the mare a bran mash, Mom. She took it all and the foal's feeding like he was starved.'

Val nodded. Belatedly she remembered her manners. 'Thank you for going to town,' she told Miss Pink gruffly. 'Now' — to Jen — 'if you can help me package this stuff — '

She hitched her horse and mother and daughter started across the yard. Miss Pink followed, intending to offer assistance, although she'd not been asked.

The telephone rang as Val reached the steps. She dived into the kitchen followed by Jen and Miss Pink. They started to unpack the shopping, listening to Val's raised voice in the living-room.

She wasn't long on the phone. 'That was Bret,' she said, returning. 'Hilton's fussing about Byer. Now he wants to know where the guy drinks in Ballard.'

'Why?' Jen asked.

Miss Pink was still, holding a box of eggs. She opened it and stared, not seeing eggs. 'Has he found something?'

'Such as?'

'His pick-up?'

'Bret didn't say. What's on your mind?'

'If Hilton's interested in Ballard it looks as if he thinks Byer isn't far away.'

After a moment Val gave a gasp of angry laughter. 'Oh, come on! Byer's done a runner and Hilton's trying to trace his movements just. The only friends that guy has apart from Skinner will be in the bars in Ballard: drinking buddies. Nothing sinister about it. And, by the way, can I ask another favour of you? Bret needs to come down here, help shoe some horses for tomorrow. Will you go up and sit with Edna a while? Jen can relieve you after she's helped me here.'

On her way to Glenaffric Miss Pink saw a pick-up approaching. This would be Bret and it occurred to her that she had had no conversation with Jen's husband. They had been in the same party on the search for Charlie and she had been a witness to that scene when he had come to the homestead thinking to take the stallion back to Benefit. She had observed him but he was no more than an image: a man who sat his horse well and dressed like an old-timer. What she knew of him was hearsay, but this man was important. He was married to a very rich woman and in view of that the police had seen fit to question him. Her mind alert for nuances, Miss Pink went into excited, slightly-batty-old-lady mode. She was already talking as they slowed to pass, their windows down, neither wearing shades but their eyes shadowed by hat brims.

'. . . morning, Mr Ryan; I'm so glad they released you, glad for Jen, I mean; she's been talking to me.'

He glanced down the track. 'I don't think she was that worried, ma'am.'

'She had to be.' Miss Pink smiled benignly. 'Mr Hilton is working on the money motive so she is the most obvious suspect.'

He looked straight at her. 'Jen's not bothered about the money.' He sounded surprised, as if this were a fact that was evident to anyone.

'The family knows that,' Miss Pink said. 'You know it, but Hilton doesn't. And then there's the personal angle. Charlie had it coming — ' A deliberate pause, leaving room for him to protest. When he didn't she went on, flustered, 'That's police thinking, anyway. It was a cruel joke of Charlie's — that is, if he intended it as a joke and not malice. It could have been both, of course.'

He was frowning. 'Not malice against Jen; he'd give her anything she wanted. You didn't know Charlie; he liked to play jokes on his family. He'd think it was funny to tell Jen Skinner was her father.'

Miss Pink gaped. 'When she'd already told him she was pregnant? He must have guessed who was responsible. You're telling me Charlie thought it amusing to let Jen think she was pregnant by her own father?'

'He didn't tell her — '

'The implication was there. She tumbled to it immediately. You have to be — ' She broke off; she'd been about to say 'weak-minded not to see the connection'. Aware that she had dropped the batty-old-lady role she collected herself and said coldly, '*You* saw the connection.'

'No, ma'am. It were a coincidence. Charlie were joking when he told her Skinner was her daddy. He had no idea the guy had made a play for her.' Miss Pink's eyebrows shot up; how far could one go with euphemisms? 'If he had,' Bret was saying, 'you think Charlie wouldn't have taken it up with the guy?'

She studied his face. 'You're wrong,' she said flatly. 'Charlie was astute . . . and cruel, from all I've heard — and what I saw of him, because I did meet him, you know. He guessed.'

'No way. If he thought it was Skinner's baby, would he ever have told her Skinner was her own father?'

'Why not? It made the joke diabolical. From what — '

'You can't believe it was a joke!'

'I believe Charlie thought of it that way.'

'Never.' He was adamant and fierce. 'You been talking to my wife like this?'

She shook her head. 'I thought you knew already. I can see why she didn't tell you, however. She knew you'd be outraged, ask questions, probe for details maybe; she wants to forget the past and start a new life. I take it the police have no idea that Charlie could have been killed for anything other than money?'

He was looking down the track towards the old homestead, his hands tight on the steering wheel. He said absently, 'They couldn't let me forget how rich Jen is now, how poor we were before.'

'That riles you?'

His eyes came back to her. 'Why should it? I didn't know Jen was to inherit everything — well, 'most everything.' He smiled. 'I want Ali, but that's different; I don't want him because of his cash value — we'll never sell him — but because he's a great horse. I want to see his foals, I mean after we take over.'

'The money doesn't mean anything?'

'Of course it does.' He was amazed. 'This rig's only fit for the scrap heap; I can have a new truck and Jen can have a proper car so we don't have to share an old pick-up — ' He stopped suddenly, thinking, then went on shyly, 'I'd prefer to stay at Benefit but I can see it makes sense to move into the big house, where the land is.' He looked morose at the thought.

'And there's Edna,' Miss Pink murmured. 'She can't live alone.'

'Edna's all right but she can't run the ranch and I wouldn't trust Byer further than I could throw him. Anyways, he's split so she'd be on her own even today without me and Sam. You got to hand it to this family: they stick together. Charlie were the only problem, he made like a dictator.'

'How did you get on with him?'

'I didn't know him, ma'am.'

'But you visited him at hunting camp.'

'You know that? I didn't stay. I'd seen a bear and he went after it.'

'Did he tell you why he wanted to see Jen?'

'It were the other way round. She wanted to see him because she'd started to wonder if after all Skinner *wasn't* her daddy. I tell her she takes after Sam but she can't see it. Any road she wanted to see one of the grandparents, find out the truth, but Charlie put her off going to Glenaffric, told her to meet him at hunting camp. I went instead, thinking to get the truth out of him somehow. But when I told him Jen and me was married he didn't want to talk about the family. I'd told him there was a bear up in the rocks and it put everything else out of his mind. He said he'd be over to Benefit next day, then we could talk, and off he went, up the meadow after that bear, which was the last I saw of him.' He looked amused. 'Guess I was the last to see him alive.'

'Does Hilton believe you?'

'He has to. No way can he prove I followed Charlie up to the rocks.'

'No proof doesn't have to mean you didn't follow him.'

'I didn't kill Charlie.' He sounded relaxed and quite confident.

She drove on. No hidden depths there, she thought. An honest fellow, obtuse, sincere, unworldly — either that or a skilled actor, and a man who could dissemble so expertly would never have been content with a hand-to-mouth existence in the backwoods of Montana. True, great wealth had come his way, but he'd had no reason to think that Jen would inherit a fortune and even if he had, he showed every sign of caring for his wife. Money to Bret meant a new pick-up and she believed him when he said there was a downside to Jen's inheritance: he had to leave his cabin at Benefit. He would be regretting the loss of his freedom: from ranch hand to, at the very least, manager of a great estate. *Noblesse oblige*. Miss Pink smiled smugly; he had been a shadowy figure, two-dimensional. The conversation had revealed his substance, filled out the image, rendered him solid. She liked what she saw.

The Bronco crept into Glenaffric's yard like a cat and she cut the engine. If Edna were sleeping she didn't want to wake her. There were two pick-ups in the yard and she remembered that Bret had mentioned Sam. He would be out with the horses.

The kitchen was empty, the Wedgwood scraps gone, the table clear. Not wanting to frighten the old lady if she were encountered wandering through the dim rooms, Miss Pink retreated outside and turned towards the corrals. There wasn't much to look at. In a paddock to the side a couple of mares stood nose-to-tail under a cottonwood, their foals flattened like dead dogs at their feet. A Sunday afternoon atmosphere, she thought, as if there was any difference in days on a ranch. A flutter of movement caught her eye, past the corrals: something pale in a pasture.

She strolled through the corrals until she had a clear view of the field and the stationary group in the middle of it. Ali stood as if for his portrait: sleek, alert, daunting in his muscular power: Alexander's Bucephalus. He was saddled and bridled; Sam Jardine was at his head while Edna ran a hand down the near foreleg before standing up and turning to Sam. They looked like experts in earnest discussion. Miss Pink leaned against a solid post and watched.

Edna walked to the fence and climbed clumsily to the top rail. What was going on? Sam brought the stallion forward, moved to his flank and pushed him towards the rail. Miss Pink had the impression that there was communication between the three of them, not just Sam and Edna; it was a picture without sound, a picture in slow motion, fraught with suspense. She saw Edna's plump leg in a shabby trainer come over the saddle, the little round body settle down and suddenly Edna was no longer an old lady but someone who fitted right there, on the back of a good horse.

Sam stood back. Ali stepped forward — and bucked. Miss Pink's hand flew to her mouth. Edna sat like a rock. The stallion started to walk: stiffly, not relaxed. Sam moved out to the middle of the small field. Ali circled him, walking. As he relaxed, stepping nicely now, he looked as if he were enjoying his own movement. Edna sat like part of the horse, never seeming to move, as far as Miss Pink could see, but then with those fat thighs what would she see? She felt a giggle rise hysterically and checked it as Ali started to weave in figures of eight about Sam. Sam said something. 'Just once,' Miss Pink heard from Edna. Back at the fence Ali broke into a gentle trot, got into the swing of it, went round once and stopped. Edna knotted the reins round the horn and, without hands, repeated the whole process until, taking up the reins again, she brought the horse to Sam and backed him. Ali responded like a ballet dancer.

They came walking towards her, unaware of her presence. Miss Pink saw what could happen when Ali caught sight of her. She turned and tried to retreat but too late. Behind her Edna spoke rather too loudly, there was a snort, a scuffle in the dust and she looked back to see the stallion in the air, unbelievably high, coming down — Sam's terrified face behind and Edna, still in the saddle, patting the powerful neck, soothing him.

* * *

She sat in the kitchen, overwhelmed by embarrassment. She'd filled the kettle, put it on the stove and now she waited, like a pupil sent to the headmistress, uncertain how Edna would behave, uncertain of herself.

Edna came in, very quiet in her old trainers. She smiled at Miss Pink.

'I can only apologise — '

'Yes, dear? Where are the women?'

'What — ? Who?'

Edna was staring at the kettle. 'The maids.' She looked lost.

'It's Sunday,' Miss Pink said weakly. 'I don't think the maids come on a Sunday. I put the kettle on.'

'What for?'

'Because I need a cup of tea. I could have killed you! I'm shocked too.'

Edna was rooting in a cupboard. 'I know we have some chocolate chip cookies someplace. I have to do some baking.'

'You ride like — as if you were born on a horse.'

'I haven't been on one for twenty years. Riding's something you never forget.' She looked rueful. 'I shouldn't have done it; Val's going to be cross.' She was rubbing her back. Her shoulders were very flexible.

'I won't say anything. I hope I haven't set Ali back: spooking him like that. I did try to get away before he came close.'

Edna looked blank. 'He's not ready yet. There's an Arabian mare — Barb — they've decided on — ' She trailed off. 'I've told Jen she's to choose which room she wants for the nursery,' she said brightly.

'What were you discussing with Sam?' Miss Pink seemed only mildly curious.

'Discussing what, dear?'

'In the pasture. He was holding Ali, you felt his near fore — to see if the swelling had gone down? Then you stood back and you said something.' Under the steady stare Edna's face started to crumple. Miss Pink said desperately, 'You and Sam talked like — like a couple of old horse dealers.'

'No!' Edna shook her head vehemently. 'That wasn't a dealer. That's Sam; he's Jen's daddy. Sam Jardine — that's it.' And she beamed, delighted because she'd remembered a surname.

18

Miss Pink stepped out of the lift at the Rothbury, glanced in the restaurant and turned to the bar where Pat Kramer was studying sheets of computer printout. Actually, Miss Pink had wanted to speak to Russell but Pat looked up as she hesitated. The bar was as empty of customers as the restaurant, the place not yet gearing up for the modest Sunday evening trade. Pat raised her eyebrows in inquiry. Miss Pink advanced. She had showered and changed, and smelled of Bronnley lemons. 'May I have a shot of dry vermouth in a tumbler of ice?'

Pat was amused. 'It's different.'

'Refreshing. There's a note in the apartment saying Sophie's gone to Irving. But she was lunching there, I knew that before I left this morning.'

'She came home and went back. With my husband. Didn't you catch the newsflash?'

Miss Pink looked blank. Pat grimaced. 'Their hand's been found in the river.'

'Hand? Whose hand? Oh, a ranch hand!'

'The Gunns' man. A guy called Byer. They took his body out of the water below Irving.

It was on the television.'

'Byer.' Miss Pink released her breath suddenly and fell silent. Pat looked uneasy and nudged the ice-filled tumbler. Miss Pink picked it up and sipped absently. 'Byer,' she repeated and then, 'why Sophie?'

'Russell's gone with her,' Pat said quickly. 'He's fond of Sophie. We both are; couldn't let her go on her own.'

Miss Pink was incredulous. 'They've taken her in? But she — she hardly knew Byer!'

'She knew him well enough — '

'You're telling me he was murdered and they arrested *Sophie*?'

'Good God, no! I'm sorry, we're at cross-purposes.' Pat gave an embarrassed laugh, threw a glance at the doors that were open wide to the street and lowered her voice. 'Sophie came back from lunching with their lawyer, put the TV on when she was in the apartment and caught the newsflash. The police were asking for help in identifying the guy. She recognised Byer straight away although he's dead. Ghoulish if you ask me: putting a dead man's face on the screen. Anyway, she called the sheriff in Irving and they asked her to go down and identify him formally. She told Russell that Clyde's too sensitive, she wanted to spare him, and I understand that his mother is — rather confused? Russell went along for company. Not a nice thing to have to do: identify a drowned man. You look puzzled. Is something wrong?'

Miss Pink caught her breath at that but she asked evenly enough, 'Is that all you know: that he was taken out of the river? Nothing about how he came to be in it in the first place?'

'I didn't see the newsflash. Sophie said nothing else. I guess he had to be drunk and he fell in.'

'So where's his pick-up?'

Pat didn't respond, evidently taking it as rhetorical, distracted at that moment by a group of people pausing at the door. She pressed a button on the wall. 'If you'll excuse me . . . ' She gathered up her papers, flashing Miss Pink a smile — but the customers were advancing and she was enough of a business-woman not to leave the bar unattended. The new arrivals were elderly, the men in showy tartan trousers, the women blue-rinsed. They took their time deciding on their drinks and Pat was already serving them when a smooth, tanned youngster slipped behind the bar and took over. 'This is Henry,' Pat told Miss Pink. 'Now I have to go and supervise the blue trout. It's chef's night off.'

Miss Pink did a double-take. 'Oh' — arresting

her as she passed — 'the trout were delicious. I hope we weren't robbing you.'

'There were heaps,' Pat assured her. 'He always comes back with a load from those lakes. There'll be more for you next time.'

The customers were served and they retreated to a table. Miss Pink observed the new barman benignly and was about to open a conversation when she was forestalled. Glancing at the door, lowering his voice like a conspirator, he hissed, 'Where are those lakes you were talking about?'

'Ah!' She beamed. 'Another fisherman. They're the Finger Lakes, at the back of the Bobcat Hills.' She gestured westwards. 'Buy the large-scale map for the Bobcats.'

His eyes gleamed. He was a handsome boy, most attractive in his enthusiasm. 'Cut-throat or rainbow?'

'Mr Kramer brought us several rainbow — apparently. I'm no expert. Why didn't you ask him?' She was amused; was Russell possessive about his favoured fishing spots?

'I've not had the chance. I'm sure he'd tell me if I asked' — but his eyes belied it — 'I had the day off yesterday so I haven't seen the boss since. In fact, I never knew he'd caught anything — didn't even know he was fishing, except this guy called and asked where he was and Mrs Kramer said he'd gone fishing. But there was a crowd in here — happy hour — I was run off my feet and I forgot all about it until you mentioned it there.'

'The Finger Lakes,' she repeated, suddenly feeling tired. 'Buy the map.' She nodded pleasantly and went up to the apartment where, to her amazement, she found Sophie ensconced at the window and drinking brandy.

'I was about to call down,' she said. 'Came in the back way but I couldn't face the bar although I knew you were there. Heard your voice.'

'Is it Byer?'

'Yes. And he's been shot.'

There was a long silence. 'Suicide?' Miss Pink asked brightly.

'No. That is, I doubt it. A rifle shot — in the chest? No powder burns. And no exit wound so the bullet's still there. They'll find out tomorrow with the autopsy.'

'How do you know all this? They wouldn't show you the chest, surely, only the face.'

'I called Seaborg. He found out. He would, of course.'

'Why 'of course'?'

'He's our lawyer. Byer was the family's employee. We're involved.'

'I hope not.'

'In a manner of speaking just.'

They regarded each other wordlessly, then both looked away, over the town roofs.

★ ★ ★

'You knew him,' Hilton said.

'Hundreds of guys knew him,' Skinner protested. 'And hookers. He wasn't particular. Ask me, someone was waiting for him in a parking lot, followed him home. Some fight over a woman.'

'What was the pick-up's registration?'

'How the hell would I know?'

'You knew the guy.'

'That don't mean I know his registration! It were new; I mean, he'd just changed the model.' Skinner looked sullen but they could smell his fear.

They hadn't waited for the autopsy. It was obvious that Byer had been shot and already they knew that, outside his employment, Skinner was the closest person to him, not that anyone was really close, but there was gossip about poaching and the two men drank together. Shortly after Sophie Hamilton had identified the body in Irving, Hilton and Cole followed her to Ballard. They'd found Skinner hitching a horse trailer to his pickup. He said he was planning on helping his ex-wife with her pack-trip tomorrow. He was sweating hard as they questioned him but the sun was hot and the air humid down there by the river, and hitching up a trailer is heavy work. Yes, he said, he had caught the newsflash, which was why he figured they'd need an extra hand either at Val Jardine's place or at Glenaffric. It was when Cole pointed out that the murder of his buddy didn't seem to bother him that he'd protested that plenty of other guys knew Byer, not to speak of hookers.

'When was the last time you saw him?' Cole asked.

Skinner thought about that. 'I can't remember. Weeks, I guess, maybe a coupla weeks. I saw him in town one Saturday, in a bar. I had a drink with him.'

They stared at him and he shifted his feet. 'So which bars did you drink in?' Cole asked.

'*Me?*' The astonishment was overdone.

'You and him.'

Skinner's mouth opened and closed. 'He favoured the Sage Grouse and the Maverick,' he said grudgingly.

Hilton glanced at Cole who retreated to the police car. 'So that's where you'd expect to find his pick-up,' Hilton said, 'at one of those bars?'

‘ ’Less someone followed him home.’ Skinner’s eyes were wide, watching Cole. ‘A rifle shot would be loud in a parking lot.’

‘Who said a rifle was used?’

‘What else would it be? Guys don’t go to town carrying a handgun. Everyone has a rifle on the rack.’

‘So we’ll find his vehicle between Ballard and Bear Creek, right?’

Skinner glared at him, the sweat running down his forehead. He wiped his eyes with his hand. Hilton looked past him to his ramshackle home, the door closed. He pondered. ‘Want to look inside?’ Skinner asked. ‘It’s all yours, man.’

Hilton studied him, then shifted his gaze to the two horses in the makeshift corral. He grinned. ‘Don’t leave town,’ he said.

‘I’ll be back in the mountains tomorrow.’ From somewhere Skinner dredged up a spark of belligerence.

Hilton sketched a shrug and walked to the car. He glanced at the guy’s pick-up as he passed but it told him nothing other than that Skinner was packed, ready to leave. There was a pile of clothing on the front seat, his saddle in the back.

‘Check with Val Jardine,’ he told Cole. ‘Find out if Skinner arranged to help with her pack-trip tomorrow. Did you contact them in Ballard, tell them to check the parking lots at these two bars?'

'They're on their way.' Cole found the homestead's number in his notebook and dialled. After a long time Clyde Gunn answered and told him to wait while he spoke to his sister. He came back and said no, there had never been any question of employing Skinner. Cole lowered the mobile and looked from Hilton to the man's trailer. 'No,' he said.

Hilton inhaled deeply. 'He might just be telling the truth. Check out Glenaffric to be sure.'

Cole went through the motions. There was no movement from inside the mobile home but they knew they were being watched.

Cole stiffened. 'Edna,' he mouthed at Hilton. He introduced himself boyishly and asked if she were about to take on Paul Skinner since she would be short-handed. He listened, raised his eyebrows in surprise at his boss . . . 'When would he start?' he asked, and: 'Would he bring his own horses?' After long moments during which he fidgeted impatiently, he cut her off with an emphatic, 'Thank you, ma'am, you've been very helpful' and lowered the phone.

'Yes,' he said. 'She's employing him from

tomorrow and he's using his own horses.'

'Shit. Get down to Ballard, see if we can find that pick-up.'

This wasn't going to be easy on Sunday evening. At the Sheriff's Department they learned that although Byer had a number of motoring offences (driving under the influence and without insurance) the registration that the police had was for his old pick-up, and the Transportation Office in Irving wouldn't be open until Monday. In any event there were no unclaimed pick-ups in the vicinity of the Sage Grouse or the Maverick so it was decided to abandon further search for the vehicle until the morning.

The detectives were about to leave Ballard when a boy of twelve and a large man in work clothes walked into the station. The man was carrying a rifle and he looked stiffly angry. The boy had the wide-eyed stare of a terrified youngster trying to appear cool. They were shown into the sheriff's office where Hilton and Cole stood aside, eyeing the rifle with professional interest that intensified with the man's first words.

'My boy found this,' he said, laying the gun on the desk.

The sheriff didn't touch it. He glanced at Hilton. 'Where?' he asked.

The man nudged his son who croaked,

cleared his throat and whispered, 'In some willows.'

This time the sheriff looked hard at Hilton who was deadpan. 'Which willows?' the local man asked.

'Upstream a ways,' the boy said. 'We didn't steal it, we found it there' — a long pause — 'laying in the reeds and we couldn't leave it, could us, not for little kids to find?'

'Is it loaded?' Hilton asked kindly.

The boy stared at him. 'It's not loaded,' his father said.

Hilton looked out at the sky. 'It's still daylight. You'd best show us where you found it.'

On the way the man explained a little more. His boy and a friend had been hunting a coyote they figured was stealing the wife's chickens and they'd come home with this rifle, that was all. Hilton guessed from the man's restrained anger and the boy's terror that the father had discovered the rifle by chance, that the kid had thought he might retain possession of it, but he said nothing. None of that mattered for the moment, the priority was to discover where it had been found.

Sitting in the front of the police car the man directed Cole to cross the river. In the back beside the boy Hilton was expressionless. This was the road to Glenaffric and to Byer's house.

'Take a right,' the man said, while they were still on the bridge. Cole's eyes met Hilton's in the mirror. It was the way to Skinner's place.

On the left now were one or two small frame houses and, to the right, the thick belt of willows and cottonwoods that lined the river bank.

'You can park here,' the man said as they approached the second house. A heavy-set woman watched them from the porch as they left the car. Neither father nor son acknowledged her but it was evident from her interest that she was the mother. The man laid a firm hand on the boy's shoulder and steered him towards the lush undergrowth and the start of a narrow path.

It was a well-used trail, the kind that had been made and frequented by small boys who had grown up here and played in this sappy green world until they were old enough to own cars and travel to the real forest. Hilton was familiar with such places. Every country boy had his personal territory, which he knew like an animal, every inch of it. They walked about a quarter-mile before the boy stopped and pointed to a patch of flattened grass. 'There,' he said.

'How'd the grass get laid?' Hilton asked.

'We stomped around, Elmer and me.' His terror was back.

'A coyote was laying up here,' Hilton said calmly. 'You can smell him. Where's this trail go now?' It seemed to continue, black and muddy as it neared the river. They could see reed beds beyond the willows and a coot called nervously.

'I dunno,' the boy said.

Hilton looked at the father who said tightly, 'It runs a half-mile or so to a fishing hole.'

'On the river?'

'There's a side channel where we find catfish.'

'Let's go.'

The boy said something to his father. 'No!' the man exclaimed. Hilton looked cheerful as they resumed their walk in single file. Cole cast a puzzled look at the flattened grass and hurried after them.

After a while the trail widened and became more soggy. The reeds took over on their right and they were so tall that they almost obscured the pick-up until they were within a few yards of it. Beyond the pick-up was a turning circle and a Jeep track.

'Someone fishing?' the father said. 'What's he doing here, off the road?'

The boy stared at the truck as if it were alive.

Hilton pushed past the two of them and glanced in the cab. He could see nothing to frighten anyone, neither there nor on the back, only the absence of something. He turned to the boy and beamed. 'You thought the truck was scrapped,' he said. 'And they forgot to take the rifle and it would make a nice present for your dad, right?'

The father gaped at him, then turned on his son. 'You took it from *here*? Off of the *rack*?'

The kid hung his head and started to snuffle.

'It's mired.' Cole appeared round the back of the truck. 'He got in deep and couldn't get out again.' He pointed. The pick-up's nearside wheels were axle deep in black mud.

They removed the documents, sent the father and son ahead of them and followed, careful to walk to the side of the track as far as the turning circle, but they could see no footprints other than those made by kids' trainers. The rain had erased any fishermen's tracks.

'No keys in the ignition,' Hilton observed,

'but the documents left. Apart from a guy not being able to shoot himself in the chest with a rifle — '

'It could be rigged — '

'There'd be powder burns. Unless it was a very complicated mechanism and I don't think Skinner's a clever guy, do you? This' — he gestured back towards the truck — 'this is a stupid guy, or one in a panic: rigging a murder to look like a suicide.'

'Why in hell did he leave the pick-up so close to home?'

They were walking along the road now, the willows on their left and, up the slope on their right, the roofs of the bright brown ranch-style houses. 'The truck's mired,' Hilton said. 'He couldn't move it. If he tried to winch it out some nosy housewife up there coulda come out to see what the commotion was about.'

'This guy's in the clear?' Cole indicated the man walking ahead.

' 'Course he is, he came in voluntarily. No, it's Skinner we want.'

They were not to find him that evening. When they reached his place it looked just as they'd left it: the horse trailer, even the horses still in the corral, but the unlocked house was empty and the pick-up was gone.

'He'll be back,' Cole said with certainty. 'He left the horses.'

Hilton snorted. 'He couldn't make a run for it towing a horse trailer. And those two animals: I wouldn't give you a thousand for the pair of 'em. Jeez! He musta followed us to Ballard soon as we were out of sight.'

'He can't be gone far. We can set up road blocks — '

'Man, he has three, four hours start on us. He'll be out of the state; he could be in Canada!'

'At least we have *his* registration — '

'And you figure he's still driving the same vehicle? First thing he'll do is change it.'

'He won't have the cash — and no way will he use a credit card.'

'How d'you know he's no cash? And what's to stop him stealing a car — stealing a car and killing the driver? He's murdered once' — Hilton's eyes were wild, he was beside himself, goaded by the memory of the lost opportunity: a few hours ago they had the man in their hands — 'maybe twice,' he grated. 'Who killed Charlie Gunn?'

* * *

Miss Pink was in bed and deep in Cornwell's *Cause of Death* when there was a knock and the door opened a crack. 'I saw your light,' Sophie said excitedly, 'and you have to hear this.' She came into the room in her robe, her face shining with moisturiser. 'Russell just called. They found Byer's truck — and now Skinner's missing.'

Miss Pink marked her place with a leather bookmark. 'You're saying there's a connection?'

'The pick-up was on the river bank close to Skinner's trailer.'

'How close?'

'Less than half a mile I'd say. Remember where you come down from the Bobcats past that sub-development, you turn parallel with the river? Near where you turn there's a place that people park to fish. The truck is there, mired. I said thieves fall out, didn't I? And Skinner left his horses behind and the trailer — which is worth more than the horses.'

'He could hardly move his house.'

'I mean his horse trailer.'

'Why do they think he's missing, then?'

'Because Hilton and Cole interviewed him and he was sweating blood. When they went back after finding the pick-up, Skinner had vanished. Oh, there was a rifle in the pick-up, but it was — what's the term? Liberated, that's it — liberated by some kids, until one of the dads found out and hauled his son to the station, with the gun — which I guess is how they came to find the pick-up. What happened was Skinner shot Byer and put his body in the river.'

'And left the pick-up there?' Miss Pink was incredulous. 'Right by his house?'

'He must have tried to turn it but it was bogged down. It could have been dark.'

Miss Pink frowned. 'Hilton told Russell this?'

'Oh, no. But Russell knows everyone and the chief reporter from the *Irving Chronicle* was downstairs in the bar. He'd followed Hilton and Cole when they came to town earlier. The media had Irving's police department staked out ever since Byer's body was found. I guess someone in the mortuary talked about the gunshot wound. The police can't play it close to their chests, anyway, there's an alert out for Skinner's pick-up. Why are you looking so puzzled, Melinda?'

'I was wondering what could make this particular pair of thieves fall out to the extent of murder.' She lied; she was trying to recall something she'd heard recently, something relating to Byer? Or to Skinner? Or both? She sighed. 'I'm too tired,' she protested.

Sophie was contrite. 'I thought you'd be interested. I wouldn't have come in, but your light was on.'

'I wasn't complaining. It's merely that I'm too tired to take it in.'

'And we've a hard day tomorrow. Odd about Skinner, though; I wonder how Val will feel: her ex turning out to be a killer.'

19

On the Monday morning Jen and Bret were to move their horses from Benefit to the improved pastures at Glenaffric. Sophie and Miss Pink had agreed to assist them once they had seen Val's pack-trip on its way. In the bustle of early rising, of packing food and other necessities for a long day, there was no opportunity to discuss Sunday's events, not that they were of much concern to the family anyway, except for the thefts, and they weren't momentous. Pretty objects, certainly, but insured and not in the same class as, say, priceless paintings.

At the homestead the yard was full of expensive 4×4s, and men and women in casual designer clothes. Horses were tied to rails while finishing touches were being put to the loads on the pack-mules.

At the last moment Miss Pink approached Sophie, who was adjusting the tarpaulin on a mule, and begged to be excused from herding Benefit's horses. Sophie was concerned, was she unwell? Just feeling the need for a quiet day, Miss Pink confessed, a gentle amble perhaps — smiling ruefully — not galloping after wild horses.

'You don't mind if I go to Benefit?' Sophie asked anxiously. 'They could do with more than two riders. Look, why don't you ride out with the pack-trip a short way, take it easy, then turn back after a mile or so?'

'What a good idea.' Miss Pink looked tired but amenable: an old lady bothered about being a nuisance, ready to fall in with any alternative suggestion.

Val said absently that of course she could tag along; she was far too preoccupied with overseeing the departure to worry about an extra body who wasn't even her responsibility. She saw her dudes mounted and, leading the way with a pack-mule, set off down the track. There was some jostling and then the customers fell in behind, Miss Pink towards the rear and in front of Clyde, who was leading the second mule.

They rode to the swing bridge, the visitors awestruck at the sight of the river boiling through the narrows, they traversed the slopes below Glenaffric, where the brood mares regarded them with casual interest, and then they entered the forest.

Miss Pink was mounted on a pinto: a skewbald mustang which, Sophie said, was an Indian pony and would go anywhere. The animal was smooth and responsive while travelling in line and his rider wasn't bothered about his behaviour when solo. She was going over her proposed actions; the horse was a minor consideration.

About five miles into the forest they stopped for an early lunch and Miss Pink turned back, assuring Val and Clyde she would be fine on her own, walking, and the pinto knew the way home; there was no chance of getting lost.

She started back at a fast walk. The horse felt her sense of urgency and it was all she could do to hold him until she was out of earshot. Half a mile away, trusting that the dust would muffle hoofbeats, she let him go. She had noted obstacles on the way in and was confident that if she could keep on the same line there were no overhanging branches and the only tricky moments would come at the creeks. The first he took like a dog, sliding down to the water on his haunches, clawing and lunging up the far bank, his rider clinging to the horn, her spectacles jumping on their cord, shirt-tails flying. She stopped to replace her glasses and twist her cap back to front yardie fashion, the better to see where she was going.

That first creek sobered the pinto. Perhaps he was intelligent enough to know that a stumble with this weight on his back could result in serious trouble; whatever the reason, he kept to a smooth and steady lope as far as Glenaffric's pastures, slowing further as he breasted the slopes below the house.

Miss Pink slid down at the back door and looked around as she stretched her legs. There were two vehicles in the yard: a pick-up and a Jeep. She remembered that Edna had been out in a Jeep on the morning of the search for Charlie. No one was visible in the corrals and the kitchen was empty, although there were signs of occupation: a newspaper opened to the Byer story, used mugs, plates in the steaming sink. There was a faint murmur in the depths of the house.

She walked purposefully along passages and through rooms. She passed the alcove where the scent bottles had been displayed and saw that other ornaments had been advanced to close the gap. She came to the den with its monstrous trophies and, surveying it at a glance, she checked. The shelf above the fireplace was bare. It should be covered with silver horses; there wasn't one in sight.

A thickset woman who was vaguely familiar was vacuuming Edna's bedroom. Miss Pink switched off the machine at the socket.

'Where is Mrs Gunn?'

'She's outside.' The maid was as phlegmatic

as if Miss Pink were a member of the household. 'Just shout, you'll find her.'

'Very well.' Miss Pink was thoughtful, taking stock of the woman. 'What happened to the silver horses in the den?'

'They was stole.'

'Naturally.' It was tart. 'Like the snuff boxes and all the rest.'

'I guess. Jen will flip when she finds out. Who's gonna tell her?' The woman looked hopefully at Miss Pink.

'I can do that. Is anything else missing? Apart from the load that Byer took?'

'I haven't noticed nothing but it's a big place and Skinner only took the horses yesterday. I guess we'll find what else is gone when we dust.'

'You're saying he took them yesterday?' Miss Pink's brain raced . . . brown paper sacks on the seat of his pick-up . . . 'She shouldn't be left on her own,' she murmured.

'Tell me about it.' The woman heaved a sigh. 'But we don't come Sundays and it wouldn't never occur to us that the family weren't gonna be here. 'Sides, Skinner were family once; who'd have thought he'd rob an old lady — there, it's his stepdaughter he's stealing from, isn't it, all to come to her now?'

Another woman was washing the dishes

in the kitchen. 'Have you seen Mrs Gunn?' Miss Pink asked, doubting it but producing an excuse for her presence.

'She went out.' Jerking her head towards the slopes at the back of the ranch.

'On foot?'

'Oh, no, she were riding. She won't have gone far.'

'She's not out alone on Ali!' Miss Pink was appalled.

'No. On her own little horse.'

'Is that wise? I didn't know — she was allowed — that she rode still.'

'She don't *ride*.' The woman was indulgent. 'She'll be walking round the pastures just. Don't do no harm. We know where she is.'

There was no sign of her in the fields beside the fenced track that led to the forest and, since she hadn't returned to the house, it was reasonable to assume that she was ahead. Miss Pink pushed her reluctant horse uphill towards the trees, increasingly uneasy.

It was the horse that alerted her. He was plodding up the long zigzags, his breathing the only sound other than the creak of saddle leather, and suddenly his head came up with a start. Miss Pink couldn't see what had attracted his attention but she was on her guard. They were approaching an elbow and, above and below, there were chutes of soil and trampled vegetation where animals — deer or moose — had ignored the serpentine trail and cut corners by plunging straight down the hill. And now something was approaching fast; she could hear it although it remained invisible.

She dug in her heels and the horse leaped round the elbow and up the gentle gradient of the trail. After some fifty yards she drew rein, turned him carefully on the narrow path and waited. Too late she realised that if this were a bear — or a mountain lion chasing deer — she was facing towards the predator when she should be facing away, poised for flight. But a lion would never attack a horse and rider — surely — and as for a grizzly, she had the advantage of surprise; she knew he was coming, but he didn't know she was there.

It was there and gone in a flash but the image was imprinted on her retina: a small black horse sliding as the pinto had slid into the creek — jumping on to the track and diving over the edge on the downhill side. And, sitting like a limpet on his back: Edna.

Miss Pink was immobile, listening to the crashing progress below. After a while she started back, keeping to the trail, filled with renewed disbelief each time she passed that precipitous chute.

Edna was in the barn rubbing down the little black horse. Sweat didn't show on that hide and in the dim light. She looked round as the animal turned to eye the visitor. 'I like to keep them looking nice,' she said amiably.

'Why's she sweating?'

'Is she sweating, dear?' Miss Pink put a hand on the wet back. 'She's been chased,' Edna said. 'One of the geldings has been giving her a hard time, which is why I brought her in.'

The mare dropped her head. 'How far did you go?' Miss Pink asked.

Edna walked round to the far side of the animal and started to hum. Miss Pink said loudly, 'I really think, if you want to ride, you shouldn't go alone. Anything could happen and no one would know where you were.'

'You'll come with me?' Edna asked brightly.

'Of course.'

Miss Pink strolled out of the barn, mounted the pinto and trotted away to the homestead. The place looked abandoned but those horses that had not been needed on the pack-trip were still in a corral. She transferred her saddle to a mouse-coloured gelding and set out on the Bobcat trail.

She came to the zigzags above the point where she had caught sight of Edna, confident in the belief that the other woman, having seen her leave for the homestead, would never suspect that she might double back on a fresh horse. Edna was up to something; no one, senile or sane, would descend a hill so recklessly, risking her horse's life, without some powerful motive.

Edna hadn't cut all the corners but still she had gone downhill fast; where springs crossed the trail fresh prints were deep and widely spaced in the mud. That mare hadn't been walking. The shoes were distinctive, an oval rather than a circle (and why did Edna keep a horse shod if she didn't ride?). It was a simple matter to follow her trail back, all the way to the old mines, but there, among the ruins and the spoil heaps, the spoor was lost.

The mousy horse was sure-footed but quickly bored. They wandered about the mines, Miss Pink studying the ground, seeing hoof prints that were not those of the black mare but probably made by her own horse two days ago. She paused above a draw and sighed in exasperation: at a fruitless quest, at her horse that wanted to go home;

thinking that Edna could have skirted the mines altogether and made for the ridge above — but why? What was there on the Bobcat ridge to attract her, except by way of a jaunt, but always she came back to the conviction that Edna had not been out for fun. Had the woman been in such a hurry in order to reach home before her absence was discovered? The maids knew, of course, but they thought she was walking a horse round the pastures.

The gelding rested a hind leg, shifting his rider's balance. She grumbled at the strain on her spine and glowered resentfully at a mound of broken beams and iron sheeting on the other side of the draw. Litter, but the land was big enough to contain it. Over there was a platform that could be man-made, it looked too level to be natural, and there was a spoil heap below. No doubt the mound of wood was plugging a shaft. She didn't like this place, there were shafts everywhere: death traps.

She moved up the side of the draw, crossed it and approached the spoil heap. There was a lot of copper in the rock and she was conscious of growing familiarity; the features were similar to that place where there was a shaky covering above a mine shaft. There would be a shaft here but there was no cover.

A baulk of timber lay across the platform, the roof collapsed behind it. It was the same place. Nature — erosion, gravity, an earth tremor — had done its work and the prop had moved.

The timber had fallen on something pale — not a stone — something like frayed filaments. She dismounted and tried to tease the object from under the weight but with no success. It looked like strands of nylon rope. On the other side of the baulk was a neat white circle the diameter of a finger. It had been cut clean with a knife.

She stood up and looked from the timber to the collapsed roof. She knew that underneath the prop was a length of nylon. Nature hadn't been at work here but someone with a rope, like the one she carried on her saddle, rope that served a multitude of purposes: to catch a cow, tether a horse, or collapse the roof above the entrance to a mine shaft.

* * *

At Glenaffric the tack room smelled of burned nylon. There were nine saddles set neatly on wooden bucks, coiled ropes on several horns. One coil had an end like a leech, shining black where it had been fused to prevent fraying.

Miss Pink crossed the yard to the house where she found the maids dismantling the den, the smaller trophies a welter of antlers and heads in the middle of the floor. Mrs Gunn, they told her, was on the patio and she was directed down the main corridor.

She hadn't seen the patio before today: a paved space on the north and shady side of the house, with chairs and a table in turquoise plastic, echoing the coloured window shutters on the house. There were *chaises longues* but Edna was sitting upright at the table, a half-full bottle of Jim Beam in front of her and a number of glasses.

'Expecting company,' Miss Pink observed, sitting down without invitation.

'It's a party; they'll be here soon.'

'Ah yes, Jen and Bret, and Sophie. They're bringing the horses over from Benefit.'

Edna poured two measures of bourbon and eyed Miss Pink across the rim of her glass. Miss Pink didn't drink; she asked, with what sounded like mild curiosity, 'Did Clyde help you put the body in the mine shaft? He was a big man. You couldn't have done it on your own.'

Edna's expression was unreadable. She had worn her usual look of vacuous good humour, now her face relaxed and the faded eyes were blank, no emotion showing at all.

Miss Pink regarded her warily. 'Bret saw someone below the hunting camp,' she said. 'It was a Saturday, the maids weren't here. You took the black mare and you galloped through the canyon. I've seen what you can do on a horse — on that horse. Charlie's death wasn't rigged to look like an accident; Ali bolted when you fired. And then you threw the gun in the river?' She stopped on the question and saw that Edna's eyes were sharp and intelligent. They reached for their glasses and drank together.

Edna smiled her fatuous smile and it reached her eyes, obscuring the intelligence. 'Do I say something now?'

Miss Pink breathed deeply. 'Byer could blackmail Val,' she said, 'because he thought it was she or Jen who had visited Charlie, but it was neither of them. It was you.'

'I never went to the cabin,' Edna said in a normal voice.

'No, of course not. It was Bret who visited Charlie and drank his coffee, but Val didn't know that when she found the mugs the following morning and washed them and the pot. She thought Jen had been there. But you weren't there?' Miss Pink considered this and nodded. 'You could be speaking the truth' — Edna's eyes narrowed — 'but it was immaterial to Byer. He didn't know the truth but what he did know was dangerous. He tried blackmail on Val and it worked. And then he tried it on you? And you shot him with his own rifle.'

Edna was amused. 'So I put him in the river and I left his truck there, and I called a cab to bring me home.'

'Clyde helped. Maybe he — '

'Clyde was fishing.'

'He wasn't. I've been talking to the barman at the hotel. Clyde called the bar asking for Russell that afternoon but it was already late; the barman remembers because the happy hour had begun. He overheard Pat Kramer tell Clyde that Russell was fishing. Clyde may well have started out for the Bobcats but he didn't spend the afternoon at the Finger Lakes. Russell lied.'

'So?'

'Skinner knew about the blackmail because he and Byer were buddies, and Skinner wanted a piece of the action. He came here and demanded the silver horses as the price of his silence, and you caught up with him' — Miss Pink checked, frowned, then went on firmly — 'and put his body down the mine shaft. You collapsed the roof by pulling out the timber with a rope.'

Edna put her plump little hands on the table and showed the unmarked palms.

'Your horse pulled it down,' Miss Pink amended. 'And you had to cut the rope because it was trapped under the baulk. I saw you. You didn't see me.'

'You saw me.' It was quiet and flat. Edna topped up her own glass and looked an inquiry at Miss Pink, who shook her head. 'It isn't Skinner in the shaft,' Edna said.

'Who is it?'

'No one. It's my snuff boxes and the little scent bottles and stuff.'

'*What?* Byer cached them there?'

'He never stole them. I took them to incriminate him.'

'But why put them down the mine? They'll be smashed.'

'If they were ever found it would be assumed Byer put them there — but they won't be found. The police think Byer passed them to Skinner who took them to Seattle.'

Miss Pink started. '*You* put the Wedgwood pieces in the creek — and the fragment in Byer's house.' She was so stunned that it had failed to register that the other was talking sensibly.

'You have it basically right,' Edna went on. 'Where you went wrong was in thinking Clyde helped. You're right: he did pick me up after I'd put Byer's truck down there by the river, but he didn't know what I'd done, why I was there, and since everyone thinks I'm senile, I didn't have to tell him why, only to say I'd been wandering.'

'That won't work.' Miss Pink was collecting her senses. 'You must have told him because you had to impress on him that it was essential to provide himself with an alibi — fishing with Russell — so he had to know why one was needed.'

'Only you and Russell know that.'

You old fox, Miss Pink thought. Aloud she said, 'And Clyde had to help you put the body in the river. No way could you do that on your own.'

'Impetus. Byer was shot on the Bear Creek bridge. I convinced him to walk out there because I said my Jeep had broken down, right there on the bridge. I shot him with his own rifle and hoisted him over the rail. He wasn't heavy.'

'And you wiped the rifle,' Miss Pink said, deflated.

'And I wiped the rifle.'

Miss Pink thought about it. 'Where's Skinner?'

'I've no idea.' Edna looked surprised. 'I don't think they'll catch up with him. You see, he did go to Seattle but like he said, he was only a poacher, selling deer meat. However, Hilton has to find someone for

Byer's murder and Skinner fits the bill, and then, of course, he's a suspect for Charlie's murder too.'

'Only if Hilton were to discover the lies that Charlie told about Jen's parentage.'

'There were other lies: that Skinner murdered his wife, for instance, that he stole the silver horses.'

'Ah, those horses. They were taken yesterday. They were in paper bags in his pick-up. You were quarrelling with Skinner when I came into the kitchen. Why didn't you mention the horses then?'

'I didn't know he'd taken them . . . I wasn't myself — '

'No, you can't revert now. I know you're not senile, that you're not a drunk either, but it was a good act. You knew Skinner had those horses and you said nothing. Why not?' Light dawned. 'You *gave* them to him. And you left the pick-up by his house. You set him up!'

Edna shrugged. 'Someone had to be the fall guy — '

'How could you — '

' — for Byer's death, because if Hilton suspected me, the whole thing would come unravelled. Byer was killed because he knew one of us was involved in Charlie's death, so eventually Hilton would come to me and then he'd have to know why I killed my husband.'

The silence stretched. Miss Pink helped herself to bourbon for something to do. Edna was waiting for her to ask the obvious question.

'Why did you?'

'Because of what he did to Jen, and Val, and all of us. Jen lost her family and hated her mother for ten years. I shot Charlie before he could do more harm. I was afraid he was about to send Jen away again.'

'How did you do it?'

'Why, you guessed. I went fast through the canyon like you said and I was letting the mare have a blow when I heard someone coming, so I got off the trail as Bret passed. By the time I reached the cabin, Charlie was away up the hill after the bear that Bret told him was there in the rocks. I caught up and shot him with his own pistol. I told him why I was doing it and he went for his rifle. He would have shot me — not that I'm excusing myself; I meant to shoot him before I started out, otherwise I wouldn't have taken his pistol. It was his own, he kept it in his night table. He'd threaten me with it sometimes for fun. I threw it in the river afterwards.'

'If you knew Charlie had lied to Jen

all those years ago why didn't you do something? You could have found her, Sam could have persuaded her to come home.'

'You don't understand what kind of a man my husband was. He would lie and retract; you never knew what was the truth. Ten years ago he said he'd told Jen that Skinner was her father, next thing he said he was only teasing me. Last week he said she'd been pregnant and it wasn't until then that I put it together: I saw Jen left home because she thought she was about to have a baby by her own daddy. I decided there would be no more of Charlie's jokes.'

She stopped talking and allowed the other to think about it. After a while Miss Pink asked, 'When you called Sophie the morning that he left for hunting camp, you told her everything?'

'No, no, not at all. I meant to' — Edna smiled ruefully — 'I was thinking of joining you for the picnic at Mazarine Lake, of our losing you in some way; I'd go down to the cabin: shoot him, push him in the river, anything — and Sophie would cover for me. But as soon as I started to tell her Charlie had known all along that Jen was pregnant, had given her money, she flipped. I let her rave for a while, but I knew that no way could I use her as an alibi. She can't conceal her feelings. Whatever I did, I had to do it alone, so I let her think that was all there was to it: Jen being pregnant and Charlie keeping quiet about it, and what should we do about this secret meeting at the cabin? When Sophie came back to Ballard I rode to hunting camp.'

'What happens when Skinner is caught? Would you let him hang?'

'Of course not. Actually, I doubt they'll ever catch him. I told him to go to Mexico; he can make a reasonable living there and the silver horses will give him a good start in a new life. He can come back when I'm dead because I'm going to leave a full confession with my will, although there'll be no mention of my true reason for shooting Charlie. However, I'll think of something, make it sound right.'

'I suppose one place is as good as another for Skinner to live.' Miss Pink was grudging. 'Suppose he were caught in your lifetime. Would you confess then?'

' 'Sufficient unto the day . . . ' but no, I wouldn't let even the man who seduced my granddaughter hang — and after all, she was seventeen. Girls should know their own mind at seventeen. If I should live that long I'll put my trust in Jen's money and a good lawyer.'

'And a plea of self-defence perhaps; Charlie went for his gun. How would you plead in the case of Byer?'

Edna pondered. 'Maybe I should plead self-defence there and think of something else for Charlie.'

Miss Pink regarded her with awe. 'You must have scared the daylights out of Skinner. How many people know of your involvement?'

'Just you, dear. Clyde had to know about Byer and no doubt the older members of the family suspect the rest, but no one's going to talk, are they?'

20

Next day, when the evening rush was over, Russell went upstairs to call on those he thought of as his ladies. He found them in party mood, drinking champagne.

'What are we celebrating?'

'A new beginning,' Sophie announced, handing him a glass. 'Starting over, as Edna has it.'

'I see. How is Edna? Any improvement?'

'She's virtually back to normal.' Sophie seated herself and splashed champagne in Miss Pink's glass. 'By that I mean she's her old scatty self — like she always was.'

'It was the shock,' Miss Pink murmured.

Sophie threw her a glance. 'Exactly — and then secondary shock kicked in.'

'Good.' He beamed at them. 'I mean good that it isn't Alzheimer's or dementia, whatever. What happens at Glenaffric now?'

'Jen's full of plans,' Sophie told him. 'Like making apartments for herself and Bret, and for Edna. Clyde too, if he wants. It makes sense for the young people to live there; they have all their stock on one ranch and Bret was only renting the property at Benefit.

Sam will have to look for a new hand — or two. That would leave him free to help out with the pack-trips and at Glenaffric.' She giggled. 'My crazy sister says she's going to start riding again: at her age!'

'She isn't seventy yet,' Miss Pink protested. 'You won't see seventy again, nor me.'

'That's different,' Sophie snapped. 'Edna hasn't been on a horse in centuries, and look at her: she couldn't get a foot in the stirrup, let alone stay on once she was in the saddle.'

'That's no way to talk of your sister,' Russell chided. 'However, I'm glad she's staying at Glenaffric; it's her home, and now that she has Bret and Jen as company and to look after the stock — ' He stopped, his eyes dancing.

'What?' Sophie barked.

'I was wondering where Charlie's silver horses are at this moment. Melted down or gracing a collector's mantelpiece in Seattle?'

'Is there any news of Skinner?' Miss Pink asked.

'Not so far.'

'And Byer?' Sophie prompted.

'I didn't think you'd want to know — '

'Of course we do. What happened with the autopsy? You know something?'

'They recovered the bullet, but they have

to wait for the forensic report. The bullet and the rifle have gone to the laboratory, but my reporter friend says Hilton is reasonably sure that the rifle — the one the kid took from Byer's pick-up — has to be the gun that fired the bullet.'

'It couldn't have been suicide.' Miss Pink looked puzzled. 'Not with a rifle, not to shoot himself in the chest.'

Russell blinked at her. 'There are no prints on the gun except those left by the kid and his dad. It had been wiped before they handled it. Obviously it wasn't suicide, it was Skinner. Byer's truck was mired just below his place and he was about to do a runner when Hilton arrived. He was actually hitching his horse trailer to his pick-up. He said he was going to work for Edna. Did you know she confirmed that?'

'She didn't know what she was saying.' Sophie was dismissive. 'She knew she needed a hand to replace Byer, so when Cole asked, she assumed she'd engaged Skinner.'

'Hilton had the guy right there, in his hands, and he let him go. And now he's vanished.'

Miss Pink's eyes glazed. Sophie said flatly, 'He'll have changed his vehicle.'

'Hilton's in a rage,' Russell said. 'Here he has two murders, he knows who done both of 'em — well, accomplice anyway — and no chance of closing the case — cases — until he catches Skinner.'

'Accomplice?' Miss Pink surfaced from her reverie.

'For Charlie's murder. It needn't have been the two of them working together but it's more likely. And Clyde always maintained Byer was unpredictable. He'd be a threat to Skinner, wouldn't he? Gives Skinner a motive — although shooting Byer could have been no more than the result of a drunken quarrel.'

'You don't need motives for that kind of low life.' Sophie was scathing. 'They'll never catch Skinner; the guy's too terrified of being brought back; we have capital punishment in Montana.'

'Oh yes,' Miss Pink echoed. 'He'll be terrified.' But not of hanging or lethal injection; Skinner would be terrified of Edna.

'She'd blow him away,' Sophie said.

Miss Pink started. Telepathy? 'Charlie *was* her husband,' Sophie insisted. 'No matter he could be a prickly bugger on occasions, it was a terrible way to go: dragged over the rocks, dying out there alone.'

'And they left him there.' Russell shook his head. 'And then' — he waxed indignant — 'not content with murder they have to start blackmailing — that is, Byer did. That would be another motive to get rid of the guy, he was playing with fire: Byer, a killer, trying to set someone else up for the murder.'

'Stupid,' Miss Pink said.

'Tell me about it. And then the thefts from Glenaffric.'

'All criminals make mistakes,' Sophie pointed out. 'And these two were only amateurs initially: poaching and petty theft — '

'There was that rumour that Carol Skinner didn't fall in the river,' Russell reminded her. They eyed each other speculatively. 'No,' he said. 'That was Charlie's slander. Forget it.'

'We have enough without it,' Sophie told him. 'More than enough motivation for Skinner to kill Byer.'

'What would be their motive for killing Charlie?' Miss Pink asked, all innocence.

'Oh, that's simple!' Sophie cried. 'He'd caught Byer thieving and was going to fire him — '

'Had told him he *was* fired,' Russell corrected.

'And Charlie had accused Skinner of killing Carol — '

' — would never let him forget it — '

'Motives enough,' Sophie declared with finality.

Miss Pink subsided, seeing the flaws, trusting that she was the only one to do so, with the exception of these two. They had only Edna's word for it that any objects had been stolen from Glenaffric and, indeed, that Charlie was about to fire Erik Byer. And what sane killer would have left his victim's vehicle within half a mile of his own home? She had been listening to a wily team constructing a scenario; they too would spot the flaws in time and work out clever ways round them.

It was ironical that Charlie, head of the family, should have derived so much pleasure out of manipulating its members, without ever dreaming that one of his jokes might misfire. Justice prevailed in the end, however primitive its form, and they'd kept it within the family, all of them, and that included Russell, a kind of honorary member, and Miss Pink: uncertain whether she was bound by a sense of fair play, or friendship, or respect for what was basically a very private concern.

Other books in the Ulverscroft Large Print Series:

HIJACK
OUR STORY OF SURVIVAL

Lizzie Anders and Katie Hayes

Katie and Lizzie, two successful young professionals, abandoned the London rat race and set off to travel the world. They wanted to absorb different cultures, learn different values and reassess their lives. In the end they got more lessons in life than they had bargained for. Plunged into a nightmarish terrorist hold-up on an Ethiopian Airways flight, they were among the few to survive one of history's most tragic hijacks and plane crashes. This is their story — a story of friendship and danger, struggle and death.

THE VILLA VIOLETTA

June Barraclough

In the 1950s, Xavier Leopardi returned to Italy to reclaim his dead grandfather's beautiful villa on Lake Como. Xavier's English girlfriend, Flora, goes to stay there with him and his family, but finds the atmosphere oppressive. Xavier is obsessed with the memory of his childhood, which he associates with the scent of violets. There is a mystery concerning his parents and Flora is determined to solve it, in her bid to 'save' Xavier from himself. Only after much sorrow will Edwige, the old housekeeper, finally reveal what happened there.

BREATH OF BRIMSTONE

Anthea Fraser

Innocent enough — an inscription in a child's autograph book; a token from her new music teacher, Lucas Todd, that had charmed the six-year-old Lucy. But in Celia, Lucy's mother, it had struck a chill of unease. They had been thirteen at table that day — a foolish superstition that had preyed strangely on Celia's mind. And that night she had been disturbed by vivid and sinister dreams of Lucas Todd . . . After that, Celia lived in a nightmare of nameless dread — watching something change her happy, gentle child into a monster of evil . . .